SHB
u

Hel~~en~~ ~~Dickson~~ was born and still lives in So~~uth~~ Yorkshire, with her retired farm manager ~~husband.~~ Having moved out of the busy farmhouse where she raised their two sons, she now has more time to indulge in her favourite pastimes. She enjoys being outdoors, travelling, reading and music. An incurable romantic, she writes for pleasure. It was a love of history that drove her to writing historical fiction.

Also by Helen Dickson

The Master of Stonegrave Hall
Mishap Marriage
A Traitor's Touch
Caught in Scandal's Storm
Lucy Lane and the Lieutenant
Lord Lansbury's Christmas Wedding
Royalist on the Run
The Foundling Bride
Carrying the Gentleman's Secret
A Vow for an Heiress
The Governess's Scandalous Marriage

Discover more at millsandboon.co.uk.

REUNITED AT THE KING'S COURT

Helen Dickson

MILLS & BOON

All rights reserved including the right of reproduction
in whole or in part in any form. This edition is published
by arrangement with Harlequin Books S.A.

This is a work of fiction. Names, characters, places, locations
and incidents are purely fictional and bear no relationship to
any real life individuals, living or dead, or to any actual places,
business establishments, locations, events or incidents.
Any resemblance is entirely coincidental.

This book is sold subject to the condition that it shall not,
by way of trade or otherwise, be lent, resold, hired out
or otherwise circulated without the prior consent of the publisher
in any form of binding or cover other than that in which it is published
and without a similar condition including this condition
being imposed on the subsequent purchaser.

® and TM are trademarks owned and used by the trademark owner
and/or its licensee. Trademarks marked with ® are registered with the
United Kingdom Patent Office and/or the Office for Harmonisation
in the Internal Market and in other countries.

First Published in Great Britain 2019
by Mills & Boon, an imprint of HarperCollins*Publishers*
1 London Bridge Street, London, SE1 9GF

© 2019 Helen Dickson

ISBN: 978-0-263-27284-0

MIX
Paper from
responsible sources
FSC® C007454

This book is produced from independently certified FSC™ paper
to ensure responsible forest management.
For more information visit www.harpercollins.co.uk/green.

Printed and bound in Spain
by CPI, Barcelona

Prologue

Arlette Dryden had been a motherless child when her father and brother took up their swords in support of the Royalist cause, leaving her alone at Mayfield Hall in Oxfordshire in the care of loyal servants. The news of a fresh battle having been fought between Cromwell's army and Royalists at Worcester meant that Arlette, now thirteen years old, had made it her mission to hide her father's horse, his precious Hector. A year before, the fine, huge, spirited horse had carried him in battle and brought him home wounded from the Battle of Dunbar, never to take up his sword again. Hector was conspicuous in the paddock. She would have to put him out of sight should marauding soldiers from Worcester come their way.

If passing strangers could be believed, having defeated the Royalists, the Roundheads now

posed impending danger, so Blanche, the housekeeper, had told Arlette not to leave the house.
She had promised she wouldn't, but, unable to
bear the thought of Hector alone and vulnerable
in the paddock, with the thought of a Roundhead
sitting on his back abhorrent to her, Arlette knew
she must defy Blanche.

Panting and breathless by the time she reached
the paddock, which stood away from the house,
she had the satisfaction of seeing Hector nibbling
the grass. Pleased to see her, the stallion nickered
and tossed his black mane, arching his neck. She
dared not risk taking him to the stables at the
back of the house. They had once housed some
fine horseflesh, but the horses had gone long
since to serve the Royalist cause. Instead she
guided him to a corner of the paddock where a
hut was almost invisible behind a clump of over-
grown laurel bushes. Urging him inside, where
there was hay and water, then petting him and
whispering in his ear that he had to be quiet, she
went out, closing the door securely, hoping he
would be safe.

Hurrying back to the house, she hoped that
Blanche had not noticed her absence. With only
a vague memory of her mother, who had died
giving birth to her sister when Arlette had been

barely two years old, and the newborn not having survived, either, Blanche had always been there for her and she loved her dearly. Arlette knew little about her mother. She had asked about her often and found it strange that no one, not even her father, would speak of her. They always side-stepped her questions and quickly talked of other matters. Perhaps, she thought—for it was the only explanation she could think of—her father had loved her mother so much that it was diffi-cult for him to speak of her.

Besides, her father had enough worries. In the past, due to her father's careful manage-ment, the estate had prospered, but the enor-mous fines imposed by Parliament on Royalists during the wars had almost crippled them. Any day now her father expected to be turned out of Mayfield Hall and the estate sequestered, which had happened to Royalist estates all over the country.

As she glanced towards the orchard, her at-tention was caught by a figure standing in the shelter of the pear trees watching the house. Cau-tiously she made her way to where he stood, looking at him with curiosity. He was young—scarcely more than a youth—perhaps seventeen or eighteen years of age. His clothes were stained and torn, his face streaked with sweat and grime and strained with exhaustion. An unmistakable smell of powder clung to his clothes. There was a bleakness to his darkly circled eyes. Dried blood stained the shoulder of his doublet.

The light from the sun was shining full on his face, and the sight of him caused Arlette a certain amount of unease. Where had he come from? she wondered. Holding her breath, she took in the beauty of him. It did not seem credible that a man could be so beautiful. He was unquestionably the most handsome male she had ever seen, with fine, clear-cut features that might have been described as feminine in their perfection but for the firmness of his mouth and strong chin. His dark brown hair, blackened by gunpowder and soaked in sweat, was clipped to just below his ears. He had strong shoulders under his dark blue doublet. His eyes were a vibrant blue that were normally filled with warmth and charm, but today burned bright with all he had done and seen with the besieged Royalists in Worcester. There was something about him that seemed familiar.

'Who are you? I sense that we have met before.'

'My name is William—William Latham—the son of Lord Robert Latham of Arlington Court in Warwickshire.' His voice was rich and polished and had the tone of a gentleman. 'This is the house of Sir Isaac Dryden?'

Arlette nodded. His name was familiar to her. He was a friend of her brother Thomas. 'He is my father. Have you been at Worcester? We were told there is a battle raging.'

He nodded, his expression grave. 'That is correct. It is over now and the King defeated. I was there. I—have news for your father.'

Arlette stared at him, her instinct telling her all was not well with Thomas. 'Is it Thomas?' she ventured to ask, fearful of what he might say. 'My name is Arlette. Thomas is my brother. He is with the King's army.'

'I know. We fought together.'

'I remember Thomas speaking of you.'

He nodded. 'We were at school together. I am here at his request. I must tell you that there is a need for haste. Will you take me to your father?'

She nodded. 'He is anxious for news of Thomas. You look exhausted—and you're wounded.' She noticed how he held his shoulder.

He breathed deeply. 'It's not easy to run for your life with a sword wound.'

'Don't you have a horse?'

'I did. Due to the wounds inflicted on him at Worcester, I had to abandon him some miles back.'

Tilting her head to one side she looked at him gravely. 'Is there someone to look after him?'

He nodded. 'I met a kindly farmer who promised me he would take care of him. Now, I don't wish to bring trouble to your house so we must hurry. The countryside will very soon be crawling with Roundheads searching for fugitives from the battle. Anyone found harbouring them will be granted no quarter.'

'I'm sorry. I'll take you to my father right away—but I must tell you that he is very weak. It is thought that he will not last much longer,' she told him in a small voice.

'I'm sorry to hear that.'

'He was wounded at Dunbar last September. He managed to make it back, but he has not left his bed since. Come, I will take you to him. He will be eager to hear what you have to say.'

Eighteen-year-old William tried to keep up with her as, light of foot, she sped ahead of him. An image of his stricken horse and the bullet with which he had put it out of its misery had been what he considered to be a humane kindness. The horse had served him well and it had been a hard thing for him to do. It was not something he could share with this innocent child. He had not lied when he had told her about the farmer. The man, a Royalist sympathiser and knowing William was trying to make good his escape from the Roundheads, had agreed to dispose of the horse.

Mayfield Hall was a fine old house. The red brick glowed warmly beneath the sun, the diamond-paned windows winking in the light. They entered through the heavy oak doors and William's boots echoed on the floorboards as he walked through the large baronial hall. Looking around him, he saw that, like many Royalist houses throughout the land, the war had left its scars. Fine furniture showed signs of misuse. Panelling and wainscoting had been ripped from the walls. Windows had been broken and left unrepaired. He made no comment as he followed in Arlette's wake.

After climbing the wide oak staircase to the upper floor he followed her along a landing where she came to a stop before a door. William looked down at her, aware of her concern. She was a child, very young—he was to learn later that she was thirteen years old. In her blue dress she looked disarmingly like some little woodland nymph. There was a strange intensity in her enormous eyes with their liquid depths, which were a cross between green and blue, and her curly mop of hair had the brilliance of sunlight.

'Please wait here a moment. I'll go and tell him he has a visitor.'

William did as she asked, hearing muted voices from behind the closed door. After a moment she returned.

'When my father left for Scotland he was a fine upstanding man. Please do not be alarmed by his appearance. His suffering has taken its toll on him.'

William entered the room where Sir Isaac Dryden lay abed. It had the smell of a sick room and vials of medicines and pots of salve littered the surface of a dresser. Despite the girl's warning he found it hard to hide his shock at the appearance of Sir Isaac Dryden. He was painfully thin. Against the pillows his flesh was waxen and clung to the bones of his face. But the eyes that studied him were sharp and shrewd and bright with intelligence. William moved close to the bed and gave a formal bow. There was no mistaking the gravity of the moment.

'My daughter informs me that you are Wil-

liam Latham—your family home is Arlington
Court in Warwickshire, which I recall Thomas
telling me about.'

'That is correct.'

'Welcome to Mayfield Hall. You are the son
of Lord Robert Latham, I believe.'

William nodded. 'He was killed during the
siege at Colchester in forty-eight.'

'I'm sorry to hear that. I knew him well. He
was a fine man.'

'Yes—yes, he was.'

'It cannot have been easy for you coming here.
News has reached us of the battle at Worcester
and that it ended in a bloody defeat for the Royalists.'

'The battle was doomed before it began.'

'My son—Thomas…?'

'Was taken prisoner.'

A great relief swept over Sir Isaac. 'Thank
the Lord. You, too, have survived the battle and
I imagine you are impatient to put as much distance between you and the victors as you can.'

A fit of coughing rendered him speechless
and left him exhausted against the pillows. Arlette moved closer to the bed, her young face
filled with concern.

'Father, you will tire yourself. You must rest.'

The trace of a thin smile touched the old man's lips. 'I'll have plenty of rest soon, Arlette.' He gave another hollow cough and when it was over he looked at his visitor. 'I am dying, sir—I've been dying ever since I was wounded at Dunbar. I have prayed the good Lord in his wisdom would keep me alive until my son came home. I see now that is not to be.' He shook his head despondently. 'Thomas was a scholar. He had no enthusiasm for soldiering.' His eyes met those of the young visitor with perfect understanding. 'Tell me what happened to him?'

William met his eyes and read his need to know. 'He fares better than most—but his treatment in the hands of his captors will be harsh.' Glancing sideways at the girl standing across the bed, he saw pain fill her eyes.

'The war has dealt ill with those loyal to the King,' Sir Isaac murmured quietly, 'my own family having lost brothers and nephews at one battle or another. My daughter Hester lives in London—she married a Parliament man—a mercer. The marriage caused a bitter divide between us. Arlette and my son are all I have left. May the Lord spare them.' His skeletal hand reached out to touch his daughter's cheek with a reverence that did not go unnoticed by William. 'So—tell me. Where is Thomas now?'

'We were both taken prisoner—along with ten thousand others. We were herded into the cathedral from where we were to be marched to London. I was fortunate. In the mayhem that ensued after the battle I managed to escape.'

Sir Isaac digested this calmly. 'How was Thomas? Was he wounded?'

'No—merely exhausted and hungry—but his spirit remains high. Food was scarce. In the final minutes we were together he asked me—if I was able—to come here and assure you that he did not perish in the battle.'

'I thank you for that. It means a great deal to me knowing he survived. As to how he will be dealt with, that is another matter, but even Cromwell's army will lack the resources to try so many prisoners. But what of you now? I imagine Roundheads will be searching for those Royalists who escaped Worcester.'

'They are. It is my belief that the wars are over, the Royalist cause in ruins. The drawn-out conflict has reduced honest citizens to beggars and no corner of this land has been left untouched by the evils of war. The world as we knew it before the wars has gone. England has suffered enough. It's my intention to go to France.'

'If Cromwell offers a pardon to Royalists willing to abide by the laws of the Commonwealth, will you accept it?'

'Never.' A fierce light burned in William's eyes. 'I did not enter the fray until my sixteenth birthday and before he was cruelly executed, I fought hard for King Charles the First. I will not give it all up now. His son, King Charles Stuart, has my undying loyalty. It is unthinkable that I desert him. He needs support now more than ever. I expect Arlington Court will be sequestered along with many other properties of those who supported the King.'

'And young Charles Stuart? Where is he?'

'The last I heard he had escaped Worcester, thank God.'

'The day will come when he comes into his own, I am confident of that—and when he does, all that has been stolen from those who remained loyal will be returned. This time will pass.'

'Will it? Do you really believe that?'

'It must. I cannot conceive of the people of England turning permanently against their King. Reason will prevail in the end. I am sure of it.'

'I pray it will be so. There is nothing we can

do but wait and see. But I must take my leave of you. Should I be found here it will not go well with you.'

'Three times Roundhead patrols have been here—you will have seen the evidence for yourself. Each time the house was searched. You are right to put as much distance between you and them as possible. But I see you are wounded,' he said, his gaze going to the blood that had seeped into his doublet. 'You must have it tended to and take refreshment before you leave, but I have a favour to ask of you and, in the light of what has happened at Worcester and my own weakness, it is most urgent. I am almost at the allotted time on this earth. What matters to me now is Arlette. I fear greatly what will happen to her if she remains here.' He looked at his daughter with loving but worried eyes. 'It is my wish that Arlette goes to live with her half-sister in London.'

Arlette gasped. 'No, Father. I will not go. Do not ask me to leave here. It's too cruel. I could not bear it—living in the house of a Parliament man. I am your daughter and my place is here with you.'

'A daughter's place is to obey her father,' her father pointed out, his voice softening.

There was an unusual flush on the girl's

cheeks and the eyes with which she regarded her father were openly defiant. 'I will not go. Do you really think I would willingly go to safety, leaving you behind to face danger?'

'Understand me, Arlette. Understand why I am doing this. I am unwilling to subject you to any unnecessary suffering should the Round-heads come here—as they will, I am sure of it. I know you haven't spent much time with Hester during your childhood, but you will be safe with her and, despite our differences, I believe her husband to be a moderate man. She is a woman of integrity and honesty and she will endeavour to do her best for your welfare and protection. Do as I ask, Arlette. I beg you.' He looked at William. 'You will take her?'

William looked at Arlette standing like a miniature statue, feeling her withdrawal from her father. Her dejection pierced his heart. He saw her attempt to struggle to mask her painful disappointment and inexplicable sadness. His gut tightened with the instinctive need to protect her.

'Will you do it?' Sir Isaac asked.

William nodded. 'I will take her,' he said hoarsely. 'I will then make my way to the coast and take ship to the Continent. My mother and sister are there already.'

Having reluctantly agreed to Sir Isaac's request, to ease his unease and to soothe Arlette's, William met her eyes and smiled, relieved when she met his gaze unflinchingly. He was encouraged by her quiet display of strength.

With a need for haste, just one hour later, after William had eaten and had his shoulder tended by the housekeeper, and Arlette had gathered provisions and a few necessities she would need to see her to London, they left, mounted on Hector.

With her small body nestled close to William's and tears clogging her throat after saying a final farewell to her father and Blanche—who had been more like a mother to her over the years— Arlette was strangely comforted and reassured by William's presence and the warmth in his voice. But knowing she would not see her father again on this earth, her young heart ached fit to burst with her loss.

As they rode away she turned and looked back at the house, drawing in a deep breath, willing the scent of the surrounding countryside and the image of the house to remain with her for the long years ahead.

It was a strange kind of existence as they travelled towards London. Arlette rode pillion behind William and when they encountered the odd traveller he implied that she was his sister and that they were going to visit family in London. They kept away from the main thoroughfares, for not only were they more likely to run into Roundheads on the main routes, but they were also notorious for thieves.

On the first night as they settled down to sleep beneath the stars, with the desolation of her loss and hopelessness at the thought that she would never see her father again, Arlette's tears had flowed. Looking at her huge eyes awash with tears, silently beseeching him for comfort, William had responded automatically and taken the distraught girl in his arms. She was remarkable. Torn from her home and thrust into the unknown with a virtual stranger at such an early age, she showed a bravery and selflessness he admired. She was also strong and healthy and the following morning the tears had dried from her eyes.

William was glad of her company. After the carnage that had been Worcester, seeing his friends brutally slain and his desperate escape which had driven him to the brink of exhaustion, it was Arlette he focused on to escape the pain of those memories. After looking back on the bleakness of that time, he totally lost himself in her sweetness, entering her world where everything was fresh and alive. Should danger confront them, he would protect her with his life.

When they finally reached London after three days on the road their weariness was beginning to tell on them both.

Arlette entered a strange time in her life. Only Hester could understand what torment she was going through, feeling the same cruel loss of her family. William's presence also gave her comfort for a short time and, whatever the future held for either of them, there would be no escaping the strong bond that had developed between them during the time they had been together on the road.

William was relieved to find Hester's husband, Richard Arden, was in the Midlands on mercer business, which reduced his fear of being turned over to the authorities. He experienced a deep concern for Arlette. Before he left he voiced his concern to her sister.

'The leaving of her home and her father has hurt her deeply. The emotional scars will be almost impossible for her to erase for a long time.'

'She will be well taken care of, but you are

right. She is bereft. It will take her a long time, but she is strong. I have every faith she will come through.'

The summer had ended and the encroaching chill of autumn was in the air when William took his leave of Arlette. He was in the yard. She went to him with a heavy heart. That day when he had arrived at Mayfield Hall, she had been meeting a stranger and was filled with anxieties and fears. Now she was facing the painful task of saying goodbye to someone who had become precious to her. She shivered, wishing this day had never come. Not only had a closeness developed between them, but also a tenderness.

William pulled his hat down over his ears and hugged Arlette, who was clinging to his hand.

'I don't want you to leave,' she whispered, her eyes wide and vulnerable and shining with tears. 'I want to go with you.'

'I can't take you with me, Arlette. I am going to join the King in France. With my father dead and the rest of my family in France, my estate in Warwickshire seized by Parliament and myself declared a traitor, I have no choice.'

'But you will come back, won't you?'

'Perhaps—in time. But I will not return to

England while it is ruled by Cromwell.' Seeing the pain in her eyes, he placed his hands on her young shoulders and bent down so that his face was on a level with hers. 'It is right that you are here with your sister.' As he held her from him, his look was earnest. 'You do understand why I have to go, don't you?'

She nodded, swallowing down the lump in her throat and blinking back the tears that threatened to flow from her eyes at any moment. 'Yes,' she whispered. 'But you won't forget me, will you?'

'You have become very dear to me, Arlette. I could never do that.'

Giving him a teary smile, she backed away from him. 'Wait a moment. I have something for you.'

William watched her scamper off, then, hearing a horse's hooves clattering on the cobbles, he saw her leading Hector towards him. He smiled.

'What have we here?'

Arlette glanced at the pathetic-looking horse her sister had managed to find for him, which Arlette rejected. 'I want you to have Hector.'

'But Hector was your father's horse. I cannot take him.'

'I want you to have him. I know it is what my

father would have wanted. Besides, Hector likes you. I know you will take care of him.'

With emotion almost choking him, William wrapped her young body in his strong arms and hugged her hard, then he took her face in his hands and kissed her forehead.

'Goodbye, Arlette. I wish you joy and happiness and luck in your life. May God bless you.'

'William,' she said as he turned from her. He looked back with a questioning look. 'Be careful, won't you?' she said hoarsely. 'With your life.'

He was silent a moment and then said, 'Of course I will. Why? Why would you say that? Is it precious to you?'

She nodded slowly. 'Yes. Will I see you again?'

He smiled. 'I do have a habit of turning up when least expected. Perhaps I may have cause to come and visit you in London—or better still at Mayfield Hall when all this is over. Would I be assured of a welcome in your house?'

'There will always be a welcome for you, William—no matter where I am.'

Lowering his head, he turned and walked away. Arlette watched him, wanting to say something more, but she couldn't. The words were trapped in her throat and tears welled up in her eyes. She had been aware that one day he would have to leave her, that his presence in her world was transitory. But it had come too soon. Sorrow and emotion swamped her, wrenching at her heart. He left her then and she watched him ride away. All that remained of his solid presence was the trace of a light kiss on her forehead, the image of his back and the painful noise of Hector's receding hooves.

Hester came to stand beside her, placing her arm about her shoulders.

'Will he come back?' Arlette asked in a low voice.

'As to that I cannot say.'

Her desolation was as acute as when she had left Mayfield Hall. 'He has to come back,' she whispered to herself. 'He has to. I couldn't bear it if he didn't.'

Chapter One

⤜⤛⤚⤙⤘

1660

Having been summoned by her sister, after spending the morning sitting by the river watching various craft moving along—which always delighted her—Arlette brushed the dried grass from her skirts, straightened her hair and hurried into the house.

Oaklands House, west of London, was a lovely house. It had been Richard Arden's family home for generations, built in better, more prosperous times to get away from the plague which descended on the city every year. Its airy halls, parlours and reception rooms were carpeted and tastefully furnished. Beyond the domestic quarters, the buttery, bakehouse and wash house could be found. The gardens were a well-kept delight and extensive, the smooth lawns dropping down to the river's edge. Hester kept the house in perfect order, ruling the servants with a firm hand.

The Ardens were hard-working mercers. The family's substantial business premises were in Spitalfields, where fabrics were stored and trained women and apprentices in leather aprons carried out the work of weaving. Hester's husband, Richard Arden, a harsh, controlling man, went into the City each day, one of the servants rowing him down river. Devoted to business and administration, not for him was life idle and carefree.

Richard had prospered in his trade before the wars and because he had declared for Parliament when the troubles began, he had been allowed to continue with his business unhindered, but it had suffered very badly from lack of trade during the Commonwealth. Now King Charles and his courtiers were returning, with nobles and their ladies flooding the capital once more, trade in finer fabrics—brocades from Milan, silks from Lucca and Venetian velvets of supreme quality—would be in demand once more. But that was in the future and Richard had no capital put by to invest.

Arlette found her sister in the parlour. With more constraints than excesses, when Arlette had come to Oaklands House, she had soon realised that life was not going to be easy for her, but she wearily accepted the way Richard treated her without complaint. In the beginning he had welcomed her into his home with a genuine warmth, glad that Hester would have the company of her sister and to have an extra pair of hands to help with the everyday chores.

Hester had a desperate yearning for a child of her own. In the early days of her marriage she had lost a child and, as the years went by and she failed to conceive another, being deprived of this natural function enjoyed by most women of her acquaintance had left her feeling deeply disappointed and inadequate in some way as a woman. She was tense at the moment—she had been for days—she was always like this when she was going to visit Richard's sister, Anne Willoughby, who had a large brood of children, which only exacerbated Hester's own sorry situation.

Hester lifted her brows and stared disapprovingly at her sister's attire, her eyes lingering overlong and with exasperation on a rip in her skirt, caused when it had become snagged

on a thorn bush. Arlette was aware of Hester's
displeasure over her friendship with James Sefton—in her sister's opinion the time she spent
with James could be more usefully spent. The
Sefton family of Willow Hall were neighbours.
With his fair hair and boyishly handsome face,
James had a precocious and open manner. Arlette valued his friendship, but their relationship
was no more than that. Direct from his travels
abroad, he had returned to England ahead of his
father, who was to return from his years in exile
with King Charles Stuart. His mother, of Puritan stock, had remained at Willow Hall throughout the wars.

'Mary said you wished to speak to me, Hester.'

'I sent for you half an hour ago, Arlette. Have
I not enough to do without worrying about you
all the time? As you well know we are to travel
into the city tomorrow and there are a thousand
and one things to be done. Anne and her husband are expecting us in good time. Since we
are to stay with them overnight I have much to
pack—which is something you can help me with
when you have cleaned yourself up.'

Arlette knew exactly what Hester was thinking when she looked at her. Her pale blue eyes

were narrowed with annoyance as she darted sharp disapproving glances at her, having burst into the house shattering the peace. Arlette knew she must present a frightful vision in her stained and crumpled skirts. Shoving the untidy mop of hair back from her face, she sank into a chair in a most unladylike pose, doing little to appease Hester's displeasure. She prided herself on being intelligent, quick-thinking and sharp-witted, but much as Hester loved her she was always accusing her of being problematical and a constant headache. She heard Hester sigh heavily, as if tired of her burden.

News had reached them shortly after William Latham had brought Arlette to London that their father had died following a visit from Cromwell's soldiers searching for Royalists who had fled Worcester after the battle. Like hundreds of Royalist properties, Mayfield Hall had been sequestered by Parliament. Neither of them had been back to Mayfield since, although Blanche sometimes wrote to Arlette with news of friends and neighbours who had been a part of her life, and the elderly Parliament man and his wife who now lived in Mayfield Hall. They had learned that their brother Thomas, along with over a thousand English and Scottish captives and some foreign mercenaries, had been sent to Barbados as virtual slaves. Whether he lived or had died they had no way of knowing.

Arlette was more beautiful than Hester had ever hoped to be, but she lived for the moment and had little interest in anything that was not to do with outdoor pursuits.

Following his ten-year stay in France, the King's exile was over. His ship, the *Royal Charles*, along with the rest of the fleet, had arrived in Dover, where he had been received with obeisance and honour by General Monck, commander-in-chief of all the forces in England and Scotland, the man who had played the most crucial part in his restoration. The King was expected to enter his capital during the next few days. It was for this reason that they were going to stay with Anne and her husband, who lived on the Strand. Anne and her brother Richard had been raised in a Puritan household and when the troubles had started between the King and Parliament they had supported Parliament, but Edward, Anne's husband, was a staunch Royalist and he welcomed the return of the monarchy and was insistent on celebrating it.

Mortified that she had upset her sister and keen to make amends, Arlette swept her hair back from her face and stood up. 'I will help you, Hester. I'm sorry. It was remiss of me to leave you to do it all. It completely slipped my mind. Was there something else?'

'Yes, as a matter of fact there is. Sir Ralph Crompton has approached Richard again. Do you forget that soon you are to be betrothed?'

Arlette's face fell. The effect of Hester's remark was like having a bucket of cold water thrown over her and was a reminder that soon she would have the mundane affairs of a wife to fill her days—soon, but not yet—and she continued to resist. 'I do not forget, Hester, but...' She sighed. 'I don't see why I have to marry him.'

'He is taken with you, Arlette. You know perfectly well he is.'

This was true. Sir Ralph was also a mercer and nothing would please Richard more than for his sister-in-law to marry an important and respected member of the guild, a man who played a prominent role in London's civic life. Along with other members of the guild, Richard had suffered because of the restrictions austerity imposed on him by the Commonwealth. He felt the humiliation of his reduced status and when Sir Ralph expressed his interest in making Arlette his wife, it was like balm to his wounds. She did not have the dowry formerly anticipated and the most worthy of the men seeking wives, those able to provide her with standing and security, would turn their attention elsewhere. Marriage to Sir Ralph would provide Richard with an important connection and raise his standing with the guild. Sir Ralph had offered a sizable stipend to be paid for Arlette's hand in marriage, which would not be forthcoming if she turned him down. Richard had readily accepted on Arlette's behalf.

The instant Arlette had set eyes on Ralph Crompton she had taken a dislike to him, but she had thought she sensed the trace of a satisfied smile on his smug face. She had moved away when he had positioned his hand on her waist as though he had the right. He had appraised her, studied her with the sure eye of someone who knows exactly what he likes and is used to getting what his desires dictate. She had never believed herself capable of stirring such a desire in anyone, but just as an animal scents danger, with the same primal instinct she knew that Sir Ralph Crompton had decided to pursue her.

'There must be hundreds of women he could choose from. Why me?'

'Just thank your lucky stars that he still wants you.'

'Of course he does. Who else would he get to take care of his two motherless daughters?' Arlette replied, unable to hide her bitterness at such a prospect.

Hester waved her objections aside. 'Nevertheless, your defiance and the gossip directed against this family, brought about by your friendship with James Sefton of late, are all too much. Your behaviour has upset Richard. If Sir Ralph did change his mind, I would not blame him.'

'Then to escape his attention perhaps I should damage my reputation some more,' Arlette retorted, tossing her head rebelliously. The moment the words had left her mouth she had cause for regret, for her flippant remark only angered Hester further.

'Do not even think of doing that,' Hester snapped, breathing deeply in an effort to control the anger that seemed to erupt more quickly of late no matter how hard she tried to temper it. 'Think yourself lucky that marriage to Sir Ralph Crompton will provide you with the standing and security you deserve.' Noting Arlette's defiance, she sighed, shoving her hair tiredly from her brow. 'You are my sister and I love you dearly and I do understand that you are set against the marriage—but...'

'Richard would be not so understanding. Where your husband is concerned, my opinion counts for nothing.' Arlette sighed. 'Worry not, Hester, I know I am duty-bound to marry Sir Ralph and I have committed myself to doing what is right. I will not go back on my word,' she said, no matter how distasteful she found the consequences.

'Richard is only doing what he thinks is best for you,' Hester said in his defence. 'You have to marry as your circumstances demand and Sir Ralph is the only one offering. It's high time you were married. This alliance is important to Richard—more than you realise. You should be grateful he is doing this.'

Arlette took a deep, tight breath. That she was being sacrificed for Richard's ambition angered her, but she had learned to know her place in Richard's house and knew better than to defy the rules and make her own destiny. All her life she had hoped she would have the freedom to choose her own husband, but, when it came to it, Richard had chosen for her. A good alliance, he called it—but the last person she'd ever have chosen was Sir Ralph Crompton.

'I had hoped you might repent of the folly of your ways,' Hester went on, 'but it seems that is not so. I have tried so hard since you came here, Arlette, hoping to find more submission in you—obedience, even—but I have come to realise it is not in your nature. With no one to steer you, you were left too much to your own devices at Mayfield Hall. I love you dearly, but you do try my patience to the limit.'

'I am deeply sorry to have caused you so much grief, Hester, truly, and I am most grateful for everything you and Richard have done for me. But,' she said, with a note of defiance, 'I am twenty-two years of age and even though I know I have to marry Sir Ralph, I would like to have had a say in my choice of husband—and Sir Ralph it would not be.'

Furious by what she considered to be Arlette's insolence, Hester was unable to curb her tongue as it began to run away with her, which was something she would come to regret later. 'You ungrateful girl. You put me in mind of your mother. You are turning out to be just like her after all. Her ingratitude, after all our father did for her, was unforgivable also.'

Arlette stared at her in puzzlement. 'My mother? Why do you mention my mother? And why should she have need to be grateful to our father?'

'Our father was a fool ever to marry her.'

'Please don't say that, Hester. I will not let you shake my kinder memories of my mother. She was my mother and I loved her dearly.'

'How could you? You scarcely remember her.'

'I was a mere child when she died—I know that. I know very little of how she came to wed our father.'

'Then it's high time you did,' Hester replied sharply. 'It's high time you knew what kind of woman she was.' Anger had brought blood rushing to her face and a hard glitter to her eyes. She looked so frighteningly angry that Arlette almost turned and fled the room. Suspecting that her sister was about to enlighten her to the more disagreeable traits to her mother's character she turned away, unwilling to hear anything to discredit her.

'Pray excuse me, Hester, but I will not stay and listen to anything you might say that is disparaging.'

'Oh, yes, Arlette, you will listen.'

She had always sensed Hester's deep dislike

of her mother, whose name was never mentioned between them. The reason for this dislike had always remained a mystery to her, but she felt it must be something deep and profound, that maybe it was because their father had taken another wife after the death of Hester's own mother.

'So our father would have you believe that she died giving birth to our sister in an attempt to hide the truth. She did not care for our father. The man she loved—whose bed she had wallowed in and whose child she had conceived while Father was away in London about the King's business—was a widower.'

Arlette was filled with an overriding horror at what Hester was telling her. The whole of her world seemed to be rocking about her. It could not be true. 'But—but that cannot be— she would not...'

'Yes, Arlette, she did. Open your eyes to the truth. Like a fool Father worshipped her—she could do no wrong in his eyes—but when he returned home after a long absence and found her nursing a child and knowing it could not possibly be his, he turned both her and her child out.'

Arlette stared at her, sick with horror at what she had been told. Feeling light-headed, she slumped into a chair at the table, staring ahead of her, but seeing nothing. There was a constriction in her throat and tears swam in her eyes. 'What happened to her? Where did she go?'

'As to that I cannot say. I do not know.'

'And my sister?'

She shrugged. 'I don't know that, either.'

'What was my sister's name?'

'I don't remember. Miranda—Matilda—something like that. What does it matter now? She was your sister, not mine.'

'It does matter to me. Very much. But why have you told me now? You could have spared me this and continued with the deception.'

'Because, Arlette, I have reached the limits of my endurance in keeping this secret,' she uttered tiredly. 'I think it is high time you knew what kind of woman your mother was.'

'Say what you like, Hester. It is easy when she is not here to defend herself. I will remain faithful to her memory no matter what you say. Does Richard know of this?'

'No—I was too ashamed to tell him.'

Arlette's cheeks burned with indignation and heated words rose to her lips in defence of her mother, regardless of what she had just been told, but her sister silenced her before she could utter a word.

'As your sister, I will continue to do my duty towards you, which is what our father would have wanted, and see that preparations are made for your betrothal to Sir Ralph as soon as possible—for the sooner you are wed with a family to care for the less I will have to worry about.'

When Arlette was able, she escaped to her room beneath the eaves to consider at length what Hester had told her. Her father was not young at the time he had married her mother, being forty years of age. His first wife had died shortly after giving birth to Hester. Arlette's mother was twenty years her father's junior and she had been told she had died in childbirth along with the newborn infant.

After what Hester had confided, she could imagine the anger and the grief at Mayfield Hall at a time when, at two years old, she had been too young to understand the goings-on in the adult world. Her father had been a good and gentle man, but the wars had taken him away from home all too frequently, leaving Arlette in the capable and loving hands of Blanche.

Because of Hester's revelation, she discovered

to her dismay that suddenly everything she believed to be stable had been upset, twisted from its course. Her mother might still be alive—and her sister. She had a sister. She could not imagine how her mother must have suffered to be cast out, away from everything she held dear—having to leave her daughter Arlette behind, knowing she would never see her again.

She sat on the bed, trying to sort out the confusion of her thoughts, the violent swings of her emotions. How could her father, Hester and Blanche have kept this from her?

She had been sitting on the bed for half an hour when there was a soft tap on the door. It was Hester. Arlette noticed how downcast she looked and very tired.

'What is it, Hester? Is something amiss?'

She shook her head. Crossing to the window, she stood looking out, her back to Arlette, a noticeable dejection about her stance, which was unusual since she was always busily employed with no time for idle chatter. 'I'm sorry, Arlette. I spoke harshly. I didn't mean to—only—I don't know what comes over me at times. I apologise if you find me unsympathetic. I realise how what I told you must have upset you—naturally so—

but what I told you was the truth.' She left the window and came to sit beside her on the bed, taking hold of her hand.

The gesture and soft words touched Arlette. Hester was never outwardly demonstrative with her or anyone else, but for all her harsh temper, she had a soft heart and Arlette had an enormous love and affection for her.

'I'm glad you told me, Hester. I only wish I had been told about my mother earlier. I do not blame you—there was little communication between us when you married Richard and came to live in London. But I cannot believe Father kept it from me—and Blanche. How could they do that? All these years I have believed my mother to be dead—when all the time she is alive.'

'He was deeply hurt by her deception, Arlette. It was a difficult time for Father. He could not forgive your mother for what she did. Her betrayal hurt him deeply. When she left Mayfield Hall, he forbade her name to be mentioned. She really was dead to him. I spoke the truth when I said that I have no idea where she went—or if she is still alive, even. As far as I am aware there was no further communication when she left Mayfield.'

'I wish I could find her, Hester. I wish I knew where to look. Do you know the man who…?'

Hester shook her head. 'No. The only thing I know is that he was a widower. Some believed it to be Lord Stanhope, from Warwick. She talked about him a lot when she returned from visiting her cousin who lived there. You went with her. It was at a time when Father was in London on the King's business, which happened often in those days before the wars. Lord Stanhope was a frequent visitor to her sister's house apparently. But it was not known for certain how close they had become. I do recall when she returned from her visit how quiet she was. She appeared to be unhappy about something.'

Arlette had no recollection of that time. She had been far too young to remember. But she stored Lord Stanhope's name in her mind. At least it was one line she could follow when she had the time.

'I would like to see you happier, Hester,' she said softly. 'There is a great deal of bitterness in you of late.'

'Circumstances change us all.'

'But there is so much that is good in life.'

'I see little of it.'

'It is a dark period we have gone through. But it is past. It is for us to build a new life.'

'There are two things that could make me happy—one is to see you settled in marriage and the other would be if I were to have a child. Why have other women been so blessed and not me? It's a question I ask myself all the time.'

She sat beside Arlette with the pallor of her face like marble, a contrast to those startling blue eyes which were so like their father's. Arlette immediately felt very angry with herself, angry at being so blind to Hester's suffering. The child she had lost had meant so much to her and Richard. She felt an overwhelming tenderness take possession of her.

'I don't know, Hester. I wish I did. But it's not too late. Why, you are still of an age for childbearing. Many women have children older than you. Perhaps you worry too much about it.' With a sigh Arlette took hold of her hand. 'I know you aren't looking forward to going to stay with Anne, who has a habit of flaunting her children in your face. Do not let her upset you—I beg of you. Concentrate on why we are going—to see King Charles enter London and to enjoy the celebrations. Why, the whole of London is gripped by the excitement of his restoration.'

'You forget that Richard is not of your persuasion, Arlette—nor Anne.'

'Then all I can say is thank the Lord for Edward. He is determined to show his support of King Charles and there is nothing that Anne can do about it.'

Hester gave her one of her rare smiles. 'No, there isn't and I will try to enjoy myself,' she said, her Royalist upbringing coming to the fore. 'Do you think there will be celebrations in Mayfield village?'

'I am sure of it. There wasn't a family who was not loyal to the King.'

'Have you no wish to go back to Mayfield, Arlette?'

'I don't know.' An image of her brother, now just a dim shadow of her past, appeared in her mind. 'I'd like to think that Thomas will come back and return to our old home. Perhaps now King Charles has come into his own he might make it possible and the property that was sequestered will be returned. We must put in a petition—which, I believe, is what Royalists who had their houses seized are going to do.' She was filled with nostalgia for Mayfield—images of childhood, tastes and smells, Mayfield village and the recollections of people she had known.

She thought about what Hester had told her, becoming quiet and withdrawn as she began to consider how she might discover further information about what had become of her mother and sister all those years ago. May God help her for she could not ignore it. Curiosity and the need to know would drive her on. But how could she go about it? There was no way that she could see. If still alive, they could be anywhere. With reluctance she had to admit that she could do nothing at this time. But she would not let it lie and was fiercely determined to pursue the matter when the opportunity arose.

Richard's sister lived in one of the grand private houses along the Strand. Following the austere years of the Commonwealth under the rule of Oliver Cromwell, when all pleasures were denied, when things had been difficult and uncertain and political tension had permeated every household, everyone hoped that with the King's return to his throne the days would follow a different rhythm. Already the dour cloak of puritanism was being shed and places of entertainment, closed during the interregnum, were beginning to open. In taverns, tankards were raised in toasts to His Majesty, to Charles Stuart, coming home at last to England and his people, Charles Lackland no longer.

It was the twenty-ninth of May, 1660, King Charles's thirtieth birthday, and the whole of London, gripped with excitement, was rejoicing. The Strand was lined with people who paraded bearing effigies of Charles Stuart adorned with flowers. There were street sellers doing a good trade and thieves looking for rich pickings. The crowd chanted, 'Long live the King!', and in taverns pot boys sped backwards and forwards with tankards foaming with ale. Cannons fired from the Tower announced that the King had crossed London Bridge and a cacophony of bells being rung in every church steeple were a joy to hear. The sky was cloudless and the sun gilded the lattice windows of the Willoughby household.

It was a large house and was filled with friends and neighbours all celebrating together, all eager to see the sights from the balcony that overlooked the Strand. Happy children managed to get under everyone's feet and Richard, testy and often bad-tempered, having resigned himself to the King's return, was conversing with a group of gentlemen, his head with its black steeple hat bobbing as he showed interest in a consignment of printed calico from India.

Trembling with excitement and eager to welcome the King along with everyone else, aware that this day was too important to be missed, Arlette stood at an open window and looked down upon the parade. For this momentous occasion she had donned her finest buttercup-yellow gown with a tight, pointed bodice, round neckline trimmed with fine lace, full elbow-length sleeves also trimmed with lace, and a sweeping skirt. She wore her honey-gold hair loose with pretty clips at the sides to hold it from her face and secure the sprigs of May blossom she had picked earlier.

Her heart was throbbing a heavy beat when the King, preceded by heralds blowing long slender trumpets, came into view. He was flanked by his two brothers. All three were attired in silver doublets. They were followed by the Lord Mayor and the Aldermen of the City adorned in scarlet gowns and gold chains. Then came the King's loyal cavaliers. Not for these gentlemen who rode into London along roads strewn with sweet-smelling flowers and herbs the drab garb of the Puritans. These handsome gentlemen who came with the King presented a vibrant, colourful spectacle: scarlets and gold braid, bright blue and green doublets, flowing locks and flamboyant cavalier hats with an array of dancing plumes and cascading lace at their throats and wrists.

They laughed and waved atop prancing horses, catching flowers that were thrown from happy children and besotted maids in low-cut gowns lining the route, pressing forward the better to see. Yet in the eyes of these cavaliers there was a hunger, a world weariness, a resolve never to be poor again. Ten years they had waited for this, ten years in exile in a foreign country, where to relieve the boredom many had turned to debauchery—a legacy they brought with them on this day of Charles Stuart's restoration.

Along with everyone else Arlette laughed and waved as the parade, which seemed never ending, passed by. She scanned every face, wishing with all her heart that her brother Thomas was here to share this time and not in bondage on Barbados. Her gaze was drawn to one gentleman in particular: a gentleman whose face was partly shielded by the brim of his wide hat. He smiled broadly, his teeth dazzling in a face so handsome she couldn't resist taking a flower from Anne and tossing it in his direction. He laughed, catching it in his gloved hands, looking up to see who had tossed it, inclining his head in the briefest of bows.

At just turned twenty-two, Arlette had the beautiful, fine bone structure as her mother, the mother she could not remember, and the admiration in this cavalier's eyes as they passed over her made her catch her breath. All her senses came alive. They stared at one another across the distance and the rapport, the communication between them was tangible. Suddenly a familiarity sprang between them, shooting from one to the other like a spark of lightning. That was the moment Arlette recognised her cavalier of old, the man who had brought her to safety before leaving for France. It was William Latham—out of sight for nine years, but forever in her thoughts. She told herself that she had clung to him as she would any protector or friend, that he had been her means of getting to London and Hester, but her heart had broken in two when he had left her. Even after all this time her memory of him and that short time they had been together had not dimmed. And now he was here. He had come back.

She saw his eyes widen as a slow realisation of who she really was made its way from memory. Pushed along by those coming up behind him he was soon past the house, but not yet out of sight. He looked back at her, craning his neck when others blocked his sight. Unable to stop herself, Arlette turned and ran down the stairs and into the wide hall, which gleamed like a mirror and smelled of lemon polish. Hester was walking by carrying a tray of food in preparation for the celebrations later. On this occasion Arlette took no notice of her when she told her not to leave the house. She had an urgent need which took her on to the street.

Pushing her way through the throng, she didn't stop until she was close to William. Hampered in every direction, he managed to steer his horse towards her. Not until he was close did he dismount, careful not to let go of the reins lest his horse got carried away. Suddenly a muscular youth in snug breeches and coarse linen shirt reeled towards her. He had broad, peasant features and untidy brown hair, and Arlette didn't like what she saw in those bloodshot eyes. His wide lips curled into a leering grin as he lurched in front of her and dragged her into a shop doorway.

'What's a lovely girl like you doin' out on her own? Lookin' for company, love?'

'Let go of me,' she demanded coldly, trying to

pull away from him as his heavy body weaved in front of her. 'You're drunk.'

'The whole of London's drunk today. Come now, have a drink with me—and afterwards, well, we'll see.'

'You're disgusting. Let me pass.'

'Not so fast, little lady,' he growled as she tried to push past him.

'I believe you're bothering the lady,' a dry voice said.

It came from behind Arlette. A strong hand grasped her arm and pulled her away. William Latham stood between her and her assailant, tall and absolutely nonchalant. The youth flushed, glaring at the intruder. William Latham stood in a lazy slouch, his arms by his sides. There was nothing intimidating in his manner, but the youth hesitated just the same, clearly uneasy.

'This is none of your affair,' he grumbled belligerently.

'I'm making it my affair,' William drawled. 'Now on your way before I make you regret bothering the young lady.'

His voice was lethargic, totally devoid of menace, yet the youth turned pale. Stumbling back a step and almost falling, he muttered something unintelligible and then turned and went on his way as fast as his wobbly legs would allow, disappearing into the crowd.

'Thank you,' Arlette uttered. 'He was drunk.'

'And I appeared just in time.'

'I'm happy to see you have survived the troubles,' she breathed, her eyes shining with happiness as they looked into his.

He caught hold of her arm and drew her into the recess of the shop doorway. At the same moment their gazes met and Arlette's heart gave an unexpected flutter. She couldn't believe he was here. William did not move. His repressed admiration was almost tangible in his stillness. His eyes burned into hers. His hand holding her arm seemed to pulsate with life, sending shock waves through Arlette. Her lips parted and she moistened her lower lip with the tip of her tongue.

An inexplicable, lazy smile swept over his face as he looked at her and held out his hand. *'Enchanté, mademoiselle,'* he said quietly.

Arlette had the impression that he actually liked what he saw. Automatically she gave him her hand, thinking he would simply take it in his, but he covered it with both of his and kept it. His eyes were warm with admiration as they looked straight into hers.

'Arlette! I cannot believe it is you—here.'

Raising her hand, he pressed his lips to her fingers.

She slanted him a smile. 'Do you make a habit of kissing the hand of every lady you meet?'

William laughed. 'The devil I don't. Only those I like.'

'I did not think you would recognise me.'

'You have grown up and you are right. I hardly recognised you. What are you doing here?'

They smiled at each other and happiness rose in Arlette's chest. 'Don't look so surprised. You did bring me to London so where else would I be?'

'Back at Mayfield Hall.'

She shook her head, her eyes clouding with sadness. 'No. Father died soon after we left and as far as we know, Thomas is still on Barbados—at least that is what we think. Nothing has been heard of him since he was taken prisoner. I am anxious about him. I hate to think some ill has befallen him.'

William frowned. 'I understand your concern. I, too, expected some news of him before now.'

'The house and estate have been confiscated. Hopefully things will change now the monarchy has been restored.'

'Every Royalist has the same hopes.' He

fell silent, looking at her as if he could not get enough of her. 'You look well, Arlette, so grown up and *élégante*. Life and London obviously agrees with you.'

'I'm glad you think so and I like London very well,' she admitted awkwardly, withdrawing her hand, annoyed with her attack of nervousness. 'Although when I came here I found it all so confusing at first.'

'And you became settled with your sister and her husband.'

'Yes, but I missed my father and my home terribly.'

'And have they prospered under the yoke of Cromwell?'

'There were times when things were difficult. When war broke out Richard turned a healthy profit in the wool trade—all those woollen uniforms—but after Worcester everything changed, for everyone, not just Richard. In the beginning I found it strange living in such a strict household—although now I don't hold a candle for either party as long as there is some form of normality and no more wars. Whatever Richard's true feelings his business and his home have survived intact and unmolested, although money is in short supply at present.' Her lips twisted with irony. 'My brother-in-law has double standards. He trims his cloth to the wind. After the death of Cromwell and thinking the King might be restored, he has become more tolerant in his dealings. Parliament man he may be, but he will not be averse to selling silks and velvets to Royalists in the name of business.'

'A wise man knows where his allegiances lie in times like these.'

'That may be so, but Richard is still of the opinion that all pleasures such as music and dancing are the work of the devil.'

'Let us hope that now the King has come home we will see better times.'

His voice was gentle. It was smooth and deep and wrapped itself winningly around his words and his powerful charm and manner radiated a rapier-sharp intelligence. Arlette was mesmerised. Lithe, tall and extremely handsome, she had no doubt there were plenty of ladies who would find him attractive. There was a vigorous purposefulness about him that bespoke impatience and an active life. With his lively eyes and quick smile, his face demanded attention and respect. The young William Latham she had once known with the boyish good looks had become a man. He presented a dazzling figure, yet there were harsh lines on his face and a tension in his manner that suggested some kind of struggle unrelieved by his return to England. His gaze scanned her face and swept down her body. Self-consciously she ran her hands down her skirts and tried to restore her wayward golden hair to some order. Confused and strangely vulnerable, she averted her eyes.

'I'm afraid you've caught me at a disadvantage. I'm not normally so dishevelled.'

He glanced down at his own clothes, travel-stained and creased from being so long on the road. 'And neither am I. Having been on the road since early morning, I am somewhat discomposed myself.'

'Is this the first time you have been back to England since you went to France?'

'It is. Nine long years—it seems like a lifetime. I wasn't alone. It wasn't what any of us would have chosen—we had no choice.'

'And what did you do for nine years, William? Did you spend all your time in Paris, enjoying all the gaieties that city has to offer?'

He laughed. 'No, far from it. When I arrived there it didn't take long before boredom set in. Along with many others who were not prepared to see out their exile in idleness, I went to the

Low Countries with the King, who founded a regiment of guards under the command of his brother, the Duke of York. We went into service under the Spanish flag.'

'So your fighting did not cease when you left England,' she said, curious to know more about those missing years in William's life and wondering what he had got up to when he left for France. She had the feeling that the adventure he had embarked upon was not all he hoped it would be.

'No. The regiment saw much service and too many deaths. Too many. It's not always easy to be a soldier and a survivor. I may still be alive, but I have lost all that is important to me. My mother passed away and my sister married a Frenchman.'

'I'm so sorry, William. That must have been difficult for you.'

He nodded, his expression sombre. 'It's a hollow victory over death—but I am grateful to be alive. I'm home now—one of the lucky ones.'

He fell silent, seeming to lose himself in his thoughts.

'William?' She touched his arm. It was the merest touch, but she might as well have branded him with a hot iron.

He forced himself back to the present and turned his gaze on her. 'Like every other Royalist who has been plotting towards this end, there are many things that need to be done. I'm tired of wandering. My years of fighting and adventure are over, but I never had any doubt in my mind about the justice of the King's cause. It is time to stop dwelling in the past and concentrate on the present and the future. From this day I intend to live out the rest of my life in England and never again pick up my sword in anger.'

'You will find much has changed.'

'I don't doubt it—although things could not have turned out better. It is fortunate that the King has come back to where he belongs. Are you enjoying the celebrations?'

'Yes. We are staying with Richard's sister overnight.'

'And Hester? She is well?'

'Yes, she is. Speaking of Hester, I should be getting back. She will miss me and scold me most severely because I left the house.'

'Of course. Come, I'll escort you.'

Curling his right arm around her shoulders, he casually guided her towards the house. Taking her hand, he raised it to his lips.

'I shall be in London for a while, Arlette. I'll

call on you later and I would like to pay my respects to Hester and her husband. I did not meet Richard when I brought you, which is probably as well. As a malignant he might very well have had me arrested.'

'I'd like to think not. You did my father a great service and I know Hester was most grateful.' She smiled up at him. 'Goodbye, William. If you are able, you would be welcome at the celebrations later.'

Standing in the doorway for one last glimpse of him, she noted that he moved with a casual grace and an air of authority that she had not encountered in anyone before. Deliriously happy, she almost skipped into the house.

Chapter Two

Taking his leave of her and mounted once more, William forced his way back into the parade. He was troubled. Thinking of Arlette, the young girl he had kept in his heart for so many years, he could not help but wonder why it was that she so easily aroused his desire, for when he had looked at her he had been instantly drawn to her.

In one quick glance he had seen the change nine years had made. She had a fine bone structure and a few freckles sprinkled her nose. He had seen classic beauty rather than sex appeal and there was a slight dimple in her chin below the curve of her rose-tinted lips. Her eyes were the colour of a tropical sea, he thought—blue-green speckled with amber. Had she been any other wench who had thrown him a rose and then come after him, he would have been tempted to draw her into his arms and kiss the full, soft mouth. But she wasn't any other wench. She was Arlette, no longer the girl he remembered, but a full-grown, beautiful woman.

It was dark when William was able to get away from Whitehall and find his way to the Willoughby house. Revellers were everywhere, spilling out of the taverns into the street, some of them collapsing in a happy, abandoned heap.

From his vantage point on the raised terrace in the courtyard at the back of Willoughby House, William idly watched the celebrations without consciously admitting to himself that he was watching specifically for Arlette to appear— and then, as if he was seeing a dream, there she was. Attired in the same yellow gown as earlier that clung to her small breasts and miniscule waist and complemented her complexion, her stance was one of quiet regal poise. Her wealth of glorious bright gold hair, gently curling, was drawn off her face and hung down her back. Everyone paused in their conversations and glanced her way. Her smile was dazzling and she seemed to bestow it on every one of those present—and did he imagine it, or did everyone resume talking with more animation than before?

His whole sum and substance was concen-

trated on her. She had an individuality that had
nothing to do with her beauty. It took William's
breath away. With her creamy white complexion she was utterly feminine. She moved with a
fluency and elegance that drew the eye. There
was an intriguing, indefinable presence about
her that made her stand out, even in the moving
kaleidoscope of colour and animated voices. It
was as if everyone and everything was in motion except Arlette. But he detected a restless-
ness about her. She looked about her with a keen
interest, her glance filled with anticipation and
bright expectance.

And then, as if she sensed his gaze on her,
her head came up and she saw him and smiled
the widest smile that warmed and lit up her features. Holding her gaze, he headed slowly but
purposefully towards her.

'William! I am most surprised to see you
here.'

'Do you mind?'

'Oh, no. I'm glad you came. The whole of
London is celebrating tonight. But come with
me. I know Hester will be most happy to see
you. I told her I had seen you in the parade—I
did not tell her I had spoken to you—but I told

her you recognised me and waved, which will explain your arrival here tonight.'

Hester was happy to see William and relieved to know he had survived his exile in France. When Anne Willoughby asked Arlette to accompany her to the kitchen to fetch more refreshments as the guests continued to pour in, she left William talking to Hester and Richard. She was kept busy for quite some time and when she returned to William's side he asked her to walk with him awhile in the garden.

She looked at him for a moment and indecision flashed across her face. Considering the propriety of taking a stroll in the garden with him, she glanced at Hester, but her sister was engaged in conversation and did not look her way. The indecision on her face turned to resolution and she smiled at William. 'If you have the time, I would be happy to.'

'I have no great desire to return to Whitehall just yet.'

They left the revellers behind and stepped on to a pathway that wound around the flowerbeds, the scent of roses and honeysuckle competing with the smell of roast meats wafting from the kitchen.

'I think this has been the best day of my life,'

Arlette told him, her eyes alight with happiness. 'I don't want it to end. Ever since you left for the Continent I have thought of you, remembering how we travelled together from Mayfield and wondering if I would ever see you again. And now here you are.'

Arlette didn't know how explicit her expression was—like an open book, exposing what was in her heart. William saw it and was immediately wary, and in that moment he realised that eliminating her from his life now he had become reacquainted with her was going to be harder than he could possibly have imagined.

Having walked as far as they could go, William guided her to a wooden bench against a high stone wall and indicated that they should sit.

'But not for long, Arlette,' he replied in answer to her remark. 'Very soon I shall head for Warwickshire—once the Puritan who took up residence at Arlington Court has been evacuated.'

'Will you be able to do that—turn him out?'

He nodded. 'The man was a regicide. His position is threatened now the King has returned. He may not have signed the notorious death warrant for the execution of Charles I, but it is widely known that he actively supported it. He will be lucky to escape with his neck intact. The King has agreed to pardon all those of conscience who appeal for his grace and favour—a generous action in my opinion. However, it does not extend to those who murdered his father—the forty-one men who put their name to that infamous death warrant. It is almost certain that all Royalist properties gained by the regicides and others who supported Cromwell will be rescinded.'

'Including Arlington Court?'

He nodded. 'Arlington Court means a great deal to me. The estate was bestowed upon one of my ancestors by the Crown for his acts of heroism and loyalty. Since my father died and the title and estate passed to me, it is my intention to see that this proud heritage is maintained in a manner that represents the grandeur my ancestor earned. I imagine my return will come as something of a shock.' He smiled down at her. 'But you need not worry about such things.'

'But I do—all the time. More so now the monarchy is restored. I pray Thomas will come home. I cannot bear to think of what he is having to endure on that island, and if—when—I have to think positively, you see—he comes home, I would like to think he has one to come home to. As a consequence of my father's actions and his failure to pay the huge fines levied against him, Mayfield Hall was sequestered. Will it be possible for me or Hester to put forward a petition?'

'You told me you've heard nothing at all from him.'

'No, nothing,' she said softly, shaking her head dejectedly.

'From what I understand, the prisoners' term of indenture on Barbados is for seven years.'

'Then why has he not come home?' Her eyes, big and dark in her face, filled with tears. Her brother's situation seemed so much worse now that England was at peace and everyone was celebrating the return of the King.

'I have no idea. I believe when a prisoner's term of indenture is over they are free to work for themselves or another employer. Those who wish to return to England will have to earn enough to pay for their passage. It is possible that when Thomas was released he decided to stay there.'

'But if so, then surely he would have written. Unless—unless he didn't survive. He's occupied my thoughts so much over the years and I have wondered what has happened to him. I know he will have been put to work on a plantation; that he might have been sold like a slave and forced to perform hard labour on the sugar plantations and treated cruelly. But no matter what has happened to him, I would still like to petition to have Mayfield Hall returned to my family. I think about the tenants and the servants a great deal: the old, the sick and the children who have served my family faithfully for generations, people who were dependent on us. How have they fared, I wonder? It concerns me greatly.'

'That I can understand. I remember the pain you suffered when you left.'

'I was fortunate to have stayed at Mayfield for as long as I did. It was a dark day for me the day I left. I felt the darkness of despair and the fear and the knowledge that I would not see my father again. The fear I felt was for the future, not knowing what was to happen. The real reason Father didn't send me to Hester sooner was because Richard sided with Parliament. We lost contact with Hester during the latter part of the wars. I was so tired of it all and the estrangement.'

'The wars are over, Arlette. The gaps are closing.'

'And you are here. I still cannot believe it.

In the brief time we were together I felt as if my spirit was alive…as if I had drunk sparkling wine—not that I knew what sparkling wine was like, but I tried to imagine it—and the bubbles were effervescing and bursting inside me. And then you weren't there any more and I felt quite desperate.'

'You had Hester.'

She dropped her gaze. 'Hester wasn't you.'

Looking at the young woman sitting beside him, at her bowed head and the dejected droop of her shoulders, something of her anguish and despair penetrated William's mind. Taking her hand he held it tight for a moment, breathing in the faint sweet scent of her, of roses and jasmine, he thought, and rosemary—for remembrance, remembrance of their time together as they had journeyed to London, when the countryside had been crawling with Roundheads searching out fugitives from Worcester. The memories stirred emotions he had long since thought buried.

Holding his hand, Arlette raised it to her cheek and held it there, her eyes brimming with tears. She had to admit to a stirring of emotions she had never experienced—the tremor in the pit of her stomach when he was near, the warming in her heart when he smiled at her—the desolation that he would leave her. She looked at him as if she could not get enough of the sight of him. They were two people, complicit and close, caught in a fragile net of feelings neither of them could comprehend, but each aware that after all the years they had been apart, when they were once again united and with the testimony of yesterday, the memory of that tragic time was etched on their hearts and minds.

William was immediately riveted upon her tip-tilted eyes and the full pink lips. She touched the corner of her mouth with the point of her tongue, which was pink and moist, wetting her bottom lip, and she smiled a little, as if at some secret thought. William stroked her cheek slowly, wiping away a tear that spilled from her eye with a tenderness that gave Arlette goose bumps and made her insides tremble like leaves on a tree caught in a summer breeze.

He slid slowly closer to her, his voice soft and his breath warm as he whispered her name. And then he opened his hand over the contour of her cheek and touched her lower lip with his thumb and caressed it smoothly, slowly. She did not move away—a mixture of terror and pleasure prevented her from doing so. He placed his finger beneath her chin and raised her face to his, resisting the temptation to tenderly cover her mouth with his own.

A shiver ran up Arlette's spine at the feel of his fingers on her cheek. She basked in his closeness and found she couldn't move—she had neither the desire nor the strength to do so. Her heart thumped so wildly in her breast that she could hardly breathe. His eyes were both gentle and compelling. The world around her seemed to vanish, leaving her locked in a circle of unreality. Her heart swelled with an emotion of such proportions she was overwhelmed. It was as if she were being sucked down into a pool of deep, dark, swirling water, a turbulence of longing—a longing she had never known before, but which this man could provide.

Recollecting himself, William pulled away. They continued to look at each other with startled eyes, a look that lasted no more than a moment and yet seemed to last an eternity. This strange turn of events was more than either of them had expected for, no matter how attracted William was by her, he had no intention of becoming involved with her for reasons she knew nothing about. He stared at her lovely face, framed by her golden hair flowing down her spine. He noticed how her firm breasts strained beneath the bodice of her gown, how her moist lips trembled as she tilted her head slightly to look at him.

'My apologies. I forgot my manners. I was quite mesmerised by you for a moment,' William murmured.

She smiled softly, raising her eyes to his. 'Don't apologise. I don't mind—I care for you, William, and I like it when you touch me—although I shudder to think what Hester would have to say about me sitting on a garden bench in such close proximity to you.'

'She'd probably thrash me to within an inch of my life,' he said, his lips breaking into an impudent smile in an attempt to lighten her comment. 'I'm sorry, Arlette. I got quite carried away—but seeing you here, I am unable to believe my good fortune that I have found you again, that I am here at all.'

'And not still in France or The Hague, where King Charles had his Court,' she whispered.

'Exactly.'

'I once told you that your life was precious to me. Do you remember?'

He nodded. 'I do. It was when I was about to leave for France.'

'It is still. You are still precious to me, William.'

William laughed softly in an attempt to lighten the moment, to dispel the seriousness from her eyes. 'And you have turned into a very beautiful young woman. I'm afraid if I don't watch my step I am in danger of letting my emotions get the better of me.'

Suddenly the darkness of the night was illuminated by a fabulous firework display, which lit up the night sky in a fantastic array of colour. Cries of awe and excitement and laughter from those watching the display destroyed the magic of the moment like someone bursting a bubble. The clarity of her thoughts now recovered, Arlette looked around, as though awaking from a dream.

'I'd quite forgotten about the fireworks. What happened to Hector, by the way? Did you take him to France?'

'I did and he served me well, until a couple of years ago when he died of old age.'

'Poor Hector. I'm glad he was with you at the end. We were speaking of the petitions being presented to the King by returning Royalists. I would like to know more about that.'

Resisting the urge to take her in his arms and bury his face in her glorious wealth of hair, William drew back a little. He must not, he told himself. A moment ago, in a moment of weakness, he had almost given in to the desire to kiss her. To do so would bind him to her in ways he would find hard to break and this he must not do, not when he was bound to someone else. But as he looked at her lovely face his thoughts were anything but honourable and he prayed he could be forgiven any impure thoughts that crossed his mind. She really did have the deepest, loveliest blue-green eyes he had ever seen and her lashes were long and dark and swept her cheeks when she lowered her eyes with a fresh naivety, which he knew stemmed from innocence. His eye was drawn to the faint shadow beneath her jaw line and the tendril of silken hair in her nape. He imagined the tiny curl around his finger, his hands at the back of her neck, just where the heavy mass of her hair lay above the lace of her gown.

Forcing himself to concentrate on her question, he said, 'Every Royalist in England wants something back, be it land, property or money. Some Royalists who are not impoverished and had their property confiscated have bought it back. Others whose properties were sold may not be so fortunate. After the enormous fines exacted on Royalists after our defeat at Naseby, many of them were forced to sell off land to pay them. As if that were not enough, the house and the rest of the land were confiscated. It is hopefully expected that everything claimed by whoever claimed jurisdiction in London will be returned to its rightful owner. Earlier you told me that Mayfield Hall has been confiscated.'

'Yes, at least that is what we understand. We had a letter from Blanche recently and she told us a man and his wife were living there. The lady of the house died a year ago and her husband lives there alone. He is not in the best of health and not expected to live long.'

'Then you may be fortunate if you petition to have the estate returned to you. But it is early days yet. Whitehall is filled to capacity with Royalists and their families wanting something from the King. But all that is for another day.'

'Will he be a good king?'

'Time will tell, but I believe so. Hester told me of your impending betrothal to Sir Ralph Crompton. He's a lucky man—no doubt he has your head in a spin.'

His words penetrated the fog of Arlette's senses, bringing her back from the languorous narcosis into which the magical evening, the moon and the stars and his presence had sent her. She felt as if something were shattering inside her; a raw, illogical panic slithered into her. She had not wanted to think of Sir Ralph Crompton. It spoiled the moment.

She stepped back, horrified that Hester had confided this to William. 'It's clear you have never met Sir Ralph.'

'No, I am not acquainted with him.'

'Clearly.' Her eyes flashed rebelliously. 'I feel no joy in being betrothed to him. He's an old man—fifty and a widower with two young daughters. Father would never have given his permission for me to marry a Puritan—a man who pledged himself to Cromwell and the Commonwealth.'

'Why not? Hester married one.'

'Richard did not declare his allegiance to Parliament until after their marriage, otherwise Father would not have allowed it, even though Hester would have no other. Richard hadn't been of any persuasion then, until he met Sir Ralph. Impressed and influenced by Sir Ralph, he soon fell under his spell.'

'And you have no wish to marry Sir Ralph. I hear it in your voice and see it in your eyes. Your life is not yours to order, is it, Arlette?'

'What woman's life is? I have lived in Richard's house since you brought me to London and the price I have to pay is obedience. An alliance between Sir Ralph and me would be advantageous to Richard—they are both in the same trade and Sir Ralph is important and powerful in the guild. Marriage to Sir Ralph is a way in which Sir Ralph would honour Richard with such an important connection—I often get the feeling that Sir Ralph has some kind of hold over him, although what it can be I have no idea. I am duty-bound to show my gratitude for all Hester and Richard have done for me since I came to live with them. Indeed, if I don't marry him, Richard has told me the consequences are too dire to contemplate.'

William was uneasy by her reply. If what she said was true and Sir Ralph Crompton was indeed an old man—as old as Methuselah to a young woman—then he couldn't blame her for having an aversion to the match. He was badly affected by this lovely young woman who had commanded all his attention from the moment he had seen her when he had ridden up the Strand. Strangely, the thought of Arlette with another man—in his arms, kissing him, lying with him, young or old—disgusted him. Looking at her afresh, he could not help feeling that such perfect beauty would be sadly wasted on an old man.

'So am I to understand that you would prefer it to be an affair of the heart when you marry?' he asked, with a teasing twinkle in his eyes.

'A love match. That's what I really want, nothing less,' she replied, meeting his eyes steadily.

William cocked an eyebrow with wry amusement and mastered a faint smile. 'Love! My dear Arlette, people rarely marry for love.'

'Oh, but you are wrong,' she enthused, her eyes sparkling with animation. 'I know many who have.'

'Then you must make your feelings clear to Richard. He may not be in accord with our beliefs, but he appears to be a reasonable man. I doubt he would force you into such a marriage.'

'He will try, no matter how hard I protest my aversion to Sir Ralph. He considers me problematical and cannot wait to get me off his hands. But it goes against the grain marrying a Parliamentarian.'

'You cannot hold that against him, Arlette. Many families were divided during the war years. For those who had faith, believing that the things they fought for were right, then they deserve our respect. They were our enemies—but honourable enemies.' He got to his feet. 'I must take my leave of you, I'm afraid. I've arranged to meet up with some gentlemen at Whitehall later. I expect the celebrations will continue throughout the night.'

'Yes, I expect they will,' she replied, disappointed that he had to go.

Arlette accompanied him to the door where they paused, stepping aside as people went in and out.

'Will you advise me about what to do to forward a petition to have Mayfield Hall returned? I really would appreciate some advice.'

'Now the King is restored the injustices will be redressed. Those who remained loyal will not find him ungrateful. He does not forget his friends, but you must give it some time, time for him to settle into a routine.'

'Of course. I understand. I'm sorry, William. I apologise. I should not ask you. You have your own troubles. What must you think of me?'

What did he think of her? He didn't know. All he knew was that he wanted to hold her and go on holding her, but it was sheer madness and dishonourable to one other to harbour such thoughts. He shook his head and lowered his gaze, knowing he would be unable to look into those blue-green eyes for much longer without beginning to lose all reason.

'I'll do what I can, Arlette. Maybe you should go and see your father's lawyer—or perhaps Hester, being the eldest. Let him sort it out.'

'Thank you. I'll talk to Hester. Goodnight, William. You will come again?'

He turned and looked at her, seeing the appeal in her eyes. 'Yes, yes, I will.'

Returning to Whitehall, William realised that if he wasn't careful his feelings for Arlette would be in danger of running out of control. He had been totally unprepared for her—how she would look now she had grown into a woman—how she would affect him. He should never have let her come so close. But, no, he thought, that wasn't how it was. He should never have let *himself* come so close. The night and the scent of the flowers and her very nearness had quickened his blood in a way he had not felt for a long time.

He couldn't let her waste one moment of her precious life thinking of him. In her innocence and naivety she had told him that she cared for him. He had done well, not letting her know how much he had come to care for her, too. But it was hard, no matter how he tried, to still his emotional rebellion against the rational reason of his mind. He had not spoken of his future bride and deep down he had not wanted to. But he knew he would have to sometime and he would do so with a great deal of apprehension and misgivings. He had told Arlette he would see her again. He would, he decided, before he left for Warwickshire.

Arlette was about to return to the celebrations when a man emerged from the parlour. Her heart sank when she saw Sir Ralph Crompton.

With the death of King Charles I, back in forty-nine, Sir Ralph had hoped the Stuarts would have been swept away into oblivion. But now his son was here, bringing with him the evil seeds of lechery and decadence that had flourished at his Court in France and Bruges. Suddenly there was too much laughter, too many people feverishly intent on enjoying themselves—no matter what the cost to their immortal souls. Mistress Dryden troubled him. He had seen her converse with Lord William Latham and he had noticed something in her attitude, something coy, almost flirtatious and frivolous. It had caused him deep displeasure.

Arlette found her crawling dislike of Sir Ralph difficult to conceal. Bobbing a small curtsy, she faced him, having made up her mind to be calm and reasonable on meeting him. He knew her to be a high-spirited girl—better if she had been more docile. Looking at her with a critical eye, he bowed stiffly, as though his joints needed oiling.

'Ah, Mistress Dryden. You are not leaving, I hope,' he said in clipped tones.

Stern and unsmiling, he studied her so intently that she felt embarrassed under his gaze. How ugly he is, she thought. How old. Slight of build and thin, with narrow shoulders and thin legs, she hated the thought of being his wife. He was wearing his usual severe black, but he had loosened his white stock. His luxurious periwig made his face look small—it reminded her of a weasel—and his eyes were grey and as cold and hard as steel. She looked at his tightly compressed lips and those eyes of his, which had always seemed to her to be able to see right through her. Could he read her mind now? she wondered.

'No, Sir Ralph,' she replied. 'We are staying with Anne and her family for the night.'

'I know. That is why I am here. Richard invited me to the celebrations. It is you I have come to see. I thought it opportune for us to become better acquainted.'

Arlette was tempted to comment that after spending the past two decades opposing first King Charles I and then his son when the likes of him had executed the first, she found it odd that he would wish to partake in the celebrations of the return of the monarchy, but thought it best not to. In Sir Ralph's opinion a woman should be servile, modest and obedient, and only speak to those superior to her when invited to do so. She thought it prudent to keep her comment to herself.

His pale eyes surveyed her, narrowing as they took in her gown and her bright uncovered head before settling on her cleavage between her creamy breasts. A vein began to throb in his temple.

'You should practice more decorum,' he said harshly. 'Your appearance is unseemly, your behaviour with Lord Latham wanton.'

Bright, angry colour stained Arlette's cheeks. 'My dress is no more indecent than any other woman's present, Sir Ralph, and you read too much into my encounter with Lord Latham.'

'William Latham and his like will rue the day they returned to England,' Sir Ralph sneered.

'His like? What do you mean by that, Sir Ralph?'

'He's a King's man—do not forget that Charles Stuart's father was executed for the tyrant he was.'

'None the less, his son is the King who it is hoped will turn England back into a place of happiness and contentment, a place of peace.'

The look Sir Ralph gave her was hard. 'You are far too outspoken, Mistress Dryden. I hope the obedience of your attitude is not a guise to deceive me.'

'I am not sinful. I have done no harm.'

'I see so little of you. I might think that you deliberately avoid me. Have I offended you in some way?'

'No,' she lied, anxious to be gone, hating the way his eyes devoured her, lingering too long on the swell of her breasts beneath the fabric of her dress, seeming to take salacious pleasure in what he saw despite his earlier rebuke. 'Hester keeps me busy for most of the time.'

'Not all the time, surely. You have the time to spend with James Sefton by all accounts.'

The reproach in his voice was evident. 'James is a friend. He makes me laugh. We are neighbours and of an age and he is fun to be with.'

'And I am not.'

'I did not say that, although I know you to be more than twice his age.'

'True, but let me give you a bit of wisdom. There is more to a man than a handsome face or pair of broad shoulders. Think about it. You know that I have always been fond of you. I find it such a delight to talk to you.'

'You are easily content, Sir Ralph.'

'Richard always speaks highly of you—of your intelligence, Mistress Dryden. You are aware of my intentions and that Richard has given permission for a betrothal between us.'

'I know that.'

'Then you might sound more enthusiastic about it. It is my wish that we be married before the autumn, so our betrothal will be soon? When you are my wife I shall be favoured twice.'

'How so?'

'A beautiful and a clever wife. I would be the happiest of men. What more could any man ask?'

'What more indeed?' Arlette murmured quietly.

'I was drawn to you the first time I saw you and blind to all other women,' he said, his voice low, as if unable to conceal the passion Arlette never failed to rouse in him. 'I will visit Richard at his house to discuss the details of the betrothal.' His eyes narrowed as he noted the flash of defiance that flared in Arlette's eyes, which vanished almost as soon as it was there. 'You do want to marry me, don't you, Arlette?'

'I thank you for your offer—it is most generous, Sir Ralph,' she replied, preferring to prevaricate than tell him what she really felt. 'Please excuse me.'

She stepped away from him. Her heart was pounding. She was not afraid of this man, but she did wonder if she should be. He was a friend of Richard's and one of whom he thought highly, yet she experienced a revulsion whenever she was in his presence. She turned to go, but he caught her arm, his thin fingers closing around it like a vice.

'A moment, Mistress Dryden. I am curious as to what you are thinking? Is it of young Sefton, perhaps?'

Turning to face him once more, she could see a darkness in his eyes. His thin lips were clamped tightly together and he had two red spots high up on his cheekbones. She knew this was anger and it was all being directed at her. His eyes were cold, like wet stones. She wasn't scared of him, but she was scared of what he would do to Richard and Hester if she refused his offer of marriage.

She withdrew her arm and said calmly, 'No, of course not. I told you. James is a friend—nothing more than that. I believe his heart belongs elsewhere. You must forgive me, but I am reluctant for the betrothal to take place just yet. Richard has only recently made me aware of your interest and I would be grateful for a little time to become accustomed to the idea. When I feel the time is right, I will give you my answer.' Her eyes unrepentant, she did not drop her gaze when he moved closer to her and his mouth curled up in a cruel parody of a smile. It was an odd sensation, Arlette thought, to feel intimidation by a slight person, but it had nothing to do with his physicality and everything to do with the waves of malice emanating from every pore of his skin. 'Now please excuse me. I promised Anne I would assist with serving some of the food.'

Without another word and with her head held high, she walked away from him. She was shaken by her encounter with Sir Ralph. Having asked for a delay in the betrothal, which to her mind was like asking for a stay of execution, she sincerely hoped he would honour her wish.

The more she dallied, the more chance there was that he would become tired of waiting and turn his attention to someone else, but somehow she didn't think so.

Hester wasn't long in finding her and took her aside, clearly anxious.

'Sir Ralph has left. He is most displeased that you have requested a delay to the betrothal. You have to marry as circumstances demand, Arlette.' Sighing despondently, she shook her head and went on, 'Things have been difficult of late, which you must be aware of. The business has suffered very badly.'

Arlette knew this was true and that everything to do with their future prosperity depended on her. 'I'm sorry, Hester. I know what it means to you for me to marry Sir Ralph and I—I will. I only ask for a little time.'

'Make no mistake, Arlette, Sir Ralph is determined to make you his wife. When he arrived and saw you with William, the way you were together... Already he sees him as a rival.'

'That is absurd. William is a friend, someone who did my father a great service when he brought me to London at the risk to his own life. I cannot forget that.'

With a concerned frown puckering her brow, Hester remarked quietly, 'I know what your feelings are concerning Sir Ralph and I am not so heartless as not to consider your happiness. But do not let your head be turned by a handsome face, Arlette.'

Arlette's face burned. 'It would take more than that to turn my head, Hester. But if my conversation with William made me aware of anything, it is that it might not be impossible to have Mayfield Hall returned to us—to Thomas—should he come home. I intend to do all I can to that end, which is one of the reasons I asked for Sir Ralph to delay the betrothal.'

Hester stared at her. She had not expected this. 'Thomas—I—I had not thought it to be possible... Mayfield Hall has been taken... How can it be got back?'

'It has to be, Hester, for Thomas. Our brother. Can you not lend me your support at this time? I don't think I can do it on my own. You can't deny our brother his heritage.'

'But—after nine years! Is there anything worth inheriting?'

'How can you say that? If the Roundheads have sacked it down to the ground it is still Thomas's home—all that he has to come back to. It is up to us to secure it for him—we have a duty, Hester. I know someone else is living there, but they will have to hand it back to its rightful owner. What if he returns and goes directly to Mayfield, as he surely will, and finds strangers living there? Have you not thought of that?'

'Yes—yes, I have and, if that happens, he will come here. Leave him to deal with it, I implore you.'

'I can't, Hester. I can't do that.'

Hester could not bring herself to look at her, to see the anger in her young sister's eyes. 'Forgive me, Arlette. I did not mean to sound so negative. You are right. We have a responsibility to our brother, a duty to do what is right. There is no one else. I will speak to Richard before he leaves for the Midlands to buy cloth—and as for your betrothal, well, I can tell you now that he will not hear of a delay.'

Unfortunately, Richard was not of the same mind as Arlette and his wife. He had no time for the Court of Charles II, which in his opinion consisted of knaves and fools, shallow and frivolous and empty-headed. His time was taken up with his imminent journey to the Midlands and he had no time to put himself forward to petition for the Dryden estate in Oxfordshire. And regardless of Arlette's wish to have the betrothal set aside for now, he refused to comply and was impatient for it to take place as soon as he returned.

Two weeks had passed since Arlette had seen William and she had heard nothing since. She became restless and impatient and found that it only intensified her situation, increasing her determination to have Mayfield Hall returned to them. But to do this she needed Richard's cooperation, which was not forthcoming, and Hester would not go against her husband.

The answer to her problem came in the form of James Sefton when she was walking by the river. His sudden appearance took her by surprise.

'Why, James! Forgive me if I seemed startled, but you surprised me.'

'Then I apologise most sincerely. But why so downcast? Are you not happy now the King is home?'

'Yes, of course I am, only...' She sighed. 'I hear Royalists are petitioning the King to have their confiscated properties returned. As you know, my own family estate became forfeit and

I want it back. The problem is how to get it back. The person I need to speak to returned to England with King Charles and he is at Whitehall Palace. I can hardly go there alone.'

'Have you not discussed the matter with your brother-in-law?'

She nodded. 'Richard won't entertain the idea of going to Whitehall Palace. He says that if Thomas comes home he must do his own petitioning.'

'And that's not good enough for you, I can see.'

'No. I have to go to Whitehall Palace.'

'Well, if I can be of help I would be happy to. I go to the Palace early tomorrow morning. I will be happy to take you. My father is staying at Whitehall for the present and I have a message to deliver to him from my mother. I don't intend being there more than a couple of hours or so.'

Arlette looked at him with sudden interest—already the semblance of a plan was beginning to form in her mind. This was better than she dared hope for. At the prospect of going to Whitehall Palace and seeing William, her heart began to beat fast and she felt a great sense of excitement.

'Do you mean it? You will take me?'

'Of course. I wouldn't have offered otherwise. But what of your brother-in-law? How will you explain it to him?'

'I won't tell him. He left for the Midlands two days before so I will be back before he comes home.'

'And your sister? What will you tell her?'

'I don't know, but I'll think of something.'

'What you are intending is reckless in the extreme. You are to marry Sir Ralph Crompton. What will he say should he find out? Have you not thought of that?'

'I care little for my reputation, James—' *or Sir Ralph*, she was tempted to add, but considered it prudent not to '—and should Sir Ralph hear of it he will be angry, I know, but it is a small price to pay to get Mayfield Hall back.'

'Very well. I shall escort you to Whitehall Palace. We will go by boat. I will call for you at nine o'clock.'

'That suits me well, but don't come to the house. I'll meet you at the privy steps.'

The following morning Arlette rose early to prepare for her outing to Whitehall Palace. She forced herself to remain calm and prepared what she would wear carefully—although she had nothing nearly so grand as the gowns the ladies of the Court paraded in—and each of those movements, which she had done a thousand times in her life without giving them a thought, took on a whole new meaning. She had an objective and a goal. It was for William that she put on her best gown—a plain blue woollen befitting the sister-in-law of a Puritan. It was for him that she decided to leave her hair loose, for him that she fluffed out the flounces on her skirt and tightened the strings at her waist till she could hardly breathe. It was for him that she perfumed her flesh. For him that she preened in front of the mirror, wanting him to see her, wanting to see him, so that she could lose herself in his eyes.

Seated with James in the boat being rowed by one of his father's oarsmen, she was apprehensive yet excited as she travelled to Whitehall Palace. The Palace, which lay to the west of the walled city, the skyline peppered with innumerable church spires, was like a great adventure. Arlette always found the city both repelling and fascinating, its vitality springing from a variety of commerce and industry within its walls. It was violent, thriving and alive, colourful and noisy, and it stirred her deepest emotions. On the times when she came with Hester she never ceased to be enthralled by it all.

The old Whitehall Palace stretched along the riverfront from Whitehall to the mouth of the Fleet. A huge sprawling mass of red-brick buildings, it was the chief residence of the Court. It was a labyrinth of streets and alleyways, of apartments inhabited by noblemen and armies of their dependants. On the whole, the Palace was open to anyone who had been presented at Court or came with one who had, but strangers filtered in all the time and wandered about at will.

Alighting from the boat at Whitehall steps, James and Arlette entered through the Palace Gate—inside there was great bustle, and lackeys and footmen in a multitude of coloured liveries flitted about. With a wide-eyed Arlette by his side, who was unable to believe she was in the Palace of the King of England, James strode confidently forward and up some stairs which he told her was the Stone Gallery. It was a long corridor and considered to be the main thoroughfare of the Court where splendid paintings collected by Charles I were hung on the walls. Here lords and ladies paraded in all their finery. Arlette gazed about her with enchantment, for never before had her eyes beheld anything as splendid. The scene was colourful and exciting and to Arlette's youthful fancy it seemed that all this glittering display of King Charles's Court could bode nothing but well for the country.

Chapter Three

'**O**h, how splendid it all is,' Arlette breathed. 'I'm so glad I came.' She felt happy and carefree as she had not felt in a long time, and reckless—unwisely so, for it would be so easy to give way to recklessness with a man like William, if only she could find him among all these flamboyant courtiers.

James escorted her through the throng. Arlette was grateful for the way he tried to put her at her ease. She was eager and full of admiration for everything she saw, devouring everything, her eyes darting about so as not to miss a thing. She was like an exotic flower trying to pick her way through a weed-filled undergrowth, her eyes searching through a sea of unfamiliar faces for the one she knew. Groups of pretty ladies stood around, eager, laughing ladies with fluttering fans in satin and taffeta gowns which rustled as they arranged the folds.

She paused when a young woman, about nineteen years of age, hurried towards them. Her green silk gown fluttered behind her and her fair hair, caught into a gold filet, fell loose down her back. James, unable to conceal his delight, seemed to forget all about Arlette. His face lit up on seeing her—a vivacious, pretty girl. Excusing himself, he took her hand and drew her towards a screen. With a smile on her lovely face, the young woman did not object—in fact, she seemed to welcome James's attention and Arlette was quite shocked to see James plant a kiss on the girl's eager rosy lips. She found this romantic incident in this vibrant palace touching and, smiling softly, she waited for James to return to her.

'I presume that is the young lady who holds your affections,' she said when he finally appeared without the young lady. 'She is exceedingly pretty. I can see why you like her.'

'I love her, Arlette, I truly do. She really is quite delightful, don't you think? Sadly she is promised to another, but I live in hope that she will be mine one day.'

'I sincerely hope that she will be, James.'

The incident was forgotten when he drew her towards a group of boisterous young bucks across the room, who welcomed him into their midst. Laughter and frivolity surrounded Arlette and she found herself responding to it automatically. James lounged in a chair and proudly and noisily introduced Arlette as Mistress Arlette Dryden. 'This is her first venture to Whitehall,' he announced.

One of his associates laughed heartily. 'Then with such beauty, we must pray it will not be her last.'

They embraced her into their circle with impudent grins and subjected her to long, lingering looks. She laughed, warming to their natural charm and easy manner.

James caught her hand. 'We are going for a game of bowls. Come with us? You wanted to see Whitehall.'

'Absolutely not,' she said. 'It would be quite improper and commented upon,' she chided teasingly, amused and flattered by their offer. 'I have my reputation to uphold. I didn't come to Whitehall to play bowls, but to look for Lord Latham.'

She failed to notice the peculiar look James gave her. But then, refusing to take no for an answer, James raised his arm. Arlette gave a couple of quick little steps to avoid his hand as it reached out for her, but, catching her heel in the train of her skirt, she tripped and lost her balance, unable to prevent herself from falling in an undignified heap in James's lap, which resulted in a gale of good humour and high spirits.

He laughed out loud, his arm snaking round her waist. 'You really are quite incredible, Arlette, and not as light on your feet as you might think. Remind me never to accompany you in a dance. I value the comfort of my feet far too much.'

Arlette was suddenly aware of a tall male presence. Having seen what was happening, William had moved across the space that separated them with such speed and the silence of a panther that she had not seen him come. At a stroke the amusement fled from her face. Her mouth formed his name, but no sound came. For a moment she forgot her predicament and looked at him with loving eyes, her heart beating with the unbelievable joy and comfort of knowing she had found him. A world of feelings flashed across her face—surprise, disbelief, happiness—but only for an instant. William's face was glacial, his mouth drawn into a ruthless, forbidding line.

Thrown off her balance, Arlette continued to

stare at him. There was nothing of the softness that had marked his expression on their previous encounter. Even as she sought in vain for something to say that would be neither stupid nor inept, she was aware of his eyes scrutinising every detail of her appearance and she resented it, as if he were judging her.

Only for an instant had William's expression betrayed what he felt upon seeing Arlette, who was too busy toppling over to see his face quicken with admiration which shone fleetingly in his eyes.

He glared down at James. 'You, sir, forget yourself.' His voice was like steel. Tempted to commit murder, he restrained himself, the iron control his military training had taught him to employ coming to his aid as he looked with freezing contempt from one to the other.

Arlette sprang up from James's lap and he quickly followed, concerned by the threatening menace emanating from the formidable Lord Latham. James's friends seemed to melt into the shadows. Arlette was rendered speechless. But seeing the way he was looking at her, the whole of him vaguely disturbing, she was filled with shame and humiliation that he should find her in such embarrassing circumstances.

'I—I'm sorry,' James stuttered. 'It was not—I was not…'

'I tripped,' Arlette remarked, lifting her head and meeting William's gaze head on. 'That's all there was to it. At least James provided a soft landing and prevented me from being injured.'

William fixed his attention on young Sefton. 'What is your purpose for coming to Whitehall?'

'To see my father. His business at Whitehall has kept him away from home for three days. I have a message to give him from my mother.'

'I saw him not half an hour since. He was in the privy garden. If you go now, he may still be there. I'll take care of Mistress Dryden.'

James's eyes flicked uncertainly from the still-glowering Lord Latham to Arlette. 'Yes—I see—although I shall be returning home after I have seen my father if you wish to return home, Arlette. If I don't see you before, I'll be at the palace gate in an hour or thereabouts, I expect.'

'Thank you, James. I will bear that in mind. I am most grateful to you.'

James nodded nervously. 'I—I'll go now.' Without further ado, he fled.

Arlette shrank back beneath the look that William fastened on her and she was aware of the anger he must feel at finding her in such a compromising situation. He would never understand the situation, for she knew how her conduct must look.

'Now, Mistress Dryden, have the goodness to explain your presence here. You are not supposed to present yourself at Court.'

He was looking at her with open contempt. Arlette experienced a welcome stir of anger mingled with her fear. 'Then pardon me. Having lived almost half of my life in a Puritan household, I am not familiar with Court etiquette. And Mistress Dryden! Why, William, what is this? Why so formal? You have never called me anything other than Arlette. Are you not pleased to see me, *my lord*?'

His lips were a tight grim line as he regarded her. 'Should I be? I had not thought to see you here with Master Sefton.'

'You are acquainted with him?'

'I know his father. James and I have met on a couple of occasions. Take my advice and choose your friends with more care. Young Sefton is a rogue who, since the King's return, floats around the edges of the Court. He's a veritable rake.'

'An affable and charming rake,' said Arlette, with an infuriating, barely discernible quirk to her lips, which William could not fail but to see and goaded him to further anger.

'A rake just the same.'

'Which you know all about, do you, my lord?'

'Be that as it may, but I may not be around to save you the next time. Sefton should have known better and I curse the lad for his foolishness and thoughtless stupidity for bringing you to Whitehall. I will ask you once more. What are you doing here?'

Wide-eyed she looked at him. 'Why, not having heard from you I thought I would seek you out. It has been two weeks now and I was hoping you would consider petitioning the King on my behalf.'

'And your sister? As the elder of the two of you, why has she not put forward her desire to have your family estate returned to you?'

'Hester is as eager as I am, but unfortunately Richard is not of the same mind and she will not cross him,' Arlette said in a low, halting voice. 'He insists that we wait until Thomas comes home and he puts forward the petition himself.'

'There may be some sense in that.'

Arlette bit her lip and sighed. 'I know that. But there are still people in Mayfield I remember—loyal people I care about who relied on the estate for their work.'

'Arlette,' he said, speaking in gentler tones. 'You left Mayfield almost ten years ago. You were a child. Much has happened since then. The world has changed. Be it for better or worse we shall have to wait and see. I think your sister and her husband are right. Wait and see if Thomas comes home. Your father had a lawyer, didn't he?'

'Yes, in Oxford. I believe there is a sick old man living at Mayfield Hall who hasn't long for this world.'

'Then it may not be difficult to have it returned to your family. My advice is to contact him and ascertain exactly what happened to the estate and the family that lived there. If Thomas were to do that, he could then request its return.'

'I can't wait for him to do that.'

'And what will you do if it is returned to you? Go and live there? Managing an estate and putting it to rights is a man's job.'

Arlette stiffened and looked at him, not inclined to argue with him, but she had to make him understand. 'I am perfectly capable of managing the estate. But you are right to point out the difficulties I would encounter, which I am fully aware of.' Her expression became grave. 'Much as I have my brother's best interests at heart, it is impossible because I am about to become betrothed to Sir Ralph Crompton.'

'And if Thomas still lives,' William said quietly.

Arlette glared at him. 'We do not know that he is dead. I will not mourn him until I know for certain. Until we learn anything to the contrary, I will continue to believe he is alive. He has to be. I couldn't bear it if he didn't come home.'

William looked away. Barbados! It was a hell hole. They might as well have given Thomas Dryden a death sentence, he thought. He would not say this to Arlette, not while she had hope in her heart that her brother would survive and come home.

'It's important to me that my family is back together again,' Arlette said—never had she felt so alone in her life.

'You have Hester.'

'I also have another sister—a half-sister—I have never met. It is only recently that Hester told me of her existence and that my mother—whom I was told had died in childbirth when I was too small to remember—might still be alive.

My father turned her out when he returned home after a long absence and found her nursing another man's child. I have to find them. It's important to me.'

'I'm sorry, Arlette. I didn't know that. I understand your need to find out what happened to them. But tell me, does Hester know you have come to the Palace to plead your case?'

Heat flushed Arlette's cheeks and she could scarcely bear to look at him. Her heart began such a rapid beat that she felt slightly sick. She shook her head. 'No. I did not tell her because I knew she would forbid it.'

'And rightly so. She will be furious, as will Sir Ralph Crompton should he come to hear of it.'

Arlette had the grace to look shamefaced. Suddenly a young woman emerged from the shadows and came to stand beside him. It was the same young woman she had seen earlier, the same vivacious young woman who had disappeared behind a screen in James's embrace, declaring her love with a kiss. Arlette stared at her, experiencing a disquieting feeling of puzzlement she could not explain. She was the same height as Arlette, the bone structure of her face fine and delicate, her form slender. William turned to her and smiled. She returned his smile with glowing eyes. Taking her hand, he drew her forward.

'Arlette, I would like to introduce you to Marian Nesbit. Marian, I would like you to meet Arlette Dryden. When she was a girl I brought her to London. You remember, I told you about that time.'

Marian frowned and when she looked at Arlette something that appeared to be recognition crossed her face, but it was gone in an instant. 'Yes, I remember.' She smiled, a warm, friendly smile, revealing small, even white teeth, and, reaching out, she placed a hand on Arlette's, obviously altogether unaware that Arlette had witnessed her amorous union with James Sefton. Her blue eyes fairly shone with a brilliance that matched her ebullient smile. There was a naivety about her, but also something that inspired trust, and Arlette was drawn to her in a strange way, although she could not have said why.

'I am thrilled to finally meet you. William speaks of you often. He has told me all about the dangers you faced on the road, from cutthroats to Roundheads searching for fugitives from Worcester and how brave you were. In praising you I was sure his assertions were exaggerated until now.'

The sudden flush to Arlette's cheeks evidenced her delight over the woman's compliment and that William had spoken of her so generously. She met Marian's eyes, which were as blue as her own. Unselfconsciously, Arlette studied her. This was just a casual encounter which she found disquieting and puzzling, one which would stay with her.

'I am surprised that he would remember that—it was so long ago—so I suppose his account of that time is a bit farfetched, considering we managed to reach London without assault from either cutthroats or Roundheads. In those days, when I rode to London with him, I was far from pretty—more like an unkempt girl whom my sister scarcely recognised and lost no time in dunking in a hot tub.'

William caught and held Arlette's gaze. 'You are mistaken, Arlette. I do remember everything about that time and I recall you as being extremely brave.' He looked at Marian, tucking her hand through the crook of his arm. 'There is something I would like to tell you. Marian and I are to be married, Arlette.'

Thrown off balance, Arlette stared at him uncomprehendingly, as if she could not have heard him right. His wife? Had he really said he was going to marry this girl? But how could that be when she had just seen her kissing James? And how could William have kept this from her? Suddenly all the glitter of the Court was meaningless as the impact of his words hit her. She felt something inside her shatter, some hitherto untouched part of her heart breaking into tiny pieces. It sent her reeling into a black hole of desolation so deep she thought she would never climb out.

'You are to be married...' Arlette's voice failed her.

Staring at them but without really seeing anything, she felt suddenly weak, lost, and there was a great emptiness inside her. So much for wishing he would fall in love with her. He had introduced her to his bride-to-be—why had he not told her before? And why should she mind that he loved another? Why should she want their relationship to be anything deeper than what it was? He had fulfilled her father's wishes and brought her to London, but that gave her no reason or right to assume she could ever mean anything more to him than a devoted friend. During their time together all those years ago, having fallen victim to her grief and reaching out, she had found William. That was all. It could never be anything else.

With an iron control, Arlette pinned a false smile to her face. No matter who this woman was, she had arrived to shatter her new-found happiness. There was no room for anything in her vision, her heart or her mind but this one enormous disappointment.

'Why, that—that is good news,' Arlette said, looking from one to the other steadily, giving no indication of her thoughts, of how much seeing William with this woman pained her. 'I—I do hope you will be very happy. Your wedding— is it to be soon?'

Marian smiled and glanced warmly at her be- trothed, her face lighting up with a broad smile. Anyone would think it was a smile reserved only for him—but Arlette knew better. Marian was deceiving William with James, but it was not her place to tell him. But she knew that in the days to come, she would agonise over keeping the secret from him.

'William is impatient for it to be soon,' Mar- ian uttered, 'but so much has happened of late that we thought we would wait until Arlington Court has been returned to William.'

'Of course. My brother Thomas was at school with William. I recall him saying it is a beauti- ful house.'

'I believe it is. William has described it to me and I am impatient to see it.'

'You—you met in France?' Arlette asked tentatively.

'Bruges,' William provided. 'Marian was there with her father.'

'Sadly, my father died in Bruges,' Marian said, a sadness clouding her eyes, 'but not before William and I became betrothed. He had been ill for some time. Having no other family, he died content knowing that I would be taken care of.'

'That must have been a comfort to him.'

'Yes, it was. My mother went to the Continent with us when we were forced out of our home. Unfortunately she caught a chill on the boat, which developed into something worse, and she died soon after arriving in France.'

'I am sorry to hear that.'

'Is this your first time at Court?' Marian asked.

'Yes, it is. After all the years of austerity under the Commonwealth it all seems so strange—so different from what we're used to seeing, so colourful and exciting, and how handsome all the ladies look. It makes me realise how hopelessly out of fashion my clothes are.'

'I'm sure it does,' Marian said, passing her

eyes casually over her woollen gown, 'but your dress is very pretty. To change one's way of life cannot be done overnight, but new dresses can be turned out if one has the means.'

Arlette smiled, liking this young woman's easy manner and friendliness. 'That is true. We had no leisure for frivolous amusements. Everything that we did always seemed to have a serious purpose.'

'You poor thing. What a miserable time that was. Why, England would shrivel up and die if it were to continue practising those wretched rules imposed on it by Cromwell. We heard that all theatres and places of entertainment were banned throughout the length and breadth of the kingdom. Even the ceremonies and festivities of Christmas were suppressed. And the maypoles, that harmless amusement of the people, pulled down—whoever heard of England without a maypole? But do not be taken in by all that you see at Whitehall Palace today. Many returning from exile are as poor as church mice. I was in Paris for a while and later with the Court at Bruges, but we heard what was happening in England. You must come back to Whitehall, mustn't she, William? It's so exciting one cannot fail to be impressed. All manner of delightful entertainments are to be enjoyed here at Court.'

Arlette noted how eager Marian had become and an animated gleam shone in her eyes. 'I would like that, but I doubt my sister will permit me to come again when she learns of my visit today.' She smiled when Marian gave her a questioning look. 'I did not tell her I was coming, you see. She would have forbidden it and I fear I shall feel the wrath of her tongue when I get home.'

'Then William must speak to her. You are acquainted with Arlette's sister, are you not, William?'

William nodded. 'I am, but Hester is guided by her husband and, since Arlette is about to become betrothed, I doubt she will allow it.'

Marian clapped her hands with delight. 'That is wonderful news. And who is the gentleman you are to marry, Arlette?'

'Sir Ralph Crompton—although nothing definite has been decided. He is a mercer in the city.'

'Then he must accompany you to Whitehall. Would he like to, do you think?'

Arlette gave her a dubious look. 'I think I can speak for him and say no, he most certainly would not.'

'Then William must have a word with your

sister and persuade her to allow you to come. You can be charming when the mood suits you, William, so I am sure you can persuade her.'

Arlette and William exchanged glances, each knowing perfectly well what Hester's answer would be should Arlette show an interest in visiting Whitehall Palace again, but not saying anything to quash Marian's natural exuberance.

'There is to be a social gathering the day after tomorrow—not a grand affair, but it will be fun. Why, if you do manage to persuade your sister into letting you come, you might even meet the King.'

Arlette stared at her in amazement. Never in her wildest dreams had she imagined meeting Charles Stuart. 'The King! Is he really as tall and handsome as everyone says?'

Marian gave her a sparkling smile. 'Oh, yes, yes, he is. There is no finer man in England. It isn't only because he's the King that everyone loves him—especially the ladies,' she said in a conspiratorial voice and with a twinkle in her eye. 'I do hope to see you again, Arlette. It would be so nice to get to know you.' She spoke with a sincerity that touched Arlette. 'If not here at Whitehall, then you must visit me at my house. William has rented a small property close to the

Palace for the duration of our time in London. It would be nice to see you there.' Suddenly Marian's attention was caught by someone across the room beckoning to her. 'Oh, there is Mrs Gardner.' Giving the woman a little wave, she turned to Arlette. 'Please excuse me, Arlette, but I really must go and see what she wants me for. I do so hope you will come the day after tomorrow.'

'Yes, yes, of course,' Arlette replied, not holding out much hope of being able to persuade Hester as she watched Marian skip away without a backward glance.

Feeling suddenly awkward and the need to be away from William now that everything had changed, Arlette bobbed a slight curtsy and backed away. 'Please excuse me, William. I really must go.'

'Go? Go where?' William asked sharply.

'Home.'

'You cannot go alone. I will take you.'

'No, William,' she told him firmly. 'What are you afraid of?'

'You need protection with exuberant young lords prowling the corridors of Whitehall like predatory animals.'

'You need not worry yourself. I have made arrangements. James will be waiting for me. I have known him for a little while now and, boisterous as he may be, I know him to be a gentleman.'

'A gentleman would not have brought you here alone and I do not trust the fellow.' Aware that courtiers were looking their way, he took her arm. 'Come, walk with me. Your presence is attracting attention and I have no doubt everyone is curious to know who you are.'

Arlette walked beside William as they moved along the gallery, trying hard to ignore the glances directed at her as she passed among the lively throng. 'Do not worry yourself on my account, William. I think your display of solicitude and concern for my well-being should be directed at your betrothed, not me.' She spoke lightly, but as if William read a hidden meaning behind her words he frowned, glancing at the young woman he was to wed who was in happy conversation with Mrs Gardner.

'Do you think I have cause to worry about her? Although I cannot for the life of me think what Marian sees in Leticia Gardner,' he growled as a hearty sound of feminine laughter came his way.

Arlette studied the woman he referred to. With her red hair arranged high and wearing a low-necked saffron gown, perhaps twenty-five years of age, she had an open flamboyance about her that was completely alien to Arlette. 'She's very beautiful. Is she wealthy?'

'Very—and meddlesome and manipulative. She's a married woman, but I believe she plays her husband false.' He looked back at Arlette, his face still creased in serious lines as he drew her into a window recess out of the way of prying eyes. 'I asked you if you think I have cause to worry about Marian. Should I have cause to be concerned, do you think?' he asked, steering the conversation back to her remark about his betrothed.

Immediately Arlette regretted her words, which might insinuate that he should be worrying about Marian, for his face took on a seriousness when he spoke.

'Not at all. How could I possibly think anything at all when I have not met her before today? She is a lovely young woman, William. I wish you joy in her. Now I really must go.' She smiled. 'Don't look so worried. Do not bother yourself with me.'

When he replied there was something in his voice which made Arlette's heart quicken.

'You are sadly mistaken if you think I am not concerned about you. It is important to me that you will be happy and safe. That you can be sure of. I can only imagine what your life has been like, living in your sister's house. I suspect that your brother-in-law has treated you harshly on insisting you marry Sir Ralph Crompton despite your obvious aversion to the man. But Whitehall is not the place for you.'

'No?' She glanced at Marian, who was still in happy conversation with Mrs Gardner, their heads together, whispering and giggling behind fluttering fans. 'Marian seems content with Court life—as does every other lady I have seen here today.'

'In Bruges, Marian had no choice but to involve herself in Court life. There was little else to relieve the boredom. She is naive and trusting. She was the apple of her father's eye and I promised him I would take care of her. Where you are concerned, Arlette, you need someone to guide you, to protect you, for you are ignorant of the realities of Court life, unfamiliar with the disciplines this will enforce on you and ill-equipped to deal with the reprobates who loiter about the corridors and halls. I am just glad I was here today, however severe and disagreeable I must have seemed when I found you in Sefton's lap.'

Arlette smiled at him, happy to see the warm friendliness in his eyes, but how she wished there was something else, something more loving, for his marriage to Marian would not erase what she carried in her heart for him. Had she imagined their closeness and that his feelings were something akin to her own when they had sat on the garden bench surrounded by the scent of honeysuckle and rosemary? She laughed with a lightness even though it pained her to do so.

'Yes, William, you were disagreeable, but I do forgive you. Now,' she said, looking around, hoping to see James, but failing to do so, 'I really must go, but I do not see James. Perhaps he is waiting for me at the Palace gate.' As the words left her mouth she had a feeling that it was not her that James would be looking for, but Marian. Clearly William didn't suspect she was carrying on a flirtation with another man and it was not for her to tell him.

'I insist on escorting you to the boat—you did come by the river?'

'Yes, and you can insist all you like, but I really am not your concern. I am not a child and I am quite capable of taking care of myself.'

'You little fool,' he said, his expression softening, deeply moved by her sudden change of mood. 'Say what you will, but because I find you here alone I feel that you are my concern. I've told you—I care about what you do, that you are safe.'

'Then don't. I must go.'

Looking down at her, something stirred in the region of William's heart when he looked into her clear eyes. 'In a moment.' Her beautiful hair was drawn off her face, revealing the long, slender column of her throat. He could not deny that what he felt for her was more primitive than anything he had experienced for any other woman before. She was looking at him, her eyes never leaving his face, and he saw past sorrow and sadness still there. He didn't give her time to say anything. Taking her hand almost without thinking, he drew her further into a window embrasure and they were hidden from view by a heavy curtain. Briefly an image of Marian flashed before his eyes and his conscience at what he was about to do assailed him, but the moment was too strong to resist—the guilt would come later.

Taking her upper arms, he drew her towards him, wrapping his arms about her. Something like madness exploded in his brain and before he could stop himself he had put his hand behind her neck and was planting a kiss on her lips that was so intense, so carnal and prolonged, that Arlette's whole being was startled by it.

He had a capacity for seduction so powerful that nothing could have contained it. She floated, she drank in the air he breathed. The heavens could come tumbling down and the world could end, and she could bear it if he were there by her side.

Her mouth was soft and sweet. They kissed each other hungrily and, shielded by heavy curtains, they were aware of nothing anymore but each other and the moment. Arlette trembled against him and he awoke hundreds of demons inside her head as she was swept along on a delicious tide of ecstasy. She forgot everything: her problems with Hester and Richard and his determination to marry her off to Sir Ralph Crompton, her worry over having Mayfield Hall returned—and even their disloyalty to Marian. What was it about this man that he could turn her life upside down and inside out? Everything about him seduced her.

Somehow she managed to pull herself from his arms and swayed slightly, dazed by what they had done—what she had done—but strangely she did not feel any sense of guilt or shame. Perhaps that might have something to do with seeing Marian being embraced by James.

She stepped away from William. 'We can't do this. It is not right.'

William stood quite still, his face full of unconcealed passion. Seeing the desperate hunger mirrored in her eyes, he nodded, understanding, and their eyes locked together. 'So,' he said quietly, 'it's like that with you, too.'

'Yes. I realise I should not feel this way. You are betrothed to a sweet girl. We cannot do this to her. It is unworthy. Do—do you love her, William?'

He didn't answer right away. At length, he said, 'Yes, yes, I love her,' but, Arlette thought, without much conviction. 'Marian and I have known each other for a long time, Arlette, and indeed I owe her father a great deal.'

'And does Marian love you?'

'I believe so.'

'You said you promised her father you would take care of her. What kind of man was he? Did you feel beholden to him in any way and felt duty-bound to take care of her?'

He didn't immediately respond so the question hung in the air for the few seconds it took him to consider his reply.

'Years before he lost his wife to cholera, quickly followed by his two young sons—his only offspring. Devastated by his loss, he threw himself into the war. He'd had his fair share of tragedy—enough for any heart to withstand in the space of a lifetime—but his capacity for love was not diminished. That was when he met Marian's mother. She helped him deal with his loss and in the process he learned to love again—to trust. When she, too, died, on the crossing to France, he was inconsolable and became protective of Marian.'

'And you and Marian? You said you owed her father? What did he do?'

'I told you the fighting didn't end with the wars here in England and I did not spend the years on the Continent kicking my heels. France was also enmeshed in its own Civil War. Along with the Duke of York and other courtiers, I joined the French army and embarked on several years' active military service. In one skirmish I was wounded. I almost didn't make it. Marian's father found me and managed to get me to safety and a surgeon. He saved my life.'

'What happened to him? Did you both make it back to Paris?'

'Bruges. Marian was in Bruges. Sadly, the constant wars had taken its toll on him. Knowing he had not long for this world and deeply concerned about Marian, he asked me to take care of her, to make her my wife and bring her back to England.'

'I see. That was noble of you, William.'

'No, not really. It was not difficult. I had become extremely fond of Marian. I was happy with the situation—if not the circumstances that brought it about.'

'Then you must carry out her father's wishes and marry her,' she said, even though it broke her heart to do so. 'Surely there is no reason why you can't marry before you leave for Warwickshire. I'm sure it's what her father would have wanted.'

'I know,' he said quietly, looking deep into her eyes. 'But I didn't imagine for one moment that seeing you again would make me feel this way. I shall probably go out of my mind with wanting you. I want you so much that a moment ago I would have forgotten one of the sweetest girls a man could ever hope to marry. But you are right. I will not—I cannot—betray her love.'

A sharp pain pierced Arlette's heart at these

words and she bowed her head in defeat. 'I would not ask you to do that.' She turned from him. The euphoria of his embrace had worn off and it was like waking from a dream, one that she had been living on, feeding on, from the moment she had seen him riding along the Strand with the King on his return to England. The kiss had changed everything—things could never be the same between her and William again. She felt that she had lost a happiness which had never been hers in the first place and, in that bitterest moment of all, she looked clearly at her situation as it was.

William was betrothed to Marian, committed to her, and until Marian told him of the feelings she nurtured for another man and broke off their betrothal, then she must abandon any hope that he would turn from Marian to her.

Moving out of the concealing alcove, Arlette was too preoccupied to note that their sudden appearance had been noted and commented upon by more than one sharp-eyed courtier eager for something new to gossip about. She was relieved to see that James had appeared in the hall. 'I must go. James will take me home so don't worry about me. Goodbye, William.'

'Arlette, wait.' She turned and looked at him. 'Will you come the day after tomorrow?'

'Not only will Hester refuse to countenance such a thing—but after what has just occurred between us, I don't think that would be wise, do you?'

Shaking his head slowly, William moved towards her. 'Perhaps not, but I know Marian would value your presence. Speak to Hester. You might be surprised. If she agrees, then send a note to me here at Whitehall and I will see that you get here.'

Excitement shone in Arlette's eyes at the prospect. 'But I have nothing to wear for such a grand occasion.'

He laughed. 'I'm sure you will come up with something.'

William bowed over her hand, then stood and watched her leave. How small her voice had sounded, he thought, pure and sincere, and this somehow pierced his armour. He remembered her father. The resemblance was quite apparent now she was older. Her carriage was refined and she had her father's same penetrating eyes and firm no-nonsense chin. She had that polished air of resilient nobility and she carried her blessings with a grace and humility others could learn from.

The sensations she had aroused in him when he had taken her into his arms surged through him anew. He told himself that only when he was married to Marian would he be purged of these feelings. But there was no denying that he was disturbed by the recollections of the graceful figure Arlette presented as she walked the length of the room towards James Sefton, who was waiting for her by the door.

For a brief moment he felt a sharp pang of regret and uncertainty that he was betrothed to Marian, for Arlette Dryden had suddenly and unexpectedly presented herself to him as an ideal candidate for a wife. But she was to be someone else's wife, a man she had an aversion to. He had heard it in her voice when she had spoken about him. Seeing her deep sadness had touched a tenderness, a protectiveness, within him.

William had seen enough of the world to know that sometimes, out of desperation and despair, people found it necessary to act in a manner they would not otherwise have contemplated. Maybe Arlette was desperate. Or maybe she despaired. If, after making curious enquiries into Sir Ralph Crompton's affairs and the char-

acter of the man himself, which threw more light
on Arlette's situation, if what he had learned was
true, then it would appear she was willing to sac-
rifice her own happiness for her family's welfare. He hoped Richard Arden would see sense
and refuse to let the marriage go ahead, but he
very much doubted it.

A picture sprang into his mind of the time
when he had proposed to Marian and how happy
she had been at the prospect of being his wife.
Now, when he looked into her eyes, because of
the feelings he was developing for Arlette, he
was filled with self-loathing and guilt. Guilt for
not having thought of her as often as he should
since he had met Arlette again and he could not
deny that his impatience for their wedding to
take place was no longer as strong as it had been.

He had the distinct feeling that he had hurt
Arlette by announcing that he was to marry Marian and, he reminded himself, Arlette was the
one person whose feelings he'd been most careful not to hurt. He should have been open and
honest with her from the start, giving her time
to get used to the knowledge before introducing them.

He did not want to hurt Marian. He owed her
father too much. He was betrothed to Marian

and he couldn't let Arlette waste one moment of her precious life believing she could be anything other to him than a friend. He had done well, not letting her know how much he had come to care for her, how much she belonged in his heart. He tried unsuccessfully to block out the image of her enraptured face, trying to forget the way it had come alive when he had kissed her.

As Arlette walked down the long room she seemed not to notice the gauntlet of courtiers, their eyes following her, some discreet, others less so, because she was swamped with disappointment. She had come to Whitehall Palace with the hope that she would be on the threshold of paradise and instead she had come directly to hell.

Chapter Four

The day was warm but overcast and thick puffy clouds covered the sky in a blanket of grey mist when Arlette—nursing a deep sadness and desolation—and James were returning to their respective homes by boat. The oarsman was straining against the oars. Occasionally the sun broke through and glittering rays of light bounced off the water.

'What do you think of your visit to the Palace?' James asked.

'It was certainly enlightening,' she replied, seeing a desolation in James's eyes and a melancholia in his manner she had never seen before. Marian clearly meant a great deal to him. 'Never did I expect anything so grand.'

'And did you see the King?'

'No, I did not have that pleasure. There is to be some kind of entertainment in two days. Lord

Latham has told me that if I would like to go, then to let him know and he will make the arrangements. Will you be there, James?'

He shrugged. 'I don't know. I shall have to ask my father.'

'Telling me you were going to Whitehall to see your father today was just a pretext for you to see Marian. I'm right, aren't I, James?' she asked.

James nodded, looking miserable. 'How else am I going to see her?'

'Are you in love with her?'

He nodded, hooking his arm over the side of the boat and trailing his fingers through the water, a light breeze ruffling his fair hair. 'We walk a dangerous line, I know, but, yes, I love her deeply. But—it is difficult.'

'That I can well imagine since she is betrothed to Lord Latham.'

'I know and I don't know what is to be done— if anything can be done.'

'Is Marian in love with you?'

'I believe so—at least she says she is—but I cannot be sure.'

'Then—do you not think Lord Latham should be told? It would be quite wrong of you to carry on seeing each other behind his back. They are to be married, James, and probably sooner than you think if they decided to wed before travelling to Warwickshire.'

James sat forward in alarm. 'Did Lord Latham tell you that?'

'Not in so many words, but it is probable.' Arlette was sorry to see the sadness in his eyes. 'If you both feel the same about each other, then you really should be honest about it. It will save a lot of heartache later on.'

'I'm not ashamed of what I feel for her, Arlette.' His expression grew suddenly grave. 'You see, when I first saw her and fell in love with her, I looked on it as a great gift—something wonderful and too precious to waste. It's the kind of love that everyone hopes for and yet no one believes in. I didn't know then that her father had betrothed her to Lord Latham.'

'Would it have made any difference if you had?'

He shook his head. 'No. It is for Marian to come to me—to tell me she cannot live without me. If she doesn't do that, then I can only surmise she does not reciprocate my feelings—that she was only toying with my affections, having fun, which she is so fond of doing—and I will have no choice but to let her go.'

'If you go about it the right way and speak to Marian—urge her to be honest about her feelings—then, if she loves you, you must tell Lord Latham. It is only fair.'

The oarsman guided the boat towards the landing jetty used by the Arden family. Arlette climbed out and looked down at James.

'Don't do anything foolish, will you, James?'

Shaking his head in dejection, he sighed. 'No, no, I won't.'

When Arlette arrived back at the house, deeply affected by her meeting with William and what had occurred between them and feeling a great need to be by herself, she went directly to her bedchamber. Standing at the window, she swayed heavily, gripping the curtain for support. Tears began to fall, making a thin shining path down her cheeks, then, as her utter sadness overcame her, they ran unchecked, the wetness staining the fabric of her dress. Her breath moaned in her throat and she sank to her knees, resting her arms on the cushioned window seat. She wept for a long time, then gradually became quiet, the storm having gone, though it left the ravages of its passing on her face and spirit. She got up and sat upon the seat, leaning her head against the cool glass.

The memory of what had passed between her and William was intolerable. She had never cared for anyone very much and certainly not enough to dream the impossible dream—that he would fall in love with her. Somehow she had lost control of the situation. In doing so she had overstepped the bounds of friendship and found herself in unfamiliar territory. When they had been in the Willoughby garden, she had told him she cared for him, that his life was precious to her, and he had just trampled on her declaration by introducing her to his betrothed, making a fool of her. How could he do that? Why had he not told her before?

But thinking about it, she swallowed down the disappointment in herself. No. She had made a fool of herself, indulged in a daydream. She had come to care deeply for a man who still looked on her as a child—a man who belonged to another woman—a woman who was deceiving him with another. And she was on the brink of becoming betrothed to Sir Ralph Crompton. Her unhappiness folded around her like a shroud and she wished with all her heart that she had never gone to Whitehall Palace, that she had not seen William again.

Wiping away all trace of her tears and composing herself as best she could, Arlette was aware that the house seemed unusually quiet as she went in search of her sister. Richard had left for the Midlands two days before and she was told by one of the servants that Hester was lying down.

'Why?' she asked, suddenly alarmed. 'Hester never takes to her bed during the day.' Her sister was always busy and never ill.

Full of remorse and regretting not going directly to her when she had arrived back, accusing herself of having upset Hester by leaving the house without telling her, she immediately went to her sister's chamber, fully expecting to be severely chastised for being absent for most of the day. She was surprised to find Hester lying on the bed with her eyes closed and her hands folded at her waist. Arlette thought how tired she looked and how tetchy and distracted she had been of late. Her eyes opened when Arlette stood by the bed, looking down at her with concern. She was most surprised when Hester's eyes met hers and she smiled.

'Hester? What is it? Are you not well?'

Shaking her head, she reached out and took Arlette's hand. 'I am quite well, Arlette, and happy. I sent for Mrs Shepherd earlier.'

Arlette stared at her. 'Mrs Shepherd? But— but she's—'

'The midwife—yes, I know. I've been feeling a bit queasy of late—not myself.'

'And?'

Hester's lips broke into a wide smile. 'I'm with child, Arlette. A baby—after all this time. Can you believe it? Out of all the heartache and anxiety of past years has come this joy. Richard will be so happy.'

Arlette sank on to the bed, still holding her sister's hand. Hester's other hand lowered and caressed her stomach. 'Hester, this is wonderful news and you are right. Richard will be overjoyed. But you must take it easy—no hard work. You must think of yourself and leave the household duties to others.'

'I will. I am doing that already which is why you find me lying down. Oh, Arlette! I am so happy about this, but worried, too. Nothing must go wrong this time. I pray for a healthy baby.'

'So do I.'

'Now, tell me about your day. What have you been up to?'

Arlette bit her lip, thinking hard. She had to tell Hester that she had been to Whitehall Palace with James. She couldn't keep it from her—if she did she would find out anyway. Better to get it over with. 'I—I went to Whitehall Palace, Hester. I would have asked you, but I couldn't find you. I—I hope you don't mind.'

Hester stared at her open-mouthed, pulling herself up. 'You to went Whitehall Palace all by yourself?'

'No, I was with James.'

'But why, for heaven's sake?'

'James was going to see his father and he asked if I would like to go with him. We went by boat.'

For a few seconds Hester continued to stare at her, lost for words. 'Oh, I see. Well, I would certainly not have approved of you going there—I am sure you know that—and Richard would certainly have forbidden it. But you are back and no harm is done, for the present, at least. But should Sir Ralph hear of this… I shudder to think what his reaction will be. Did—did you see the King?'

'No, Hester, but I saw William—my reason for going there was to see him—to ask his advice on having Mayfield Hall returned to us. There is some kind of entertainment taking place the day after tomorrow and he asked if I would care to go. The King is to be there.'

'Goodness! And? What did you tell him?'

'That I would love to go, but I would have to ask you. William is betrothed, Hester. He introduced me to her. Her name is Marian. She is charming. You would like her. If you agree, I have to send a note to him at Whitehall Palace and he will arrange for a coach to fetch me. Will you allow me to go, Hester? I would so love to see the King.'

Hester considered Arlette's request at length, then to Arlette's immense surprise she agreed.

'What about Richard?'

'He isn't here to ask. When he gets back from the Midlands in the next few days and I tell him he is to be a father he will grant you anything you ask for. Besides,' she said, lowering her eyes, her expression grave, 'it will be too late for him to do anything about it, although should Sir Ralph hear of it things could become— unpleasant.'

Arlette stared at her. 'I have not yet given Sir Ralph my reply to his proposal, Hester, so whether I go to Whitehall or not is not his affair.

Everything inside me recoils at the idea of being his wife. Do my feelings count for nothing?'

'Of course they do, Arlette. Sir Ralph is not the man I would have chosen for you. You are so full of life, so spirited and bright. You deserve better than an ageing widower with two young daughters for a husband. But you do not understand how it is. There is a good deal more to Richard's acquaintance with Sir Ralph than he would have you know.'

Hester's expression sent dread crawling up Arlette's spine. 'What is it? Tell me.'

'I will, when Richard returns from the Midlands. For now I have no issue with you going to Whitehall, but please be discreet, Arlette.'

Arlette knew there was no use arguing with Hester. Unwilling to upset her, she would not press her on the matter.

In the privacy of her room, Arlette hugged herself tight. She was unable to think of anything else but her forthcoming visit to Whitehall Palace and the convoluted relationships between William and Marian and the love James bore for Marian—and now her own feelings for William. She knew she should be happy for William, that after all his years as an exile he had found some-one to share his life with, someone to love.

Where Marian was concerned she could not tell William about the closeness between her and James. It was not her place—besides, the teller never came off well in these situations. Think-ing of her own relationship with William made her feel ashamed, for herself, for all of them. Whatever the outcome, Marian must tell Wil-liam of the feelings she carried in her heart for James herself. If she didn't do this and she mar-ried William, then they would go on and make a family, and that thought left a hollow empti-ness in Arlette's heart. But keeping something of such importance from William was tearing her apart. She didn't like secrets. Nothing good would come from it, that she was sure of.

As she prepared for her next visit to White-hall Arlette struggled to get William out of her head, not to recall his warm breath in her ear and the tender touch of his lips on hers. She fought with all her strength to resist and she lost. There was nothing she could do to impose ra-tionality on the uncontrolled attraction he made her feel.

She felt quite wretched and was unable to see her way forward. She would like to leave London, to go to Mayfield Hall, but she should not even think of it with her betrothal unresolved and Hester with child. She had to do something, she thought wretchedly, otherwise it would be too late and she would fall hopelessly in love with William. She must put an end to something that had hardly begun.

The gathering at Whitehall Palace was a study of lavish elegance, the room into which they entered a burst of brilliant, vibrant colour. The moment Lord Latham with his lovely betrothed and the delectable Mistress Arlette Dryden, attired in a simple but tasteful pale green gown, her hair dressed in perfect curls and gleaming like a shining light, arrived in their midst, they commanded total attention. A group of painted and bejewelled courtiers soon surrounded them, their eyes drawn to Arlette, much to William's chagrin. The appearance of a fresh female face at Court always attracted interest.

Rivalry was rife at Court. The stylishly dressed unattached young ladies eyed her from behind their fluttering fans. Some had seen Arlette when she had made a fleeting visit to Whitehall two days before and others had all heard about her beauty, fearing and admiring her at once. The married women watched her with the greatest disapproval, their eyes cold as they subjected her to searching scrutiny, their eyes hard and uncompromising. There was nothing extravagant about her dress, but this only accentuated her beauty.

Dancing was already in progress, the dancers, both male and female, looking like brightly coloured peacocks. Goblets of wine were handed around by footmen and tables were laden with every kind of delicacy imaginable. Before disappearing to speak to an acquaintance, Marian eagerly pointed out courtiers of note to Arlette: the Duke of Buckingham—a handsome man who was close to the King—the beautiful Barbara Palmer—the King's mistress and of no uncertain desires or ambitions—and the Duke of York—the King's brother—whose bewigged dark head was bent as he listened with quiet amusement to some witty comment the lady by his side had just made.

Suddenly there was a distraction when, attended by his retinue of noblemen and ladies, the King entered the large hall.

Surrounded by all this pomp and circumstance of royalty, Arlette's heart quickened. She had never felt so excited, so eager or so scared.

The King paused now and then to acknowledge the bowing, curtsying courtiers, speaking to some and all the while coming closer to where they stood.

Smiling, William took Arlette's hand and with due ceremony led her forward. When the King stopped in front of them, Arlette thought her heart would surely burst, it was pounding so hard.

'Why, Latham,' the King said, with the familiarity of long acquaintance, 'it's good to see you here.'

'Sire, might Your Majesty grant me the honour of presenting to you Mistress Arlette Dryden? This is her first visit to Court.'

With a typical flamboyant and courtly gesture, the King leaned forward and picked up Arlette's handkerchief that had fluttered to the floor. He lifted it to his face to smell its perfume before handing it to her with a slow, lazy smile that was so strangely tender.

'The honour is all mine. I am charmed to meet you, Mistress Dryden. And what do you think of our Court?' His voice was rich and deep.

'I am quite lost for words, Your Majesty, but I am certain it will be the most memorable day ever,' she replied, spreading her skirts and sinking into a faultless curtsy, lowering her head gracefully. Her hand was instantly taken and she was raised up to look into the King's dark eyes that were full of melancholy. Suddenly the wide, full, sensual mouth broke into a smile and he bowed his head slightly, kissing her hand, his eyes never leaving hers. She felt the colour mounting in her cheeks beneath his close scrutiny and sensed first-hand his legendary affability. He possessed an easy-going countenance everyone who knew him loved because no matter how distorted a rendition they drew, no one ever mistook his effortless warmth and amiable smile. His eyes mirrored sincerity and dignity at all times.

'I am delighted to make your acquaintance. It is always a pleasure to see a new face—particularly when one is blessed with so rare a beauty. You must come again. I cannot remember when I last saw such a pretty face at Court.'

The low intimacy of his voice caused Arlette to flush softly, for she was unused to such adulation.

The King looked at William. 'You must bring her again, Latham. I shall hold you to it.' He winked at a flushing Arlette and gave her hand an affectionate squeeze before walking on.

Arlette watched him go with enchanted eyes. 'How handsome he is. He told me to come again. I wonder if he will remember me.' In her excitement she had altogether forgotten William just beside her, silent and unmoving, a dark scowl on his face.

William observed the effect Arlette was having on the King—a man renowned not only for his exalted position, but also for his love of women. He took his love where he could find it. When William saw the King look back at Arlette and observed the slow smile of appreciation on his fleshy lips as he looked at her and the way his eyes swept over her, absorbing every delectable aspect of her slender form, his gaze lingering overlong on the tantalising display of creamy flesh above the bodice of her gown, he experienced a new, shattering pain. For by this very deed the King had given him cause for jealousy and made him regret bringing Arlette to Court.

William looked down at her lovely upturned face, feasting his eyes on those glorious twin orbs of blue-green. 'I know. How can he forget such a pretty face?' he murmured dryly, quoting the King. In spite of the deep friendship that existed between the King and himself, he had not been able to quell the rush of resentment and jealousy rising inside him when Charles had looked at her with obvious interest.

Arlette, with a start of surprise, gave him a look of exquisite pleasure, her eyes shining like jewels. 'With so many handsome ladies at his Court, William, I am sure he will.' She laughed happily. 'When I came here today I did not for one moment think I would be introduced to Charles Stuart himself.'

'Then you will have plenty to tell Hester when you return home.'

Arlette was self-consciously aware of the rush of attention she had aroused and it was with immense relief when the King moved on and attention was focused elsewhere. But she could see that she was not the only one who had drawn the eyes of everyone present. Attired in a rich dark blue velvet coat slashed with gold, with lace at his throat and wrists and his breeches of matching blue velvet, William looked quite splendid. His commanding presence was awesome and there were far too many ladies looking at him like predatory felines. A blinding streak of jealousy suddenly ripped through her and she had to remind herself that he didn't belong to her but Marian, who was engrossed in conversation with James Sefton across the room.

'Everyone was looking at us,' she whispered.

William looked down at her upturned face, feasting his eyes on those glorious green eyes. 'I am aware of that. And if you have any sense at all, Arlette, you will think twice about spending much of your time at Court where you will have every lord who is not in his dotage panting after you.'

An unconsciously provocative smile broke across her lips. 'Are you worried that I might encourage them?'

'Should I be?'

'Not at all, although I am quite certain that Marian would be should you be tempted to succumb to one or more of those lovely ladies whom I observe are looking at you as if you are their next meal.'

'That is very astute of you, Arlette,' he complimented quietly, 'but there is absolutely no fear of that.'

The music had ceased when the King entered the chamber. Finally, having acknowledged those he chose to speak to, he gave a signal and the music swelled once more. The King, with a large capacity for amusement and settled into a routine—although no Act of Parliament could wipe out twenty years of civil strife—certainly knew how to enjoy himself.

His character and personality were as glittering as the rings on his fingers. Partnered by Barbara Palmer, the imperious man danced the stately and graceful parade of a coranto with other couples, his black eyes alight with pleasure and his lips parted in happy laughter.

Arlette was amazed by everything she saw. She was as one hypnotised. 'Why, I cannot believe that such flamboyant intimacy with the King is allowed.'

Marian, who joined them at last, laughed. 'It often oversteps the bounds of decency. It is a hotbed of intrigue where courtiers vie for supremacy and for some, who have fallen from grace, insecurity becomes a fact of life.' She looked at James when he came to stand beside them. 'See, William, people are taking their places for another coranto. Arlette, you must dance with William.'

'If she is willing,' William murmured, his bright eyes offering a challenge, daring her to refuse.

Arlette suspected Marian had made the suggestion so that she could dance with James, but at that moment she was too happy to care what mischief Marian got up to. An unconsciously provocative smile broke across her lips and her eyes twinkled mischievously. 'Why, yes, I would like to dance—although I am sadly out of practice and will no doubt make a complete fool of myself, if not both of us.'

William laughed. 'I'm willing to risk it if you are. Come, let us take our place.'

William took her hand and led her on to the floor.

'I can see you are enjoying yourself, Arlette. Are you glad you came?'

'Yes, immensely. I wouldn't have missed it for anything.'

As they danced she'd kept her eyes directed in front of her, amazed that no one had seen the deep and abiding feelings she carried in her heart for William, for she was convinced it shone like a visible light from her eyes each time she looked at him and as she spoke his name.

When the dance ended Arlette was immediately surrounded by an admiring coterie of young bucks and she danced with several. They complimented her outrageously, vying with each other for her attention. Arlette could not fail to be aware of her growing popularity and looked to see if William was aware of it also. With immense satisfaction she saw he was, for he was scowling darkly.

Knowing this would be the one and only time she would attend the Court, with the musicians blowing and strumming, round and round she went with an energy that left her breathless. Her behaviour was daring, but she didn't care. For once in her life she wanted to be daring, perhaps even a little shocking, and this might be her only chance. She had the rest of her life for regret.

The room was a blur of colour and noise as she danced. She was tantalising and gay, claiming the attention of all the gentlemen, who appeared to have lost interest in the other wilting young ladies. She loved the atmosphere and the raw, pulsing energy that seemed to emanate from the King himself. The restraints that had been forced on her during the years of the Commonwealth broke free, as she felt the fierce thrill of the Court. She chatted, she laughed and she danced, for the first time in her life aware of herself and the enormous power of her attraction over the gentlemen of the Court.

* * *

With his shoulder propped against a pillar, William idly sipped his wine, his dark brows drawn together in thoughtful concentration as he watched Arlette being led by the hand by her partner into a quickly forming circle as couples merged together. The steps were simple enough to follow as she began to demonstrate her talents and abilities in time with the music, doing a sprightly jig or a tapping of a toe and heel as she moved around in a never-ending wheel of cavorting dancers, her smiling face evidence of the pleasure she was savouring. So engrossed was he in watching Arlette that he failed to see what was going on around him—in particular he failed to notice how many dances Marian, who had a fondness for amusement, danced with James Sefton.

Tonight Arlette looked different. She was not attired in a fantastic gown, nor was she decked out in diamonds and rubies, but there was an aura about her, an inner light that gave her more lustre than diamonds. She was like a superbly crafted gem that shone with a radiance that put every other woman present in the shade.

William stood with his associates, idly conversing with them. His smile and words were for them, but the hot glint in his eyes rarely left

Arlette. They dwelt on her as she bent her head to listen to something her partner said to her. He became distracted by the curve of her mouth, the soft swell of her pouting bottom lip and the curve of the upper one. He found himself wanting to press his mouth to hers, to follow its shape with the tip of his tongue—as he had when he had kissed her.

Heat burned in his blood. This was madness! Why did he torment himself like this? He didn't know how long he could stand being near her and nothing could assuage the guilt he felt for thinking of Arlette when he should have been thinking of Marian. His heart and his mind understood the harsh reality that, while he was betrothed to Marian, there could never be anything between them, but his mind tormented him with the same insatiable desire he'd always felt. Drinking deeply of his wine, he tried to cast the sensations away. Casting his glance about the chamber at the merrymaking courtiers, he looked for Marian, asking himself what it was about Arlette that made him momentarily blind to his betrothed.

And then it was over. William decided it was time that Arlette went home. When he sought her out and drew her aside she thought he wanted to dance with her again and her face fell when he told her he was taking her home.

'It is time already?' she said incredulously, for already another young lord was taking her hand to dance. 'But it's still early.'

'It is time, Arlette.'

Arlette's eyes flamed rebelliously and for an instant she thought of refusing, but thought better of it. Smiling sweetly at her partner, she watched him reluctantly walk away. 'Do we really have to go so soon?'

'Yes. I promised Hester I would have you home just after dark. Best not to get on the wrong side of her.'

Accompanying him out of the chamber, Arlette swallowed down her disappointment, aware of the whispers following them. Colour flamed in her cheeks. She felt like a little girl who had misbehaved and was being taken home by a cross parent. Marian didn't seem to mind leaving. Inside the coach as it bumped on its way she chatted constantly.

'You were clearly enjoying yourself, Arlette. You must come again.'

'Yes, I did enjoy myself, Marian. I can't believe that I've met the King. Thank you both for taking me. It is something for me to remember when you have retired to Warwick.'

Marian took her hand and laughed. 'But we're not going just yet, Arlette. Why, you must come with us again to Court, is that not so, William?'

William remained silent as Marian continued to chatter away. Arlette caught his eyes in the light from the coach lamps. Neither of them listened to what Marian was saying. Arlette thought of the past few hours in which she had existed in a state of wonderment, reaching a peak of happiness, and she could think of nothing else. She felt that she was poised on a pinnacle of her life and she didn't want to look back or forward. Life had suddenly become a glorious adventure and she knew that nothing could ever be the same again.

When Arlette awoke the following morning she felt refreshed and, though she might have been imagining it, it seemed that the atmosphere of the house had changed—a change brought about by the forthcoming child. Hester had been in bed when she had arrived home with William and Marian. She had gone to say goodnight to Hester, giving her a detailed account of her time at Whitehall Palace. Hester listened in awe as she told her of her introduction to the King and made no secret of the fact that she would like to have seen him for herself.

There was no communication from William the day after her visit to Whitehall Palace so Arlette tried to put it from her mind as she devoted herself to reducing Hester's workload.

One thing she did not expect was that Sir Ralph would call on her. It was mid-afternoon and Arlette was alone in the house—Hester was taking a short walk with Mary by the river. Arlette felt the hairs in the nape of her neck rise and was tempted not to let him in, but he stepped past her into the hall. He made no move to approach her, but his expression was taut with anger as he seemed to be struggling with some inner turmoil. Despite the repugnance he inspired in her, Arlette forced a smile to her face.

'Sir Ralph! You take me by surprise. If it is Hester you are here to see, she is walking by the river.'

'It isn't. It is you I am here to see. I heard you went to Whitehall Palace. Oh, yes,' he snarled when her breath quickened with alarm. 'I may despise the King and all he stands for, but I have connections at Court who could not wait to enlighten me as to your dalliance with Lord Latham—how the two of you shared an amorous interlude hidden from view—and that "oh, so noble gentleman" betrothed to another.'

Arlette felt a frisson of fear and alarm. There was something intimidating about him that she did not like, something almost predatory. Never had she seen his eyes burn with so much wrath as they did at that moment when he fixed them on her accusingly, feeding on his own righteous rage. But what had occurred between William and herself was their affair and she would not discuss it with Sir Ralph.

'I do not advise you to go there again,' he said, his voice silky smooth and Arlette took a step back, sensing a threat. 'You slut,' he hissed. 'Did you think I wouldn't hear of it—you, the woman I have offered marriage to, attending that palace of wantonness and debauchery, flaunting your charms for all to see. Succumbing to the temptation to go there, you have gone over to the side of the devil.' His eyes travelled over her with contempt. Her uncovered hair shone brazenly in the light from the windows and her high, firm breasts were sinfully exposed above the scooped neckline of her dress. 'Have you learned nothing in the past ten years? I cannot rejoice in the return of Charles Stuart as you seem to do and I will not have my future wife associating with his adherents—flaunting yourself like a strumpet at the line of strutting peacocks.'

Arlette was momentarily shocked into paralysis by his aggressive behaviour, but then she forced herself to face up to him. 'It wasn't like that. I think you may be letting yourself be influenced by a purely personal resentment, Sir Ralph. I know you have no liking for Royalists and do not welcome their return. But they are here and there is nothing you or anyone else can do about it.'

Sir Ralph glared at her, his small eyes glittering hard, then, gripping her arm in a pincer-like grip, words began to spill from his lips as though a long pent-up dam had suddenly burst.

'You can't say I haven't been patient—waiting for you to come to me to tell me you will be my wife, wanting you. You torment me, do you know that?' he snarled, his grip tightening on her arm. 'Has that damned Latham turned your head—or is it Sefton? What will you do? Sell yourself for rubies and a place at Court? Is that why you went to Whitehall? To do that—to see him—Lord William Latham? I've seen you together. If you think he will marry you, then think again. He's close to the King and already taken. He's not going to wed some beggarly Puritan mercer's sister-in-law.'

Appalled, Arlette stared at him. 'How dare you say that to me?'

'I dare, Arlette,' he growled savagely, making full use of his threatening gaze.

'I think you have said quite enough. I think you had better go.'

'I will leave when I am ready. Has he told you that he loves you? Is that it? And are you fool enough to believe it?' He eyed her insultingly. 'No doubt his years of exile have been spent in debauchery, telling every woman he beds that he loves them—until the next pretty face comes along. What do you have to say for yourself?'

Something of the venom in his tone penetrated Arlette's mind. His arrogance and the injustice of the accusations he was flinging at her stirred her ire and her eyes flared. 'Nothing to you. Nothing at all.'

'Oh, but you will—when you are my wife. Refuse me and I will expose Latham as the philanderer he is. His reputation will be ruined and his intended shamed by it. But that will be nothing to what your family will suffer. Mark my words,

Mistress Dryden, they will bear the brunt of it. Think about that when you turn to him.'

'Please leave, Sir Ralph,' Arlette said, hating the way her voice trembled. 'I have nothing further to say to you. Now please take your hand off my arm. You are hurting me.'

'I will, when it pleases me,' he said, thrusting his face close to hers, spittle foaming on his lips. 'I am not your servant to order about. You have made a fool of me—a laughing stock. Everyone has watched me drooling after you like a lovesick dog. You may congratulate yourself on being the first woman to do that—you will certainly be the last. If you refuse me, then you can be assured I will make you pay for what you are doing to me. I will find you when you have only one path to take—and that will be past me.'

His warning sent icy shards of dread shivering through every fibre of Arlette's being, causing her heart to leap in sudden fear. She expected further argument and was surprised when he released her arm and stalked out of the door. She was left shaken by the encounter as she stood and rubbed her painful arm, and very much afraid that he would carry out his threat he had made concerning William, which added even more pressure on her as she agonised over keeping secrets from him.

Looking round, she saw Hester standing in the doorway, a stricken expression on her face.

'You heard what he said, Hester?'

She shook her head. 'Not all of it. He is angry, Arlette, and impatient with waiting for your reply to his offer.'

'Offer? If I do not marry him, he will expose William as a philanderer—and he told me that you and Richard will suffer for it. What did he mean by that, Hester? Has he some hold over you? Is that it?'

Hester nodded. 'Yes, it is true. Richard is in his debt, but I beg you not to ask me any more. We will speak to Richard when he returns.'

'I have no wish to marry Sir Ralph, Hester. I cannot sustain living with such a man. There must be some way out of this.'

Arlette's heart was filled with dread in anticipation of discussing the matter of Sir Ralph with Richard when he returned home from his journey to the Midlands. He arrived the following day. She waited until the three of them were together. Hester had already told him that she was with child and he was elated. Arlette regretted having to mar his homecoming.

'Sir Ralph Crompton came to see me yesterday. He—he made threats which he will not hesitate in carrying out if I refuse his offer of marriage. I don't want to marry him, Richard. You must know that.'

Richard paled. 'What is this? Tell me you didn't refuse him?'

Arlette shook her head, wishing she could escape her brother-in-law's questioning, accusing eyes. 'No—at least not yet. I do not like him and I will not be beholden to a man I cannot honour.'

'Why are you behaving like this, Arlette? Is it because of Lord Latham? I cannot help but notice the change in you since his return with the King.'

'My decision has nothing to do with William, Richard. Besides, he is to be married shortly.' She glanced at Richard. She could tell from his set features that he was not prepared to indulge her. He looked extremely angry. 'He told me you will suffer if I refuse to marry him. What did he mean, Richard?'

From his seat by the fire, Richard glared at her, his eyes angry and accusing. 'You have to marry him. How can you not—after all we have done for you? This is not a good time for me. Things are bad—they could not be worse.'

'I know and I am sorry.'

'You silly girl. You don't understand how it's done.'

His expression sent dread crawling up Arlette's spine. 'Then tell me.'

'I owe Sir Ralph. At the start of the wars I hit some trouble. I failed in a speculation after I married Hester. Sir Ralph helped me out on the understanding that it was a loan. I knew I had to repay him, but times were hard and the interest increased.'

'And now Sir Ralph has called in the loan,' she whispered.

'It is his right. You know there is no dowry and he has even offered to cancel the loan when you become his wife.'

'I do not like him and I do not want to be his wife.'

'Sentiment has no place in marriage. You must accept how things are. If you don't do this, then the consequences of your decision will be immediate. We will lose everything. We will be beggars hoping for alms. He has made the deal clear enough. He will forgo the debt when you become his wife. Do you understand?'

Arlette glanced away, her chest clogged with so many emotions she was having difficulty controlling. She looked back at him. He had always been a dictatorial, opinionated man—she had kept her views to herself all the years she had been living in his house out of consideration to Hester and now she could not think why.

'I understand perfectly,' she said tightly.

'You have lived in this house for nine years, eating the food at my table. I've provided for you as my guest and you are brazen, stubborn and without one shred of gratitude. Come, Arlette. Sir Ralph is sober and well respected and prosperous. What more do you want in a husband?'

Arlette sighed. He did not profess concern for her well-being and happiness at all. She could expect nothing less. 'This deal he has made with you,' she said in a low voice, 'is wicked.'

'I know,' Richard said heavily.

'He is buying me with blackmail. How can he want me when I go to him under such a threat to you?' She turned away. A lump formed in her throat and she felt as if she would never swallow again and her eyes, so strangely dry one moment, stung painfully the next. Walking slowly to the door, she paused and looked back at them.

'I will give it some thought,' she said in a quiet voice, deeply distressed as she sought to find some ray of hope in a painfully dark future. It seemed there was no more to say.

Another few days went by, days in which Arlette felt herself to be in a state of waiting without knowing why. The atmosphere was strained in the Arden household. It was as if the very house was holding its breath, waiting, waiting for her to say she would marry Sir Ralph.

She knew the time would come when William would come to see her and that there would be decisions to make.

Another few days passed before she saw him. It was during an afternoon. Richard was in the city and Hester had retired to her room for some rest. Arlette was in the parlour. Mary, one of the young maids, was helping her to alter some of Hester's clothes for when her pregnancy began to expand her waistline. She was also taking the opportunity to make a new gown for herself—the fabric Hester had provided as a sweetener, Arlette thought, as a feeble attempt to ease her own conscience in not standing up to Sir Ralph and Richard on her behalf and hoping it would go some way to make her decision to marry Sir Ralph easier. It was a subtle shade of yellow with a gossamer-fine gold embroidery. After working on it for days now, with just the sleeves to be attached, it was almost complete. The bodice was fitted and decorated with lace. At her small waist was a belt of gold satin.

'Oh, it is lovely,' Mary cried when she had fitted it on Arlette. 'I told you the colour is perfect for you. It suits your colouring and your figure. Go and look in the mirror and tell me what you think. With just the sleeves to stitch on it will soon be ready to wear.'

Arlette padded across the floor in her stockinged feet and her reaction when she saw her reflection was all the maid could have asked for.

'Yes,' she gasped, laughing happily, genuinely impressed, allowing herself the luxury of running her hands down the folds of the sumptuous skirt before doing a twirl. It was cool to the touch. 'It's perfect, Mary. I feel as though I've been dressed in such dour clothes for so long I've forgotten I have a feminine side.'

'I assure you that, considering your evening at the King's Court, no one else has.'

The deep, masculine voice caused Arlette to

spin round to find Willian on the threshold to
the parlour, leaning against the doorframe. Her
heart gave a traitorous leap at the sight of his
darkly handsome face. His crooked smile and
the sparkle in his blue eyes almost sapped the
strength from her knees. She dropped her lashes
in sudden confusion as his voice wound around
her senses like a coil of dark silk.

'William! You take me by surprise. I did not
expect you.' Conscious of the bruises on her
upper arm, she half turned from him, but not
before he had seen for himself the damaged
flesh. A frown puckered his brow, but he made
no comment.

'I thought it was about time I paid you a visit.
Forgive me for letting myself in. I couldn't make
anyone hear.' He glanced about the room. 'No
Hester?'

'She is in bed, resting.'

'Not ill, I hope?'

'No. She is with child.'

He raised his eyebrows. 'I see. That is good
news. Richard and Hester must be very happy.'

'Yes, they are. They've waited so long for this.
Please excuse me while I go and change. I should
hate to spoil this gown before it's had an airing.'

'It's a lovely dress, although,' he said, raising

an eyebrow, 'I can't help questioning its brightness in a Puritan household.'

Arlette laughed. 'Thankfully Richard is not as devout as some. Besides, knowing he is to be a father at last, he has his head in the clouds just now so he hardly notices what I wear.' She shot Mary a glance. 'Would you fetch some refreshment, Mary, and show Lord Latham into the garden?' She smiled at him. 'Do you mind? It's such a lovely day and the garden is a delight.'

Chapter Five

Walking on the grass admiring the flowers, he paused when Arlette entered the garden. He was arrested by the sight of her, by the sheer beauty of the picture she made, with her dove-grey gown falling in soft folds to her feet and surrounded by clambering pink and white roses. With her hair falling in a glorious tumble about her shoulders and her chin tilted with a quiet pride, she seemed alluring and elusive, and lost and lonely and vulnerable.

As she walked towards him, her eyes fixed on his, all her anxieties about what had transpired between them at Whitehall Palace returned. With his white shirt worn beneath his open black doublet, he looked incredibly attractive and, as he strode towards her, she noticed his limbs were strong. Despite how hard she struggled against it, each moment she spent with him she grew closer to him emotionally and her mind fiercely warned her to draw back.

William's eyes looked directly into hers, his expression unreadable, neither warm nor cold. The torment in Arlette's mind showed on her face and, seeing it, he guessed at the questions there.

'I confess that I am surprised to see you, William. I thought we'd said all there was to say at Whitehall.'

'Not quite, Arlette. There will always be something between us no matter how hard we try to deny it. Come and sit down. I want to talk to you.'

'Have you come by the river?' Arlette asked when she sat beside him in the flowering confines of an arbour.

'No, I rode here.'

Mary appeared, carrying a jug of cold lemonade which she placed on a small table in front of them, pouring some into two cups before leaving them to talk.

'You looked fetching in your new gown, Arlette. You need not have changed.'

'I had to. It's not yet complete, but the King's return calls for a new gown.'

'I approve of your attitude. Why, you should be dressed in the finest of silks and brocades with lace at your throat and ribbons in your hair, not those dour clothes adopted by the Puritans.'

Flattered by his words, she laughed lightly, knowing full well what Sir Ralph would have to say about that. 'I agree with you,' she said, banishing all thoughts of Sir Ralph, 'and the whole of England should rejoice. Why are you here, William? How—how is Marian?'

He frowned. 'It is Marian I have come to speak to you about. I'm hoping I can count on your support.'

Arlette looked away, having hoped he had come to see her and not to talk about Marian. 'Me? But how can I do that when I hardly know her?'

'I understand that, but she was quite taken with you.'

'I liked her, too. Indeed, who would not? She is quite charming.'

'She is young, like a sprite.' Tilting his head to one side, he looked at Arlette. 'There are times when she reminds me of you.'

'Really? Has something happened?'

He sighed. 'Nothing I can put my finger on, but I've observed a change in her of late. Her smile is no longer spontaneous and her laugh, once unselfconscious, sounds artificial. I cannot pretend that I am not disturbed by this change in her. She's in no hurry to leave for Warwickshire. I feel there is something troubling her.'

'And why is that, do you think?'

'I have no idea.'

'Have you asked her?'

'No.'

'Then don't you think you should? Perhaps if you did then your anxieties and fears may be at an end. Or are you afraid of what she might say?'

'No, of course not.'

Arlette felt the confusion press around her heart. When she had seen him leaning against the doorframe, the joy of spending time alone with him was indescribable. She had never been happier. But realising he had come to talk about Marian and primarily not to see her, she was hurt and more than a little resentful. She didn't really know what to do, how to feel or what to say, which was most unlike her since she had always done and said the first thing that came into her head, but her female instinct told her to be careful, not to divulge something that was not her place to do so, to guard her tongue.

She paused a moment, but then drove out the question. 'William, do you still want to marry her?'

He drew a deep breath and looked at her strangely, his eyes slightly narrowed. For a moment he made no answer and then, softly, he said, 'As to that I can honestly say I don't know any more.'

'Then don't you think you should think about it before it's too late?'

'I've done nothing else but think about it,' he uttered. 'I would betray her trust if I walked away. I do love her. Perhaps not in the way I should—but I admire her. I love her gentleness, her sense of fun and her purity. We have a mutual respect and understanding. What more is there?'

'What more indeed? With such qualities as these how could you not love her? I am quite the opposite—so Hester is always telling me—being too impressionable, too difficult for my own good, and as obstinate and stubborn as a thousand mules. She also says that any man who marries me will be welcome to me.'

'Come now, Hester adores you and you know it.'

Sipping her lemonade, Arlette looked across

at him. His eyes were clear and shone with past adventures while his dark hair ruffled in the breeze. For a moment she hated the way he looked, hated the fact that he had come here to talk to her about Marian when she, Arlette, wanted him for herself. How she wished she could dislike her, but she couldn't.

'The way I see it, you are under obligation to marry her,' she said somewhat irrationally, a glitter of anger in her eyes. And then she lifted her head and looked at him directly. 'You feel that you owe her father a debt of gratitude because he saved your life. He placed you in a difficult position by asking you to marry his daughter. I'm sorry, William, but to my mind that was asking too much of you.'

William's face hardened. 'I don't think so. Lord Stanhope was a good friend of mine. I was happy to do what I could.'

Something in Arlette's mind stirred at his mention of Lord Stanhope. Hadn't she heard that name somewhere before? Hadn't Hester referred to someone by that name in connection with her mother? Giving William no indication of her thoughts and the unease this caused her, she said, 'Perhaps Marian is having second thoughts about marrying you. Have you not thought of that?

Aware of the circumstances that brought you to-gether in the first place, would she really want to spend the rest of her days with somebody who was only there out of obligation?'

'It isn't like that.'

'No? It seems like that to me. Do you think she is having regrets?'

'No—I don't.'

'You sound so sure of that, yet the last time we were together you were so enamoured of me that you quite forgot your promises to Marian.'

'I apologise for my behaviour on that occa-sion. I'd hoped I was forgiven,' he answered stiffly.

Arlette averted her eyes. How could he remain so calm and unconcerned by what had happened between them at Whitehall Palace—something that had meant so much to her? But because he had spoken in such a casual, matter-of-fact way it had confirmed her fears that he cared little for her after all. Since his kiss she had dreamed of little else.

Fearing that he would guess her thoughts, she lowered her eyes, afraid to meet his penetrating gaze lest he should lay bare the hopelessness of the feelings she carried for him in her heart. But she was angry at herself, angry that she could have succumbed so easily to the embrace of this unfeeling man. The kiss had altered everything between them. The agony she had felt when she had left him had receded to a dull numbness. All she wanted to do was to go away and never look back, to forget everything. All her attention must be focused on that, on forgetting that she had ever met William Latham and that she had been foolish and vulnerable enough to fall into his arms like a common strumpet. In control of her feelings once more, she looked across to where he lounged on the bench beside her, watching her like a cat watching a mouse, waiting patiently for her reaction to his question.

'Having no knowledge of your exploits where ladies are concerned, your behaviour took me by surprise. And as for apologies—well—it is a little late in the day to withdraw what happened, don't you think? However, you may put your mind at rest. You are forgiven. My memory of the incident is extremely hazy. As far as I am concerned, it never happened.'

William gave a laugh of unbridled amusement, doubting the truth of her statement. 'Your generosity embarrasses me, Arlette. Indeed it does.'

His amusement irked Arlette somewhat, but

she smiled softly. 'I would not have thought a man of your phlegmatic character capable of embarrassment,' she said with a hint of sarcasm.

'By that I take it to mean that I am not easily excitable, dispassionate, even.' His eyes narrowed and glittered meaningfully and his voice softened. 'Come now, after what occurred between us the last time we were together, I think you know me better than that.'

A silence fell between them, broken only by birdsong. William's blue eyes remained fixed on Arlette's face with just the trace of a smile. It was she who broke the silence.

'So, how do you think I can be of help with Marian?'

'I would like you to go and see her. Talk to her. Will you do that, Arlette?'

Arlette looked into the bright blue eyes and the refusal she'd been about to voice died on her lips. Knowing what she did about Marian and James, it made sense that she should go and see her, and if she could be of help, it was the right thing to do.

'Very well,' she said, feeling a weight settle against her chest. 'I'll do what I can. Where is she staying?'

'I've installed her in a house off the Strand

with a housekeeper to take care of her needs. I have rooms at Whitehall.'

'Is there no one else you can ask?'

'She has no one else, Arlette—no one close—no family that she knows of.'

'I see. Very well. Shall I go there or would you like to bring her here for a visit?'

'I think you should go and see her. If Hester is agreeable, I will take you there.'

'She must have been very young when her father took her to France. I recall you saying that you were together fighting in the French wars. Who took care of her?'

'Her father always made sure she was taken care of.' William stood up to go. 'I know I don't have any right to ask you to do this—'

'No, you don't.' Arlette stood up and faced him.

'I can think of no one else. There are too many bad influences at Court. You and Marian are of an age.'

They started to walk slowly back to the house. Turning to look at her, William recalled seeing the angry bruise on her upper arm.

'How did you come by those bruises on your arm, Arlette?' She turned her head sharply. 'Forgive me. I couldn't help noticing them when you were trying on your new gown.' Gently taking her arm, he shoved her elbow-length sleeve up to her shoulder, uncovering the bruises that stained her delicate skin, one of them on the inside of her arm that looked very much like fingerprints. Uttering a violent curse, William settled his angry gaze on her face. 'How did this happen? Who did this?' The cold fire in his eyes bespoke the fury churning within him. 'Was it Crompton?'

Arlette nodded. 'Yes.'

William held himself on a tight rein until the rage cooled. What was left was a gnawing wish to see Ralph Crompton dangling from the end of a rope. He was not a man, but a rabid beast with a twisted mind who had abused her.

There was a silence for a while as his deft fingers examined her arm. It clearly caused her pain for her face grimaced when he pressed too hard. At first she wanted to pull away from his questing fingers, yet at the same time she felt alarmingly vulnerable and exposed. Something stirred in her chest, making it suddenly difficult to take a breath. Every nerve in her body piqued at the feel of his touch, which was like a brand of fire against her skin, and a searing excitement ran through her breast. She felt overpowered by his nearness. Her whole body throbbed with an awareness of him, but she would not give him any hint of her weakness.

His snug-fitting doublet and high boots accentuated the long lines of his body and she noticed again the incredible blue eyes intent on her arm. It was impossible not to respond to this man as his masculine magnetism was dominant. His face was creased with concentration, his fingers strong and soothing. His touch was impersonal, as if he were examining an object, yet it was gentle and Arlette did not feel like an object—far from it. She felt cosseted. Her whole body felt as if it were unwinding, growing weak with the pleasure of his ministrations. Vividly conscious of her close proximity to him, she abruptly turned her thoughts away from this new and dangerous direction and averted her head, before he could realise just how much he affected her.

He had made it plain what his intentions were and they did not include her. In which case she did not want complications, and, she suspected, neither did he—she was almost ashamed to acknowledge her feelings as she watched him. *What kind of man are you, William Latham?* she wondered and realised she had no idea at all.

'Did he hurt you anywhere else?'

She shook her head. 'No.'

'Arlette,' he murmured. 'Tell me you are not going to marry Crompton.'

Arlette turned and looked at him as he pulled down her sleeve. 'Why, William? Why do you ask?'

'Because I am concerned. The man is clearly a brute.'

'It is important to Richard that I marry him. There is more to it than I realised. Apparently Sir Ralph loaned Richard some money in the early days and he has called in the debt—which he will forgo if I become his wife.'

As he towered over her, William's lean, hard face bore no hint of humour. His lips curled with bitterness and a coldness entered his eyes. 'How noble of him. It is not Richard who will suffer the indignities of being his wife. Do not be forced into it. Promise me you will do nothing rash.'

Gnawing on her bottom lip as if she could not quite make up her mind, she shook her head. 'I'm in no position to make promises, William. Sir Ralph is not noted for his patience.'

'Your arm bears testimony to that. Fortunately there is nothing broken and some witch hazel should be applied to the bruising.'

'You seem to know what to do.'

'My years as a soldier taught me many things, one of them being that a soldier may owe his life to his knowledge of tending wounds.'

'Then I thank you for your concern, William, and I am certain the bruise will fade in a few days. In the future, should I be in need of some healing powers, I shall know who to approach.'

When he unexpectedly smiled broadly, Arlette noticed how white and strong his teeth were and how the tiny lines at the sides of his sharp eyes creased attractively. For a moment she was confused and found herself striving for normality. It was difficult to organise her thoughts when those amazingly blue eyes were focused on her so intently. Before the rogue thoughts could progress further, she lowered her eyes, quickly shaking off the strangeness of the moment that caught her unawares.

'I am grateful for your concern, William, but there is no need for you to feel that way.' How she wished she could lay bare her feelings and tell him how much he had come to mean to her, how alone she felt and how the secret she was compelled to keep from him concerning his betrothed was tearing her apart, but words failed her. Yet here, alone in the garden, she felt a closeness between them that she had never felt before and suspected he felt it, too.

Arlette was correct in her assumption—William's thoughts disturbed him deeply. Yet when he thought of Marian, this anguish and betrayal he felt filled him with profanation and made him feel even more wretched and contemptuous of himself. But he could not resist reaching out and taking Arlette's hand. At his touch her fingers trembled beneath his and she felt it hard to meet his eyes. She had not realised that his fingers could be so strong, yet at the same time comforting.

'Nevertheless, I am concerned. You will take care, won't you?' he said, knowing his duty lay with Marian and yet feeling reluctant to leave Arlette. His gaze slipped slowly over her upturned face, seeing the luminous tenderness in her eyes. She looked so defenceless, so childlike and pure that he felt a strange urge to protect her from whatever it was that plainly troubled her.

Arlette swallowed hard, her eyes never wavering from his intense gaze. 'I've told you, you need not concern yourself with me. I shall await your instructions regarding Marian.'

William's fingers tightened before he released her hand. 'Thank you,' he said hoarsely, not trusting himself to say more or to remain with her any longer.

He strode towards his horse and looked back to where she stood. 'I will call and see you in a day or so.'

As William rode away from Oaklands House, he wondered why fate should have brought them together in such a cruel way.

He was drawn to Arlette in a way he had never been to any other woman—not even Marian—but there was nothing he could do. It was too late. The fact remained that he and Marian were promised to each other and she loved and trusted him implicitly. He could not abandon her. He had no right to make her suffer because of what he knew he was capable of feeling for Arlette. With her, he must make a deliberate effort to put up all his defences.

Arlette watched him ride away, bemused by their meeting and prey to all the emotions he had aroused churning inside her. She could appreciate his virile good looks, his seductive blue eyes and sensual mouth, but that was where it must end, she told herself, and sincerely hoped he was not going to fall into the habit of dropping in whenever the fancy took him. But then again, she didn't want to stop seeing him altogether, she thought as she made her way into the house, pausing a moment and staring into space as she remembered how his expression had softened and he had looked at her with unbearable gentleness and tenderly touched her arm, and how the simple touch had sent her emotions to war so fiercely inside her that for one second she had actually considered bending her head and placing her lips on his hand.

Deliberately turning her thoughts to other things, she cast her emotions aside, for something he had said stirred something deep in her memory. Lord Stanhope! He told her in passing that it was a Lord Stanhope that had been by his side in battle, that this man had saved his life, that this man was Marian's father. Suddenly and from somewhere far back, came Hester's voice saying her mother had made the acquaintance of a widower in Warwick—Lord Stanhope. She thought it strange that she should remember this just now, but as realisation dawned on her, of the shape her confused thoughts were beginning to take, she froze. Hester had said the

child Arlette's mother had conceived was called
Matilda, Miranda, or some such name. Could it
be Marian? They bore similarities and Arlette
herself had experienced a feeling of familiarity
on meeting Marian.

Unable to think of anything else, she hurried
to Hester's room and entered without knocking.
Going to the bed, she looked at her sister who
was propped against the pillows, her face having fullness and a rosy hue that had been absent
before her pregnancy.

She smiled when she looked at Arlette. 'Is
something the matter, Arlette? You look worried about something.'

'Hester, when you told me about my mother,
that the man she was seeing lived in Warwick,
what was his name?'

'I didn't know for sure, but I believe he was
Lord Stanhope of Warwick—a widower who had
lost his wife and children to cholera.' She gave
Arlette a questioning look. 'Why?'

Arlette stared at her for a long moment before
she could speak. Everything around her disappeared into a haze, leaving her insensate, her face
drained of colour as she stared in disbelief at her
sister. *No*, said a tentative message travelling up
to her brain, *It isn't possible. It cannot be*. But

the more she thought about it, she knew that it was highly likely that Marian was her half-sister.

Having no wish to voice her suspicion to Hester just yet, wanting time to come to terms with this disturbing realisation that her sister had appeared without any effort on her behalf, she merely smiled and said, 'Oh, no reason. It's just that—well—William happened to mention that he knew a Lord Stanhope in France.'

'Well, if it's the same Lord Stanhope your mother knew then it is hardly surprising they know each other since they both lived in Warwickshire.'

Arlette breathed deeply, hesitant to ask the next question that would confirm her suspicion. 'I never knew my mother's name before she married my father. No one told me. You must know, Hester.'

'Of course—although I find it strange that you weren't told. Her name was Nesbit. Elizabeth Nesbit.'

Arlette thought about confronting Marian. She thought about it a great deal and in the end she decided she would keep the knowledge to herself for the time being, since not only would it affect Marian, but William also.

* * *

That night she was unable to sleep with all the questions she wanted to ask Marian spinning around inside her head and for the next two days her mind was in a confused and bewildered state. Whenever she thought of Marian being her half-sister, the stark realisation of what it would mean overwhelmed her with emotion.

She was also angry that they had been deprived of each other. All her life she had believed her mother had died in childbirth, only to be told by Hester that this was false. It had given her hope that she would find her, but then to discover that she had died saddened her deeply. It was like losing her twice. William had told her that Marian was alone in the world. How lonely she must have felt when their mother had died. She wanted William to come for her, to see Marian, and she was disappointed that another week went by before he came.

William arrived at Oaklands House, looking forward to having Arlette to himself for the journey into London to see Marian. He had sent word that he would be arriving at ten o'clock and he was pleased to see she was waiting for him. His eyes softened with appreciation as he looked at her standing before him. She was an enchanting sight in her wide-skirted dark blue costume. The short, tight-fitting jacket was piped with a paler blue satin. Bright hair gleamed from beneath a provocative matching bonnet embellished with a small curling white feather—her one small act of rebellion against the strictures of ten long years of austerity. Her lovely eyes burned with an inner glow and her creamy skin was flushed to a faint rose colour.

There was a look of unconcealed appraisal on his face as he looked at her, tracing with his gaze the classically beautiful lines of her face, the brush of lustrous ebony eyelashes. She was quite extraordinarily lovely. He had never seen the likes of her and the depth of his feelings for her were disturbing. Even now she had that untamed quality that he had seen when he had first seen her at Mayfield Hall, running in dangerous undercurrents just below the surface, a wild freedom of spirit that found a counterpart in himself.

Arlette was happy to see William and relieved that Hester had no objection to her accompanying him into the City. When she had told Hester what she knew about Marian, Hester had been so surprised and relieved that the problem of Arlette's mother and sister might have been resolved that she had readily agreed to let her go and see her, expressing her own wish to meet her in time if it turned out that she was indeed Arlette's half-sister. Richard was not approached on the matter. Still simmering over Arlette's refusal to wed Sir Ralph, he appeared to have washed his hands of her.

'Arlette! You look lovely,' the fascinated William said, taking her hand and leading her to the coach. 'Are you ready to see Marian? She is at home. I have told her to expect you.'

The air was sweet-scented as they set off. Arlette felt wonderfully happy. Everything seemed different when William was around.

'How are you, Arlette?' William asked.

'I'm am quite well. Why do you ask?'

'I was concerned when I last saw you because of the bruises on your arm. Have you seen Crompton since then?'

'No. He hasn't been near me.'

'And his proposal?'

'Nothing has been decided. Much as I hate being used as a bargaining tool, I have Hester and Richard to consider. I thought when

Charles Stuart returned to his throne things would change, but committed Puritans like Ralph Crompton will never change. Unfortunately, Richard is much like him.'

'I think you might find that in this new England, things will be different. If Richard is anything of a businessman he'll put aside his prejudices and take advantage of it. When Royalists come into their own, the dressmakers will be clamouring for fine fabrics to dress them.'

'I do so hope you are right. Now, tell me about Marian.' Arlette had decided not to divulge her suspicions about Marian being her sister until they had spoken.

'She is subdued and refuses to accompany me to Court. I'm hoping you will be able to cheer her,' he said, voicing his concern, but failing to tell her how Marian had changed towards him, sensing a layer of deceit and subterfuge here which he was struggling to understand.

They soon entered the outskirts of the city with its tall, tightly packed and overhanging houses and festering gutters. The hawkers rushed up and down the streets, crying out their wares in loud, raucous voices and thrusting their goods beneath the noses of the annoyed people.

'I'm so glad I live well outside the city. I much prefer the pleasant spaciousness of Oaklands House, the fragrant clover-studded green fields, the fragrance of hedgerows and wild flowers and the leafy trees to the smoky, cramped conditions of the city.'

'I have to agree with you.'

Arlette was so engrossed in the scene before her, then slowly she felt a tension evolve inside her. William was seated across from her, his knees almost touching her own. She was aware of his closeness. Her cheeks dimpled in a smile, wishing the journey to see Marian would go on and on and this rare moment of intimacy between them would never end.

William gazed across at her. Arlette was so lovely when she smiled. For him it was as if a shutter had been flung open and the sunlight rushed in. It was a smile compounded of luminous tenderness in her lovely eyes, yet in the lift of her lips, her perfect teeth and the tiny dimple near her soft lips there was a hint of seduction.

Neither of them spoke and neither knew what was going to happen next. The scent of Arlette's gentle perfume filled the coach with a subtle fragrance that was as potent as the sound of music and there was a strange magic in the warm air. William was aware of an overwhelming impulse to reach out and take her face between his hands and draw it to his own. He caught his breath, wanting to breathe in the scent of her flesh, to hold her close, to feel the softness of her body. But he could not. He dared not. He was betrothed to Marian.

But within the confines of the coach Arlette was irresistible. She was young and ardent and willing to love. He thought of the kiss they had shared at Whitehall Palace and when his heavy-lidded eyes settled on her lips he knew he wanted to kiss her again, to rekindle the glorious sensations he had felt then. All he had to do was reach for her and when he looked into her eyes and at the plump softness of her lips, he knew he had to kiss them. He wondered about her allure, for it was more than her face or her body that drew him to her. She had a gentleness that warmed him and a spirit that challenged him. He found the prospect of what he was about to do infinitely appealing, even though when they reached their destination he would undoubtedly regret having taken things so far. On the other hand, if he was going to have regrets, he might as well have something substantial to regret.

Quickly he crossed the small distance that separated them, sitting beside her.

Arlette looked at him with considerable surprise, and for a long moment could not look away. She looked into his eyes and she could see real hunger there. Mesmerised, she stared into the fathomless depths. She was unprepared for the sheer force of the feelings that swept through her and she knew, with a kind of panic, that she was in grave danger, not from him, but from herself. She wanted to tell him how much she cared for him, and how important he was to her, but she did not want to break this moment of closeness. She was trapped and she knew it and she felt her heart suddenly start pounding in a quite unpredictable manner. He was looking into her eyes, holding her spellbound, weaving some magic web around her from which there was no escape.

The darkening of his eyes, the naked passion she saw in their depths, seemed to work a strange spell on her and conquered her and, without knowing what she was doing, moving

within his arms, her entire body began to tremble with desire and fear.

'Are you going to kiss me again?' she whispered.

'Do you want me to?'

She nodded slowly. 'Please,' she breathed.

'And how many times have you been kissed?'

'Just the once—by you. I've never met anyone else that I wanted to kiss me.'

There was nothing she could do to still the
quiver of anticipation as he lowered his head and
covered her mouth with his own. His lips were
cool and surprisingly smooth as they brushed
lightly against hers. The shock of his lips on hers
was one of wild, indescribable sweetness and
sensuality as he claimed a kiss of violent tenderness. She felt again the fierce thrill of being in
his arms once more as she was half-sitting, half-
lying across his lap. Her eyes fluttered closed
and, for a few seconds, time ceased. She was
totally innocent of the sort of warmth, the passion he was skilfully arousing in her, that poured
through her veins with a shattering explosion of
delight. It was a kiss like nothing she could have
imagined. He kissed her with ardour and passion and she could think of nothing but the exciting urgency of his mouth and the warmth of

his breath, the feel of the strong muscled body against her own. His hands glided restless, possessively, over her breasts, her waist, pressing her tightly to his hardened body. A jolt slammed through her as his lips began to move on hers, thoroughly exploring every tender contour.

Half-stifled, her head reeling, she found herself imprisoned against his chest and there was little she could do to escape—not that she wanted to, for what she was feeling was beyond her imagination. As she trailed her hands up his chest, feeling the hard muscles beneath his jacket and sliding her fingers into the crisp hair at his nape, inside her an emotion she had never experienced before began to sweetly unfold, before vibrantly bursting with a fierceness that made her tremble. With a quiet moan of helpless surrender she clung to him, lost in the sweetness of overpowering surrender and immense and indescribable joy, devastated by what he was doing to her, by the raw hunger of his passion.

William's mouth left her lips and shifted across her cheek to her ear, his tongue flicking and exploring each sensitive crevice, then trailing back to her lips and claiming them once more. His kiss became more demanding, ardent, persuasive, a slow, erotic seduction, and Arlette became lost in a wild and beautiful madness.

After what seemed an eternity they drew apart, stunned by the depth of feeling they had aroused in each other. Gazing at him, Arlette felt she would melt beneath his scorching eyes. Slowly she brought one of her hands from behind his neck and her finger gently traced the outline of his cheek, following its angular line down to his jaw. His gaze held hers with penetrating intensity. She had no immediate thoughts. She had only the memory of something immense, of incredible joy, beyond which nothing was comparable. Their breathing was rapid as they looked at each other as they had never looked before.

'I never meant this to happen,' William said softly, gazing passionately at her lovely face upturned to his, her raw emotions and feelings shining from her eyes.

'No, I did not, either,' she replied in a shaken whisper.

'It seems that where you are concerned I can't help myself. I want you, Arlette—you know that now—and I believe it's the same with you.'

She nodded. 'Yes, but we cannot do anything that would hurt Marian.'

At the mention of Marian's name a look of frustration mingled with guilt came over William's face and, sighing, he turned from her and moved to sit across from her once more. All the softness had gone from his blue eyes, which were now hard, and when he spoke it was with precision.

'I know. We would only hate and despise ourselves afterwards. I am betrothed to Marian and we cannot either of us forget that. I wish I could say that nothing else matters but us, but I can't. There is such a thing as honour and decency. It would not be right. I could not do that to Marian—she does not deserve it. But what I feel for her has nothing to do with you and me. I know that I want you so much it's sheer torture. I always believed I was strong where women were concerned, but with you it is different. I am so bewitched by you that if I am not careful it will poison what I feel for Marian and I cannot—must not—let it happen.'

Arlette said nothing. She merely stared across at him, at the broad set of his shoulders and the anguish on his lean, handsome face. He had said he would not betray Marian, yet she was betraying him with another. She nodded sadly, eventually speaking in a soft whisper. 'Yes, you are right. We must not let what we feel for each other interfere with your relationship to Marian.'

His expression softened and he sighed on seeing the misery in her eyes. 'At least we both understand what we have to do. But we cannot deny that whatever happens a spark has ignited between us, lighting a flame that is not going to be easy to extinguish—and who knows, we may not be able to. This is all so difficult for me. I didn't just promise to take care of Marian, to make her my wife—her father made me her guardian. It was a position I did not ask for, did not even want, but there was no one else.'

'And you gave him your word because you felt beholden.'

'Something like that. I also did it for her sake. I am committed to her, Arlette.'

Suddenly the coach came to a halt and, looking out of the window, William saw they had reached their destination without him realising earlier.

'We have arrived,' he said, leaning forward and opening the door. He turned and looked at her, coming down to earth from where her kisses had sent him. 'I'm sorry it has to be this way, Arlette.' Why had he behaved like that? he asked himself angrily as he helped her out of the coach.

The fact was that, flushed with the heat inside the coach, her subtle perfume and her close proximity, she had looked so delectable and desirable that he had wanted her with a recklessness that he had been unable to control.

Arlette looked at him mutely, her mouth tinder dry and her heart written all over her face. William's eyes met hers, tortured, imploring silence, but every line of his face admitted that he understood the truth of what her eyes told him.

'Worry not, William. I will not speak of it. What happened between us will remain just that.'

William's fingers tightened before he released her hand. 'Thank you,' he said softly, not trusting himself to say more or to remain with her any longer.

By silent, mutual consent nothing else was said and Arlette braced herself for her meeting with Marian. She watched William climb back into the coach and it drive off and she thought her heart would burst with her emotions and a deep hurt. That was the moment she knew the hopelessness of despair, that while ever William was promised to Marian, what was in her heart must remain unspoken. But he had taken her in his arms and kissed her. Had she misread the signals that he cared for her after all?

Chapter Six

On seeing the coach arrive from the window, Marian came to the door. Her face was composed, pale, but her eyes were troubled. She hurried towards Arlette, taking her hands in her own and placing a welcoming kiss on her cheek. In her rose-pink gown decked with ribbons and bows and her fair hair flowing free about her shoulders, Arlette thought how pretty she was and how young she looked as she searched for signs of a likeness to herself. With their fair hair and blue eyes, there was a resemblance.

'Arlette! I am so glad you have come to see me. I can't tell you how much I've been looking forward to it, how much I appreciate it.' Her eyes went beyond her to the departing coach. 'Why did William not come in? He brought you here, didn't he? I saw him help you out of the coach.'

'Yes, Marian, he did. He will return in a short while to take me home. He told me you have not seemed yourself of late and that my visit might cheer you.'

'Oh, it will. Of course it will. But come into the parlour and we will talk. Mrs Cracken will bring us some refreshment.'

She led the way into a comfortably furnished room with a fire burning bright in the hearth despite the warm weather. A brown-and-white spaniel ran forward to greet them, wagging its tail happily.

'This is Toby,' Marian said, scooping the little dog up into her arms and burying her face in its soft fur as it wriggled frantically. 'William gave him to me in Bruges. I adore him and he doesn't like it when we are parted. Do you have a dog, Arlette?'

'We have dogs at Oaklands House and a fair number of cats to catch the mice, but they belong to us all. He's a fine pet, Marian.'

Marian put him in his basket and gave Arlette her full attention. 'You look concerned, Arlette. Have you something on your mind?'

There was a fascinating charm to Marian that drew people to her. Despite the fact that she was betrothed to William, Arlette's opinion of her

had not changed. She liked Marian—although
it would have been easier for her if she didn't—
but it was difficult not to like someone who exuded so much warmth and friendliness. She did
note that the sparkle that she had seen in her that
day at Whitehall Palace had gone—little wonder William was concerned about her. She had
agonised over whether or not to tell Marian that
she knew about her close friendship to James.
Should she speak to her, tell her what she had
seen at Whitehall? Her body recoiled from the
thought of such a confrontation but, unable to
stand by and do nothing, she decided that is what
she would do.

'Yes, yes, I have. I am anxious about you. It
concerns you, Marian; you and James Sefton.'

Marian stared at her, aghast. 'Me and James?
Why? What about us?'

'It is not my intention to pry, but I have good
reason. I saw you with James at Whitehall Palace. I saw the way you greeted each other. I got
the impression that you were more than friends.'

Marian blanched. 'Oh, I see.'

'I accompanied James to the Palace that day.
Do you deny you have feelings for him?' Arlette
asked gently.

Marian looked mortified. As she collected her

thoughts it was a moment before she spoke. 'Oh, what must you have thought of me? No. I do not deny it—I cannot. Has—has James spoken of this to you?'

'Yes, he has.'

'And William?'

Arlette shook her head. 'William doesn't know,' she was quick to assure her. 'But he should. He does not deserve to be played false.'

Marian's eyes flew to Arlette's in alarm. 'No, he doesn't, but he mustn't know. You can't tell him.'

'Rest assured, Marian, I won't say a word to him. It is not my place. But if your feelings for James surpass those you feel for William, then he must be told.'

Marian shook her head. She looked quite desperate. 'I can't tell him,' she uttered wretchedly.

'But I don't understand,' Arlette said slowly. 'If you love someone else, then why don't you want to be with him?'

'Oh, but I do,' she said earnestly, 'so very much. I met James in Bruges at a time when I needed a friend. We were attracted to each other from the start and after a while we couldn't bear to be apart. Because I was betrothed to William, I couldn't tell anyone about him, so when we could snatch some time together I wanted to capture every precious moment so that I could relive it when he wasn't there. William has been so good to me. This will hurt him terribly.'

'I'm sure he will understand, Marian, and consider your happiness above all else.'

'My father wanted me to marry William so much—he was determined that I would—and William has been so good to me. He promised my father he would take care of me and he has kept his word. But, oh, Arlette,' she cried tearfully, 'you don't know what it has been like these past months, having no one I could talk to. No one.'

'Marian, listen to me,' said Arlette, reaching out and gripping her arms, looking hard into her eyes in an attempt to force some sense into her. 'You must tell William. James is quite miserable, thinking you don't love him enough to leave William.'

'But I do,' she cried.

Arlette's heart went out to her. Taking both her hands in hers, she drew her down on to the sofa, facing her. There was a long drawn-out silence as both were fighting an internal battle. Finally Arlette made a decision—not one she had been intending to make just now, but she thought that perhaps this was the right moment.

'Forget about William and James for a moment. I have something to tell you—something that affects us both and persuaded me to speak out about what I know about you and James. It will come as a surprise and will be a shattering experience for you, so please listen to what I have to say.'

'Why, Arlette, what on earth is the matter?'

'The day we met at Whitehall Palace I—I felt that I knew you. For some strange reason you seemed familiar. I couldn't explain it and put it from my mind. But now I know there was a reason for it. When I was a child and William brought me to London I learned shortly afterwards that my father had died. The only family I had left was Thomas, my half-brother, who had been taken prisoner to Barbados after Worcester, and Hester, my half-sister. When their mother died and Father married again, I was born not long after. I do not remember my mother—I was told she died giving birth to my sister, who also died. Not until recently did Hester tell me that what I had been told was a lie, that my mother did not die and that she and my sister could still be alive.' Still holding one of Marian's hands she looked at her. 'What do you know of your mother, Marian? You see, my mother's name before she married my father was Nesbit—the same as yours. It did not escape my notice that you did not take your father's name.'

Marian stared at her. 'Arlette—what are you saying? You think we are sisters?'

Arlette nodded. 'Half-sisters.'

Totally bemused, Marian shook her head slowly, trying to comprehend what it might mean. 'Please, you must tell me everything.'

Arlette did, often stumbling over her words, at times driven to tears, but she did not fall silent until she had told Marian everything she knew.

'What a terrible thing your father did,' Marian whispered, deeply affected by what she had been told. 'Our mother must have been terribly unhappy to turn to my father.'

'She probably was. That I will never know. It was the beginning of the conflict in England and my father spent a good deal of his time away from home, often for long periods, as did a lot of men at that time. But he was not a bad man, Marian.'

'But not so nice if it made our mother turn to someone else.'

'He was principled and proud, and according to Hester he could not forgive our mother her betrayal. When I was a child I would ask about her, wanting so much to know what she was like—anything would have been nice—but no one would speak of her. At the time I thought it was because my father had loved her so much that it hurt him to speak of her. Sadly, that was not the case.' Arlette felt heavy-hearted for a moment when she thought of herself growing up without her mother. 'I feel envious of you.'

Marian glanced at her with a look of genuine surprise on her face. 'You envy me? Why?'

'I envy the fact that when I thought I'd lost my mother, all the time she was with you.'

'But she never stopped loving you, Arlette. She wouldn't.'

Arlette smiled sadly. 'Maybe not. I still wish she hadn't left me. I didn't even know her name before she married my father until Hester told me. That was when I knew without doubt that you are my half-sister, born two years after me.' Tears filled her eyes. 'I am so sorry that she died. I would like to have known her. You were fortunate to have her guidance when you were a child. You will have to tell me about her.'

'I will. I will tell you everything. But how she must have suffered for so long in silence, thinking of the little girl she had left at Mayfield Hall. It must have broken her heart to leave you behind. It saddened me that my parents never married. I didn't know why, they were devoted to each other.'

'My father died just after Worcester. She would have been free to marry again.'

'Yes, if she had known. If she had found out, I am sure they would have married when they reached France, but she became ill on the crossing and died soon after that.' Marian smiled, a softening entering her eyes, which were awash with unshed tears. 'You and I are not unalike in some ways and you are very much like our mother. I can see that now. In spite of her folly she was a loving person, gracious and gentle. Now we have found each other we will not be parted again.'

'And William? Will you tell him about James, Marian? He knows something is wrong. It is only a matter of time before he finds out for himself. Have you forestalled your marriage vows?' she asked tentatively. 'Are you and James lovers?' Marian's face suffused with colour and she lowered her eyes. Arlette knew that she had. She sighed. 'Oh, Marian, what is to be done?'

The unhappy Marian shook her head. 'I don't know,' she whispered. 'And not only that—I am with child.'

The silence that followed was thick between them. There was no suitable response to this and there was no time to ponder as William had returned and chose that moment to enter the room.

Two pairs of blue eyes turned towards William when he pushed open the door. They looked slightly shocked and was it tears that brightened Marian's eyes? He was puzzled by it, but pretended not to notice.

'I trust I am not interrupting.' Neither of them looked all that pleased to see him and he wondered what they had been talking about when he'd walked in.

'Of course not,' Marian said, standing up and walking towards him, drawing him further into the room, her lips curving in a smile—a little forced, he thought—that left him even further bemused. 'It's been lovely having Arlette to talk to and I must thank you for bringing her here. She will come again, is that not so, Arlette? And she has invited me to Oaklands House to meet her sister. You will take me, won't you, William?'

'I would be happy to,' he replied, looking at Arlette keenly. She had slightly more colour in her cheeks than she had earlier, but she did seem on edge. He was aware of the tension in the room and both Arlette and Marian looked slightly uncomfortable as if he shouldn't be there. What had he interrupted?

They filled a five-minute gap with small talk about the warm weather and matters at Court. Then Arlette ended it.

'I am ready to leave when it is convenient,' she said, standing up.

He nodded. Anything, William thought, rather than stay in this emotionally charged atmosphere. 'Would you care to accompany us, Marian?'

Shaking her head and avoiding his eyes, she scooped Toby up into her arms. 'No. I can feel a headache coming on so I'm going to lie down for a while and later I'm going to take a hot bath.'

Taking her hand, William looked at her with concern. 'I trust you will soon feel better. I will call on you later.'

'Thank you, William. You are always so considerate—but, really, there is no need. I'll be perfectly all right after I've taken a nap.'

He nodded, unconvinced. 'If you're sure.'

When William went ahead of her into the hall, Arlette went to Marian and hugged her before holding her at arm's length. 'We must talk some more, Marian,' she said softly. 'I'm concerned about you.' While Marian's eyes were no longer damp with her tears, there was a new determination about her.

'Please don't worry about me,' she murmured, squaring her shoulders and giving her a wobbly smile.

'Have you told James about your condition?'

'No, not yet. I have only just realised it myself.'

'Did James force himself on you, Marian?'

'No, he would never do that. I was not unwilling,' she replied, having the grace to lower her eyes as she confessed quietly to what Arlette might consider to be a sin.

'Then you must tell him—and you will *have* to tell William—and soon.'

'I know, but nothing I say or do now can make any difference. What's done is done. But emotionally I feel an obligation to people other than myself.'

'You mean your father and William?' Marian nodded. 'And James. You have an obligation to him now.'

'I know. I have written a letter to James, begging him to come to see me,' she said, producing a sealed letter from the pocket of her skirt. 'Will you see that he gets it, Arlette? I have to talk to him.'

Arlette stared at her, aghast at the request. 'You want him to come here?'

'Yes. He must.'

'And what if William should be here?'

'I'll face that if it happens. Please do this for me, Arlette. I wouldn't ask you, but there is no one else—no one I can trust.'

There was such a note of desolation in Marian's voice and a lost look in her eyes that Arlette's heart ached for her. After a moment of indecision and with William about to enter the room at any moment, any idea of refusing her request flew out of her mind.

'Very well, Marian. I'll see what I can do,' she said, taking the letter and shoving it into her pocket. Aware that William was waiting for her, she gave Marian a swift hug. 'Try not to worry. If you need me, send a message to me and I will come right away. Maybe we could arrange for me to come and stay with you awhile. Would that be acceptable to you, Marian? Perhaps you would not feel so alone and it will give us the opportunity to get to know each other better.'

'Yes, yes, it would,' she answered eagerly. 'I would really like that.'

As the carriage moved away Arlette looked back at Marian standing in the doorway, holding Toby close to her chest. Arlette could see Marian's veneer of determination had seeped away and she seemed to have retreated into herself once again. Arlette felt a deep sadness for her half-sister and was determined to come and stay with her as soon as it could be arranged.

Seated across from him, Arlette came under William's scrutiny. Her head was inclined and she was twisting a ring on her finger, seeming unable to look at him. She was trying hard to be calm and composed, but it was not working out that way. Out of earshot and watching them both intently, he had observed Arlette's farewell to Marian. There had been an undercurrent in their exchange that he couldn't quite grasp. The expression that had flitted across Marian's face when he had entered the room had been indescribable—was it fear he had seen or something else?'

'Did you find plenty to talk about?' William asked when they pulled away from the house.

'Yes, we did. I will come and see her again very soon. She appears to be rather lonely despite having people around her when she goes to Court.'

'Is there something I should worry about?' he asked, watching her closely. 'I sense something is the matter. Is it something I've done to offend you?'

Arlette glanced at him at once. 'No, of course not. Please don't think that.'

'Then what is it? Tell me. Come. When I leave you I don't want to remember you with a long face, much rather the lovely smiling one.'

'There is nothing wrong,' she murmured.

'Don't take me for a fool, Arlette. There is something wrong. Has something happened to upset Marian?' The mood that had gripped them on their journey into London had been broken.

Arlette was struggling to remain in control and increasingly she didn't want to lie to him. 'I—I don't know, William. It's not for me to say, but she does have one or two personal matters that only another woman can understand.' She hoped he would be content with that, but he was looking at her enquiringly, clearly sensing something was wrong and wondering what it was they had been discussing before his arrival, yet reluctant to ask.

William glanced questioningly at her, but she

refused to meet his eyes and was looking out of the window—a definite habit of hers when she wanted to disguise her thoughts. Recognising that her explanation was not an answer, nor was it intended to be, he probed a little more.

'If Marian is to be my wife, I have a right to know if anything is amiss, Arlette.'

'Then ask her,' she was quick to reply, looking at him at last. 'You said *if* Marian is to be your wife. Is there some doubt that she won't be, William?'

Her question caught him unawares and his recollections of the journey into London earlier came rushing back. He was unable to shake off the feel of Arlette in his arms. She was lovely. By God, she was lovely and he wanted her with a fierceness that almost shattered him. Even when they were not together there was something invisible and powerful flowing between them, drawing them together. Her gaze seemed to sap his will, throwing him off balance, but only for a moment before his iron control took over.

He'd promised himself not to touch her again. During that one reckless moment he had lost his mind and forgotten who they were and why he couldn't have her. For that brief time he had seen a woman who was reaching inside him to a place no one had touched before, not even Marian. He brought Marian's face to mind and in desperation tried to find a connection with the woman he was going to spend the rest of his life with and failed. What was happening to him? His mind struggled for answers that wouldn't materialise.

The look on his face changed. His eyes darkened and his voice became thick with passion. 'It was a slip of the tongue. Of course I'm going to marry Marian. I may have forgotten her when I held you in my arms, but even though I tell myself that I cannot allow it to happen again, I cannot help wanting you, Arlette. I can't get you out of my mind.' He let his gaze wander hungrily over the strained beauty of her face which emphasised the largeness of her eyes and the long, slender column of her neck. 'May God forgive me, but I desire you. You do not know how hard you make it for me to resist you. Whatever secrets you and Marian share, I still have the misfortune to want you.'

'And I you, William,' she said brokenly, hot tears burning the backs of her eyes. 'But don't you realise how difficult this is for me? Every time you kiss me I weaken a little bit more, knowing there is no future for us together. You are committed to Marian,' she said, while knowing that their betrothal would be broken when William became aware of her association with James and that she was carrying James's child. 'For pity's sake, if you have any feelings for me at all, why can't you leave me in peace?'

With recognition of their mutual yearning, William accepted this. With just a small space between them he wanted to reach out and touch her, but he made no attempt to do so. Drawn by the misery in her eyes, which looked enormous in her white face, all the deep emotions and feelings that burned in his heart for her almost overwhelmed him. 'Please believe me when I say that I never meant to hurt you, Arlette. I have told you how things are between Marian and me and I am committed to her, you know that.'

Arlette hadn't wanted to tell anyone that Marian was her half-sister just yet. It was something she wanted to get used to herself first, but having no wish for him to find out about Marian's transgression with James, maybe now was the right time to tell him. She looked at him steadily, preparing herself for his surprise.

'You were right to suspect there is something amiss, William. It would be foolish of me to conceal it from you since you will find out anyway.

It's just that I wanted to keep it to myself for the time being.'

'What? What is it?'

'Do you really not know? Can you not see when you look at us both? I remember you telling me that she reminded you of me. Have you not looked at us together? Seen the resemblance?'

William stared at her, a sudden dawning in his eyes as he realised what she was trying to tell him. Before the thought formulated in his mind, she told him.

'Marian is my half-sister, William—the sister I told you about. She is of my own flesh and blood.'

William's face showed his astonishment. 'Your sister? Yes,' he murmured, 'you are right. I have been blind. I should have seen it myself when you told me that you had a sister you had never met. Does Marian know?'

Arlette nodded. 'I told her today. She was as surprised as I was when I found out.'

'And how did you find out?'

'When you let slip that Lord Stanhope was her father—Francis Stanhope. Hester told me he was the man my mother became close to in Warwick. I thought it strange that Marian did not share her father's name. My mother's maiden name was Nesbit.'

'Good Lord! Little wonder Marian looked out of sorts when I arrived.'

'I am sure she will tell you herself when you next see her. I must say she was quite shocked, which is why she must have seemed upset. She was as much in ignorance as me when she was growing up that she had a sister. My regret is that I never got to see my mother. We would like to get to know each other better and we thought it would be nice if I went to stay with her for a while.'

William nodded. 'Why not? You have many years to catch up on before Marian and I have to leave London.'

Fully aware that there was no longer any future for William and Marian and feeling that the deception would be difficult to continue until Marian told him about James, Arlette lowered her eyes. She longed to give vent to her own bitter pain. Never had any man appeared so attractive to her and never had her heart called out so strongly to another.

Whether his heart was entwined with Arlette's or not, she wondered how he could have kissed her so ardently on two occasions. She should have repulsed him, which was what any good, decent, God-fearing young woman would have done. But that wasn't what she had done. No, indeed. Instead she had encouraged him, revelling in those moments when he had held her in his arms.

As soon as Arlette arrived at Oaklands House she went directly to find Hester. She was seriously worried about Marian. Marian had dropped her predicament on her so suddenly she had been visibly shocked by it and had no time to adjust her thinking before William had entered the room. She made up her mind to return as soon as possible for she hated seeing her new friend and sister's unhappiness and felt the weight of it sitting on her shoulders.

Hester was in her chamber, laboriously arranging a layette for the birth of her child. She looked up when Arlette entered, frowning when she saw her, knowing by her dejected look that all was not well.

'What is it, Arlette? Is something wrong?' She patted the bed beside where she was sitting, a small pile of neatly arranged baby smocks beside her.

Arlette sat beside her, inhaling heavily. 'Oh,

Hester, everything has suddenly become so complicated.'

'It has? Now why is that, do you think? Has it got anything to do with William by any chance?' Arlette nodded. 'Then perhaps you had better tell me. Have you done anything you have cause to regret?'

Arlette averted her eyes, knowing what Hester was asking and trying, unsuccessfully, to hide the truth and her pain when she spoke of him. 'There is nothing to tell. We are just two people thrown together by circumstances, that is all. I owe him a great deal for bringing me safely to you. Please believe me when I tell you we have never been lovers—or are ever likely to be,' she finished quietly.

Hester stared hard at her for several moments. Reaching out, she placed her fingers gently beneath Arlette's chin, tilting her head so that she was forced to look at her. 'But I suspect you would have it otherwise if it were not for Sir Ralph. And can you look me in the eye and say truthfully that there is no emotional entanglement between you two?'

Arlette shook her head. 'No, I cannot. But with Sir Ralph's proposal of marriage to consider it can go no further. Besides, I have told you he is betrothed to someone else—and this is where it becomes complicated.'

'Why? Who is she?'

'She is Marian Nesbit, Lord Stanhope's daughter. My suspicions were correct, Hester. She is indeed my younger sister. I liked her at once. There are similarities between us.'

'How long has she been betrothed to William?'

'I don't know—possibly a year, I think—ever since her father died in Bruges. They became acquainted on the Continent. William was close to her father, who was very ill. Knowing he would not be there to take care of her, he made William Marian's guardian. William felt obligated to Lord Stanhope for saving his life in some battle or other when they fought in the French army.'

'I am curious to know why William has delayed the marriage for so long. Can it be that she no longer holds his heart?'

'Oh, I believe he loves her and, whatever his feelings are concerning me, he is still determined to marry her,' she said softly, but she could not hide the hurt and bitterness in her voice.

'I am not blind, Arlette. I am aware of the feelings you have for William. If I'm honest, I saw it that first night he came to London and sought you out. If he has feelings for you and goes ahead and marries Marian, then he will be doing so out of duty and honour and for no other reason, and these two things can be a heavy burden to bear.'

'I know. I also know he is impatient to leave London for Warwick as soon as he has news that his home has been given back. There is something else, Hester. Unbeknown to William, everything is about to change. It is something that Marian told me just before I left. I already knew that she was romantically attached to James Sefton—they also met in Bruges. I saw them together and questioned her about it. She told me that she loves him and is to bear his child.'

Hester gasped, truly shocked. 'Oh, that foolish girl.'

'William has no idea, but I know he suspects there is something amiss. He asked me if Marian had said anything to me. I—I couldn't tell him, Hester. It is not my place. But Marian is so miserable—so desperately unhappy. She has no one she can turn to—no one close. I thought I might go and stay with her awhile. Would you mind?'

There was a silence between them as Hester considered what she had told her, aware of her misery over William and her sadness caused by Marian's situation.

'What can I say, Arlette? If you would like to spend some time with her than that is what you must do—although it's not going to be easy explaining Marian's infidelity to William.'

The following day Arlette went to Willow Hall to give James Marian's letter. He wasn't at home so she left it with a servant, who promised to give it to him personally.

It was several days later that she left Oaklands House to go and stay with Marian.

Marian was expecting her and, looking at her, Arlette knew her decision to come had been the right one. Although Marian's smile was one of genuine delight, her eyes were shining not with the pleasure of seeing her, but from recently shed tears.

They gave each other a fond hug and then Marian took Arlette's hand and pulled her into the parlour. Sounds could be heard coming from the kitchen and a gentle smell of roses drifted in through an open window from a small garden.

'It's so lovely to see you, Arlette, and I can't

thank you enough for delivering my letter to James.'

'How are you, Marian? I've been so concerned about you since you told me… I've been unable to think of anything else.'

'I'm quite well considering. I can't tell you what it means to me that you've come and I hope you're going to stay awhile.'

'That was the arrangement,' Arlette said as Hester's coachman dropped her trunk in the hall before returning to Oaklands House.

'Mrs Cracken has prepared a room next to mine, although this being a small house it's the only one, I'm afraid.'

'I am sure I'll be quite comfortable. Tell me. Have you seen James?'

Marian nodded, looking down at her lap. 'Yes. As soon as he got the letter he came immediately. When I told him about the baby he insisted that we marry right away. I've told him not to say anything to his parents at present, not until I've told William.'

'That's sensible. It would not do for William to find out from another source. When do you expect to see William?'

'He said he would try to visit me today, although he wasn't certain what time. I don't know what to do, Arlette. The last thing I want is to hurt him. I'm confused and unhappy. But I've got to be positive, I know that, and try to focus on constructive thoughts before I see William.'

James came to see Marian in the early afternoon. He never came to the house in case he encountered William, but since Marian had told him that she was expecting his child, his concern for her was so great that he was prepared to risk anything. Besides, he considered it was time that Lord William Latham knew of their romantic relationship.

Arlette was in her room unpacking her trunk when he arrived. When she came down to the parlour she found Marian and James seated side by side on the sofa, facing each other. James jumped up and faced her, giving her a somewhat nervous smile, clearly finding it awkward that after their previous conversation she should find him openly visiting Marian at her home.

'Arlette. I'm delighted to see you. Are you going to join us?'

'If I'm not intruding. I saw you arrive from the window and thought I should make myself known. Has Marian told you I am to stay with her for a while?'

'Yes, she has, and that you two are sisters. I can hardly believe that you had no knowledge of each other until recently.'

'I assure you it is real enough and we are half-sisters,' Arlette corrected him, sitting in a large winged chair opposite the sofa and straightening out her skirt.

Mrs Cracken, a middle-aged widow with a warm, friendly nature, appeared with a jug of lemonade and three glasses. She placed them on a low table before leaving. James poured the lemonade, handing a glass to Arlette before resuming his seat beside Marian.

'Marian has told you...?'

Arlette fixed him with a level stare, not at all pleased at the almost impossible circumstances he had created. 'That she is with child? Yes, James, she has told me. It's too late now for recriminations. I only hope you are prepared to face Lord Latham with the truth. In the circumstances he has to be told and the sooner the better.'

'Yes—yes, of course. And I will.'

'He will be furious,' Marian whispered, clearly close to tears.

'As will my parents,' James replied. 'But when

they get used to the idea and know that we are to marry, I know everything will be all right.'

'When shall we tell William?'

'Soon. There is nothing to fear, Marian,' James said, taking her hands in his own, trying to reassure her. 'We will tell him together.'

Arlette sat back in her chair, sipping her lemonade. Marian had told her she was expecting William to call and it didn't look as if James was in any hurry to leave. She felt an anxiety in her stomach that was tightening as the minutes dragged by and she knew her conversation sounded forced, then she heard voices in the hall as Mrs Cracken opened the door to William.

Arlette heard him speak to Mrs Cracken. There was no denying the reality of that achingly familiar deep voice and shock waves at his unfortunate timing shot down her spine. Although on second thoughts perhaps it was all to the good. Best to get the situation out in the open and then everyone could move on with their lives.

When he strode in, splendidly attired in scarlet and black, joy exploded in her heart at the sight of his handsome face. For a moment he stood there. They looked at one another from across the short distance that separated them and once more, as though their minds were linked by some invisible thread, their eyes and hearts spoke to one another. The moment lasted just a couple of seconds and a faint smile lingered on his lips before taking in the scene before him, before realising what he had walked into hit him with full force.

William took in the tableau that presented itself to him: Arlette seated across from Marian and James Sefton sitting close to Marian, holding one of her hands in his own, a table with refreshments between them. For a moment he was unable to absorb the full shock of why Sefton should be holding the hand of his betrothed.

Slowly he moved into the centre of the room, a long string of colourful oaths running through his mind. He watched as Sefton's arm snaked round the back of Marian to what looked like him an act of possession and only then, as he stood and watched, did it finally dawn on him what it meant and that he was being forced to play the part of the betrayed bridegroom in this bizarre drama that was about to unfold in this room.

For a long moment there was total silence filled with tension, then William spoke.

'Would one of you mind telling me what is going on?'

He continued to keep his eyes focused on Marian and James. Seated close together, they seemed to be drawing strength from each other as they almost imperceptibly held hands and they exchanged looks in that age-old way of lovers.

'Tell me,' he ground out.

'Please, William, please don't be angry,' Marian whispered. 'As you see, James and I, we...'

'We love each other,' James said with a sudden show of bravado, 'and my dearest wish is to make Marian my wife.'

William raked his gaze over the young man with insulting thoroughness, narrow and assessing. 'That's an odd thing to say when Marian is betrothed to me,' he said with condescending sarcasm.

Marian nodded slowly, too full of emotion to speak. James sat looking at her, looking at the sad droop of her shoulders, seeming to realise what a culmination of feelings were going through her mind. She was such a tragic figure. Reaching out, he placed his hands on hers.

'Marian, it will soon be over. Come, don't upset yourself. Look at me.' He turned her face to his. Her cheeks were awash with tears and she made no move to stop them. While William looked on, James, obviously deeply affected by her anguish, did the thing which at that moment seemed so natural. He folded her in his arms, her head cradled against his breast, while she cried brokenly.

After a moment she seemed to pull herself together and took a long, quivering breath, a sodden handkerchief clutched in her hand. She was deathly pale and Arlette was amazed at how difficult it must be for her to hold herself together as she started to speak quietly, as if the shame of what she had done was rising up to overwhelm her. The sobbing had stopped, but tears continued to stream down her face.

'Do you think I wanted this?' she whispered wretchedly. 'I couldn't help falling in love with James. It just happened—to both of us.'

'And my affection for Marian deepened during the many days she was alone in Bruges.' James's eyes passed lovingly over her strained features and he raised her hand to his lips, gently placing a kiss on her fingers. Her lips trembled in a smile as she gave him a look of gratitude.

Arlette could see that William was working

hard to contain his anger in this outpouring of affection between the woman he had expected to wed and James Sefton. If he was feeling guilt brought about by James's remark about Marian's loneliness she could not tell, but she suspected it had hit its intended spot. She stood up, thinking it best to leave Marian to explain the entirety of her predicament herself. 'I think I should leave you.'

'No,' Marian uttered in a strangled voice on a note of desperation. 'Don't go, Arlette. I want you to stay for when I tell him…' As if realising the enormity of what she was about to disclose, she looked wildly at William. 'Arlette knows everything. In telling her I made her an unwitting accessory and I am sorry if this has affected her. She has been a tremendous source of strength, but I never thought it would be an issue for her.'

Arlette sank back down on to her chair. When James looked as though he were about to stand up William shot him a dagger of a glance.

'Stay where you are,' he commanded shortly, looking at Marian. 'What else do you have to tell me, Marian? Come, out with it. It would appear that you have made everyone privy to your sordid secrets but me.' When she remained silent, her eyes downcast, he looked at Arlette. 'Well? Since you know all there is to know, tell me.'

Arlette glanced at Marian, who nodded her head, indicating that Arlette could speak for her. Arlette realised that emotionally Marian was weak and that she shrank from any unpleasantness, and telling William what she had done was terrifying her.

Taking a deep breath, Arlette said, 'Marian— she—what she has to tell you is that she is with child.'

Chapter Seven

William's entire body stiffened and his brilliant blue eyes were as wide and savagely furious as a wounded beast's. He stared at Arlette with incredulity, his eyes boring into her. In frigid silence he accused her of complicity and treachery, before his face hardened into a mask of freezing rage. They faced one another and William knew of the awful truth. Unable to quell the cauldron of emotions that were seething inside him, his fury escaped him, vibrating around her.

'You! You knew of this?'

'Yes, but I pledged not to reveal it.'

'Come, Arlette. I expected better from you. Well, it cannot be mine. I know that for a fact.'

In angry frustration he combed his hair back from his brow with his fingers and turned from them. After a moment of struggling to gain control, he turned back to them.

'And is there more, Arlette? Are you going to explain why you of all people kept this from me?' That she had known this all along and not told him, knowing how it would affect him, was like a dagger thrust to his heart.

Arlette didn't like William's tone, but she couldn't entirely blame him. She was too familiar with his private code of honour and she knew the disappointment and pain this confession had brought him. They both looked at each other for a long moment. For reasons she couldn't explain, she felt deeply ashamed, as if she were personally responsible for Marian's affair with James and the resulting pregnancy.

'Marian told me in confidence. It wasn't mine to share.'

Now the truth was out in the open, Marian held herself rigid. To show one moment of weakness and she would crumble.

William's hard eyes settled on James. 'How long have you known about this?'

'Not until I received Marian's note requesting to see me.'

William's eyes shot to Marian. 'You wrote asking him to come here? When was that?'

'Just—just a few days ago. Arlette...' The words dried up in her mouth when she realised she was about to implicate Arlette even further in her subterfuge.

'Arlette what?' William demanded scathingly. 'Arlette delivered the letter for you?'

William's eyes darted to Arlette as the import of what he was hearing slammed into him, the pain that Arlette had kept this from him hurting him more than Marian's infidelity.

'You colluded in this—this charade?' He stared hard at her, as if convinced she was the mastermind behind the whole sordid affair, yet despite all the evidence, he could not find a trace of guilt or guile in those flashing eyes of hers or the angry face turned to his. Tearing his eyes from her, he again fixed them on the two people who could not sit any closer to each other if they tried. 'And when were you going to tell me?' he demanded in a fury. Marian was still holding on to James Sefton as if for dear life. 'I am awaiting your explanation. If you have one to offer.'

'We were waiting for the right moment,' James provided, eyeing the tall, powerful man warily.

'The right moment? Confound it, Sefton. How dare you treat Marian as some kind of strumpet and how dare you make a cuckold of me? Your behaviour is nothing less than scandalous. You disgust me. You may thank God that her father is not alive to witness this. And before I close this distasteful subject you owe me an explanation. How long have you two been carrying on behind my back? Well?'

'A-about four months,' Marian whispered.

'Four months and I never suspected—not for one minute. And you are sure you are with child?'

Marian nodded. 'Yes,' she whispered with apparent meekness, lowering her eyes in acquiescence and flushing, not totally without shame. 'I am so very sorry, William. I did not mean it to happen. The last thing I want is to hurt you.'

'Being sorry changes nothing and does not make it right.' His eyes took in her fair hair and sweet face, stricken and frightened, her body clothed in a pretty blue-sprigged day dress that gave her a mistaken look of innocence and naivety. He had always thought her pure of heart, full of laughter and brightness, and discovering that she was no longer pure, that she'd played him false, was like being kicked in the chest.

The room fell silent once more. Arlette couldn't even hear the sound of her breathing and realised that she at least was holding her breath. Marian spoke and the spell was broken.

Admitting what she had done was one thing, but to explain it in detail was far harder. As she spoke, William listened, staring at her with a look of absolute fury. His mouth sat in a bitter line, his black brows drawn in a straight bar across his brooding blue eyes. Marian couldn't meet his eyes.

Arlette sat and listened, watching William. Whenever he spoke, his deep voice scraped against her lacerated nerves and, on the occasion when he glanced at her, apprehension made her quickly look away. Suddenly he turned his back on them, crossed the room to the window and stood looking out. For what seemed an eternity, Arlette sat perfectly still, existing in a state of jarring tension, struggling to remain calm. He looked relaxed and in control, yet there was an undeniable aura of forcefulness, of power, restrained for the moment, but gathering force, just waiting to be unleashed.

He turned and fixed them with an angry stare. 'Your father entrusted me with your guardianship so I will take the initiative. This is what you will do and I would advise you to think very carefully,' he said, looking directly at James, 'before you go off and do anything stupid such as abandoning Marian. You will regret it, I promise you.'

Despite the icy sound of William's silken voice and clearly offended that he should be accused of doing anything so base, James lifted his chin. 'I would not consider leaving her. I love Marian. She is to bear my child and I will marry her.'

'As her guardian I insist that you do just that. To avoid the disgrace of bearing a bastard child, to allay suspicion and to cover the shame, you will marry without delay. I will arrange it, so if you have not already informed your parents then do so and prepare yourself. I will call on you tomorrow.'

As if he couldn't bear being in the same room as them a moment longer, with purposeful strides he walked out.

Excusing herself, Arlette hurried after him. Not until the door had closed behind them did she call his name.

His entire body tensed and his jaw clenched so tightly that a muscle began to throb in his cheek. Slowly he turned his head and looked straight at her, cold, dispassionate and completely in control. His gaze snapped on her face and his expression hardened. He surveyed her coldly, his hands on his hips and his eyes holding a deadly glitter. There was something in their depths that Arlette could not read. Something that went deeper than anger. She faced him with as much composure as her shaking limbs would allow, but the eyes meeting hers gave her no reassurance. She could have faced the blows from his hands better than the furious intensity of his gaze. Her usually robust self-confidence began to weaken and the facade which she wrapped around her in a protective layer of armour began to fall away as her stiff self-control went spinning away from her in waves of pain.

'What is it you want, Arlette? Have you not said all there is to say, or is there something more you have to add to this sordid tale?'

'Please don't leave like this, William. You—you are upset and angry...'

'I am furious, and justifiably so, don't you agree? You knew,' he said accusingly. 'All this time you knew what was going on behind my back and you said nothing. When I held you in my arms you knew. When I kissed you, you knew. That day in the garden at Oaklands House you should have told me then instead of watching me make a complete and utter fool of myself.' His anger scorched her. 'When was Marian going to tell me? Has she no sense of guilt whatsoever?'

'Of course she does. She truly did not want to hurt you.'

'Hurt? I am outraged by her conduct.'

His hostility was like a tangible force. Arlette's first reaction was numbing fright at the terrible, utter rage on his face. Such a transformation had come over his features that she recoiled before the change. All that had ever been good-humoured, teasing and attractive had given way to fury. Wetting her lips, Arlette took a deep, steadying breath. Even if the fact of Marian's infidelity didn't have the power to hurt as it would have if he loved her deeply, Arlette could well understand his anger at and humiliation by it all.

'All this is unpleasant. I do realise how difficult all this is for you,' she uttered quietly, in an attempt to defuse his wrath. 'I couldn't tell you, much as I wanted to. Please believe that.'

'My compliments to you, Arlette,' he reprimanded contemptuously, 'on your duplicity, your deceit and your disloyalty. You should not have involved yourself in something that was not your concern.'

His voice was like a razor slicing into her.

Her heart wrenched with pain at the unfairness of the accusations he was flinging at her. 'It became my concern when she told me about her love for James. My conscience and my sense of duty would not allow me to walk away.'

'It is obvious to me that some misguided sense of honour caused you to feel duty-bound to aid your sister in her subterfuge and deceit, and you are condemned in my opinion when you became intoxicated with that particular sentiment.' His sense of outrage at her collusion was compounded by her deception. The sense of betrayal he felt was as powerful as anything he'd ever felt in his life. 'How could you have allowed yourself to become involved—to become a go-between delivering messages? As far as I am concerned you were all in this together, conspiring behind my back.'

Arlette was beginning to feel her own form of rage as she listened to him unfairly malign her. Bristling with resentment at his highhandedness, her face flamed with indignation. 'How dare you say that to me. In the same situation you would have done exactly as I did. Marian confided in me. She had no one else. It was not my place to tell you what she told me in confidence, but I did advise her to tell you. And, yes, I did agree to take her letter to James, just the one, because quite rightly I believed he had a right to know, that the sooner it could all be sorted out the better. I have done nothing that I am ashamed of, William. Nothing to deserve this kind of treatment from you of all people.'

'And how would you have me treat you, Arlette? It has not escaped my notice that now I am no longer committed to Marian the field is open for you. Was that what you thought? Was that why you agreed to collaborate in their subterfuge and deceit?'

William was fighting her, Arlette knew, trying to shut her out, and he was succeeding, but she would not stand accused of aiding and abetting Marian in her romantic liaison with James in an attempt to procure William for herself. Upon her soul, she had never been spoken to in such a harsh and brutal way and she could hear over and over again the words he had so cruelly flung at her: *duplicity, deceit and disloyalty.* His blue eyes seemed sheathed in ice. At the moment she would have said or done anything to reach him. She could not believe that this cold, remote stranger was the same tender, passionate man who had kissed her so tenderly—that he could be doing this to her. He spoke sarcastically, with a kind of cold contempt in his voice. Anger welled up suddenly in Arlette's heart, flushing her cheeks and bringing a sparkle to her eyes. She took a step towards him.

'How dare you accuse me of something so base? Please don't flatter yourself, William. You made it quite plain that there is no future for us together. As far as I am concerned nothing has changed—and does it escape your mind that in all probability I am about to become betrothed to Sir Ralph? Despite the weakness I have shown on two occasions when I have found myself alone with you—which I have now come to regret—I have never had any aspirations where you are concerned and my pride would not allow me to be second-best for any man.'

Her apparent lack of contrition fuelled William's anger. 'You were never that. Have you no sense of fairness?'

Arlette saw the harshness in his taut features and sighed with helpless understanding. 'I know how dreadful this must be for you,' she said quietly. 'But it is right that James and Marian marry.'

'Because Sefton has been unable to keep his hands off her it is the only solution. The combination of your silence about Marian's relationship with Sefton and your collaboration makes me acutely disappointed in you. I was about to make Marian my wife, for God's sake! I trusted her, loved her and she has betrayed me—'

'Yes, William, just as you betrayed her with me—Marian's own sister,' Arlette reminded him fiercely, her eyes flashing with anger. 'Were you thinking of Marian then?'

'Exactly. Somehow that makes the situation a whole lot worse and more sordid, and on top of this and other emotions there is the inevitability of a huge sense of humiliation.'

'And hurt pride,' she stated coldly.

William stared at her through narrowed eyes. Arlette shrank, trembling beneath the blast of his gaze. Her mouth went dry and her heart began to beat with a terrifying dread as she sensed that he had seemingly withdrawn from her for good. His expression was one of controlled anger. It was as if the passion and tenderness they had shared had never existed. This was a stranger, a terrifying stranger.

William continued to stare at her, almost as if he didn't know her. After several moments of silence that Arlette didn't feel she should break, he spoke.

'Are you to remain with Marian until I have a date and time for the ceremony?'

When she replied, Arlette tried to keep her tone level, but inside, her emotions were in turmoil. After all that had happened that day, what she wanted to do was curl up and hide in some dark corner. But she had to get through this.

'Yes, of course. Marian is in no condition to be left alone just now. She needs me here.'

He nodded. 'I will arrange everything and after that I shall leave for Warwick without delay.'

He held her gaze in silence, his eyes burning with anger and an unspeakable hurt. He backed away from her, his face becoming almost lost in the glare of the sun.

'William!' Arlette spoke his name with a plea for absolution, raised from the well of her own despair.

He turned from her and paused, his back to her. 'You should have told me,' his said, his voice a hollow whisper. 'I trusted you of all people to be open and honest with me. Relationships are built on trust and you have just shattered that trust.'

Like the rush of an owl's wings in the darkness of the night, his words reverberated in Arlette's mind, punishing—long after he had left her.

* * *

With a terrible sense of hurt and betrayal by the two people who meant more to him than anyone else in the world, William strode away from Arlette in a torment of emotions. He returned to Whitehall, coolly polite to those around him, wishing he could find a scapegoat to crush to ease the intensity of the fury and pain that refused to abate, that became a deepening void that made each hour more unbearable than the last. Surprisingly, Marian's deception didn't hurt as much as Arlette's failure to tell him something that was of such immense importance to him that he could not forgive her.

Yet how well he had come to know her. He could still feel the fragile warmth of her body in his arms, in his senses, recall the delicate fragrance of her flesh, the taste of her on his lips, and see the luminous blue-green eyes that had gazed into his with such soft, trusting candour. The memory was both a lifeline and a curse.

Having no wish to dwell on what was done, the following days became a flurry of activity as Arlette and Marian made preparations for Marian's marriage to James. Marian had fallen into a moody, dreamlike rhythm of listless malaise.

She punished herself, riven with guilt for the pain she had caused William, and it was only with Arlette's clear-headed thinking that she was made to realise that she must accept what had happened and get on with things and prepare for her wedding. But Marian wanted desperately to see William, to explain, to beg his forgiveness, but of William there was no word.

Initially, Arlette—always considerate of Marian's condition and worried that her distress might harm the baby—was supportive and willing to be of help in all aspects. But inside— infected by William's punishing recriminations and her own overwhelming sense of guilt for having kept Marian's relationship with James from him—Arlette was trying to deal with a hurt the likes of which she had never experienced. How could pain that had not been inflicted physically hurt so much?

But as the days passed, days filled with sewing Marian's wedding finery—the bales of cloth provided by Richard as a wedding gift—and she and Marian getting to know each other better, Arlette noticed a definite change in herself. A stronger, more resilient Arlette emerged. For the first time since William had gone she began to realise that one could punish oneself for only so long. Sooner or later a person of strength must either succumb or accept the situation. She had done nothing wrong, so why did she feel like the victim? William had gone and he did not deserve that she should abase herself for him. Yes, he would appear to give them details of the wedding ceremony and be present when it happened, but then he would leave and not return.

While Arlette was staying with Marian she took the opportunity to visit Anne and Edward at Willoughby House further along the Strand. Everyone was pleased to see her, especially the children. She was away for the whole afternoon and when she managed to tear herself away and return to Marian, she was surprised when Marian told her that William had called to inform her of the arrangements he had made with James's parents for the wedding. His visit had been fleeting and Arlette was disappointed that she had missed seeing him, but in another way she was relieved. She didn't think she could face any more unpleasantness so it was best they avoided each other.

The wedding was to take place the following week at the small house chapel at Willow Hall, which was just half a mile from Oaklands House. Now everything was out in the open James was a frequent visitor and on one occasion Marian accompanied him to Willow Hall to make the acquaintance of his mother. She had already met Lord Sefton in Bruges. Lord Sefton had met her father on several occasions during their years in exile and he was pleased with the match—and the fact that his son was to leave his wayward way of life behind and settle down with a wife and child was an immense relief to him.

But unbeknown to Marian and Arlette, Lady Sefton had not been so accommodating when William had visited them. The conversation had been conducted in a polite and civilised manner, but Lady Sefton, with her Puritan upbringing and rigid moral principles, had left him in no doubt of her displeasure over this forced marriage between her son and a young woman who had been so foolish and lacking in morals as to give herself to a man before marriage. Not even the generous dowry Marian's late father had provided for his daughter on her marriage could compensate for this.

Arlette accompanied Marian and James on the journey, but did not go all the way to Willow Hall. Taking the opportunity to see Hester at Oaklands House, they arranged to call on the return journey so that Marian could be introduced to Arlette's older sister.

Hester came out of the house to meet Marian and James. Arlette made the introductions. Hester stopped and gazed at Arlette's younger half-sister, the warmth in her eyes giving way to a frank stare. 'I am delighted to meet you, Marian, and I can't tell you the relief I feel now that Arlette has found you. Your existence has been a long-held secret which I deeply regret. Whatever I expected when she told me, I was not prepared to see such a strong likeness between the two of you. There's much of your mother in you both and you've the same tilt of your chin as Arlette. I am happy to meet you, Marian—you don't mind if I call you Marian?'

'I would not have you address me by any other name, Hester. You do not mind that I have come?'

'Mind? Of course I don't mind. If you knew how I miss my family…'

Marian smiled. 'We both have a connection in Arlette. I cannot believe how lucky I am to find I have a family after so many years of believing there was just me and my parents. When James and I marry, we will be neighbours and see each other often.'

'There will be a welcome at Oaklands House anytime you wish to call. But what am I doing, leaving you standing out here like this? Come inside,' Hester said, ushering them into the house to partake of some refreshment.

Following them inside, Arlette felt a sudden surge of relief and gratitude towards Hester for welcoming Marian with such sincere warmth and acceptance. Knowing Hester would never feel anything but bitterness for their mother's betrayal of their father and the pain he had suffered because of it, Arlette had been anxious about her meeting with Marian, but she could see she need not have worried. But not until Thomas came home would their family be complete.

The day of the wedding dawned bright and clear. Marian was a graceful figure in a beautiful muted blue-and-gold silk brocade gown with matching adornments of blue silk ribbons. Arlette had arranged her hair in ringlets with a wisp of curls on her forehead. She was the epitome of pure perfection and the sight of her brought tears to Arlette's eyes.

'You are so pretty, Marian. You make a beautiful bride.'

'As you will one day, Arlette. I look forward to that day.'

As soon as they arrived at Willow Hall—a large mansion, elaborately ornamented with decorative plaster and stonework and armorial glass—Arlette felt the cold atmosphere inside the chapel. Her carefully held nerves prior to the ceremony were already strained by William's arrival to escort them to Willow Hall. The parlour suddenly seemed too small for William's height. He stood facing Arlette and her heart set up its familiar wild beating as she looked up into his face. The lines about his mouth and eyes were testament to the strain he had been under since Marian had confessed her love for James.

She had fought her unease on seeing him again, smothering the wave of shock that washed over her, reminding herself that she had done no wrong. Her proud, disdainful eyes met and held his without flinching. She was discovering, agreeably, that now she was face to face with him once more, their last unpleasant encounter that had haunted her since she had last seen him had vanished. He was aloof and she suspected he was still under considerable strain himself. When the ceremony was over he would leave for Warwick and she sincerely hoped he would take heart, knowing he had done his best where the daughter of his close friend Lord Francis Stanhope was concerned, even though James Sefton had not been Lord Stanhope's choice of bridegroom for his daughter.

When he had entered the house in town earlier his gaze had fallen on Marian. A hard glint of approval kindled in his eyes, then it was gone. His voice was strained when in flat tones he complimented her on her gown and enquired as to her health. Arlette could only guess at the intensity of his feelings from the way his strong fists bunched and un-bunched at his sides.

'You are to accompany Marian to Willow Hall?' he asked Arlette.

Arlette looked at him directly, his manner setting her on edge. As though some stranger inside her spoke, she heard herself say witheringly, 'Surely my attendance on Marian at her wedding has never been in any doubt. She is my sister. I am to be her maid of honour. Naturally I am to go with her. Afterwards I will return to Oaklands House. My trunk has been sent on so I shall have no reason to return here.'

He merely nodded, his expression grim. 'Then there is no reason for us to delay. We will leave for Willow Hall.'

Marian stepped forward, placing a steadying hand on his arm. 'I beg you for a moment of your time, William.'

He looked at her and nodded. 'What is it, Marian?'

'I would like to explain. I know I don't deserve your consideration after everything I've put you through,' she said with deep sincerity. 'I never meant to hurt you and I truly am so sorry.'

Arlette stood back, watching them both. William looked so strong standing there, so in control, but whether he loved Marian or not, his bodily strength couldn't protect his heart from the pain.

'I know how it must look,' Marian went on, 'and I have been unintentionally selfish. You and I…we were drawn together by circumstances. I—I didn't know the man I became betrothed to—any more than you knew me. You were always preoccupied with matters concerning the King. You should not have agreed to marry me—nor I you.'

'Then why did you, Marian? I did not pressure you into marrying me.'

'I know, but I did so for the security I needed on suddenly finding myself alone.' She smiled. 'I didn't know the man I was betrothed to. I think we were both trying to do what my father had wanted. It was the wrong reason for us to marry. You deserved better. I doubt our friendship would have been strong enough for a happy marriage.'

'And you think marriage to James will?'

'Yes. I know it will. James and I found something in each other that we needed. At first we tried to ignore those feelings, but the more we saw of each other, the more they strengthened. I'm sorry I broke my promise, William. I didn't mean to let you down. All I can do is pray that you will remember our early friendship and learn to forgive me some day.'

William looked at her for a long moment and then he sighed, reaching out and cupping her chin in his hand. 'I already have, Marian, and you are right. We were both trying to do right by your father, but I think he would have approved of you marrying James. Your happiness came above all else.' He smiled. 'Now come along. We have a wedding to get to.'

The journey to Willow Hall was not as strained as Arlette had expected since William declined to accompany them in the coach, preferring instead to ride. As they travelled over the rutted

thoroughfare she tried to assimilate what was
happening. She was disappointed that William
continued to thrust her away.

Glancing at him out of the window, seeing
how he rode beside the coach in a frosty silence,
she felt a surge of anger. She had kept Marian's
confidence out of loyalty to her, but judging by
the violence of William's reaction he obviously
continued to think she shouldn't have. None of
what had happened was her fault, yet he was
blaming her. The more she thought of this injustice the angrier she became. If he thought
for one moment that she would forget the cruel
things he had said, then he didn't know her as
well as he thought. How dare he treat her like
this?

To Arlette's relief the wedding was a sedate
affair, with few guests outside the family and
none of the usual frivolities. In the chapel, she
tried not to look across the wide space that divided her from William, but now and then she
found her eyes drawn to him like a magnet.
Attired in stark black, he presented a daunt-
ing figure.

William's gaze drifted across the chapel to
Arlette. He stared at her lovely face as if seeing

her for the first time and he could not look away. It was one of those unique faces that makes everyone else look commonplace. She was wide-eyed and vulnerable, and her golden tresses drawn back from her face and rippling about her shoulders were like a beacon in the fitful light that struggled through the windows of the small chapel. He silently contemplated her eyes. They were calmly focused on the young couple speaking their solemn vows at the altar, but their depths seemed to spread the longer he looked. Her irises were complex, touched by different shades of green, turquoise and peacock blue, and as exotic as a tropical ocean that lapped on the sun-kissed shores of foreign lands.

The anguish of his own sorrow and a heavy load of self-recrimination for the accusations which he'd hurled at Arlette overwhelmed him. The words were cruelly unjust and he'd known it even as they left his mouth. How could he? He understood she must have been as shocked as he was when she'd found out about Marian and James Sefton. A protected upbringing had taught her honesty and loyalty to others. He could not fault her loyalty to her sister or condemn her for it, which was what he had done. He should have seen the signs of Marian's indiscretions himself, but he'd heard no gossip or idle rumours, which seemed to be the fragile bedrock the Court of King Charles was built on.

The responses over, James drew his wife into his arms and kissed her gently on the lips. Arlette's heart ached for Marian. She was to take up residence at Willow Hall and Arlette did not envy her at all. Lady Sefton was a cold, seemingly unfeeling woman.

The wedding breakfast was a stilted affair, the conversation limited. Lord Sefton was genuinely pleased to welcome Marian into his family, feelings which his wife did not share as she cast a critical eye over her new daughter-in-law, whose face was alight with happiness and whose banter livened up the meal. It was an ordeal for Arlette—made a thousand times worse because of William's presence. Throughout the ceremony he had been a towering, masculine presence in the chapel. He wore the same grim expression as when she had last seen him. Arlette was happy for her sister. She quietly noticed how Marian's eyes sparkled and there was a glow about her, a bloom she had not seen before. She looked happy, a woman in love with her husband, which only intensified her own sorry situation.

When the guests had eaten their fill and toasted the happy couple, everyone began to take their leave.

To his own vexation, William's gaze wandered to Arlette's slim figure throughout the meal, the boned bodice of her ivory silk and brocade gown revealing the swell of her firm breasts and miniscule waist, the folds of material billowing to her dainty slippered feet. The meal and the wine had brought a rosy flush to her cheeks as she leaned forward, the curls warm against them when she moved her head.

When she rose from the table to accompany Marian to the bridal chamber, William went to accost her. He couldn't define the mixed emotions he felt as he watched her move gracefully across the room. A ray of light fell on her, giving her an almost ethereal beauty that belonged to another world and stole his breath. Her hair was a hundred different shades of dazzling lights. She was pale, slender and utterly breathtaking. He remembered how she had felt to hold, loving and warm, and his heart ached.

He caught up with her as she was about to leave the room.

'Arlette?'

* * *

Hearing William speak her name, Arlette paused and turned. William stood before her. It was impossible not to respond to this man as his masculine magnetism dominated the scene. A curious sharp thrill ran through her as the force between them seemed to explode wordlessly. They faced one another now and, although neither abated one ounce of their dignity, or their continued opposition, the attraction between them was almost palpable.

He cocked an eye at her, the flame of the candles that had been lit to light the gathering gloom wavering and setting strange shadows dancing around them. The light flickered over his thick dark hair and outlined his face.

'You look lovely, Arlette,' he said, with a cool nonchalance that didn't seem appropriate considering the volatile encounter of their previous meeting. 'I had to look twice before I could decide which of you was the bride.'

Arlette smiled dryly. 'Thank you for the compliment, William—if that's what it was. If you're still angry with me and intend berating me further, I will leave you now. After that unfortunate affair and what with all the preparations for the wedding over the past days, my nerves are in shreds and I am extremely tired.'

William looked down at her in impassive silence, his eyes as calm as the sea on a fair day. 'I am not angry, Arlette. I was merely commenting on a fact. You really are quite lovely.'

'So is Marian. She made a beautiful bride. James is a lucky man. It was a quiet affair, which was what Marian wanted.'

'When I spoke to Lady Sefton she insisted on forgoing any kind of festivity. Considering the circumstances that have brought about this union, she did not think celebrations on the scale Lord Sefton would have liked to be appropriate.'

'Marian had no preference for an elaborate wedding. I sincerely hope that her marriage to James will be a success.'

'They profess to love one another, so there is no reason it won't be,' he replied dryly.

'Have you made your peace with Marian? She is deeply sorry for everything that has happened. You cannot leave her with ill feeling between you.'

'Do you have such a low opinion of me that you believe I would do that? My feelings for Marian have not changed and her marriage to

James does not mean that I have relinquished all responsibility where she is concerned. She knows where I am should she need anything and I will write to her occasionally.' He moved closer to her, his eyes boring down into hers. 'But what of you, Arlette? Are you happy?'

'Of course I am. Why shouldn't I be? I have acquired a sister whom I am growing to love dearly—and living so close we will see each other often. I expect you'll be leaving London soon.'

He nodded. 'In about a week or so.'

Arlette had a vague, momentary hope that he would offer to take her with him, but why would he? Why would he want to be with a woman he could not trust?

'How long do you intend to remain here?' he asked. 'If you are ready to leave, I would be more than happy to take you to Oaklands House.'

Two spots of high colour appeared on Arlette's cheeks. Never had any man looked so attractive or so distant and never had her heart called out so strongly to anyone. As she continued to look up into his eyes, they were unfathomable. All at once she knew she must fight her attraction for him. He was leaving for Warwick. It would be madness to pursue it further. Only one week ago Arlette would have been overwhelmed by William's show of consideration for her, but she was struggling to decide if he was motivated by a guilty conscience or if this was a genuine act of caring and trying to make amends. But she could neither forget nor forgive the cruel things he had said to her and needed time before she could put on the performance he expected.

'I'm sorry, William, but I am not yet ready to leave. I promised Marian I would stay with her awhile. Please excuse me.'

She saw a brief flare of disappointment in his eyes. He clearly thought that with just a kind word and a smile she would forgive him. But as she turned away to go to Marian, in a moment of weakness her heart told her to stay, not to reject his offer of an olive branch, if that was what it was, and go back. She was angry at this sudden weakness. Was he just trying to break down all her flimsy defences?

Determinedly she continued on her way without a backward glance.

The bedchamber Marian was to share with James was large and heavily scented with lavender. With a fire burning in the hearth the room was lovely and warm. With two chambermaids laughing and fussing round her as they

stripped off her wedding gown and prepared her
for the marriage bed, Marian turned and her eyes
sought out Arlette as a flimsy nightgown was
pulled over her head. She immediately shooed
the maids away and they disappeared into an
anteroom. Arlette smiled and went to her, while
taking in her surroundings.

'This is all very fine, Marian. I do so hope
you will be happy living here.'

Marian laughed lightly. 'Despite my new
mother-in-law being something of a dragon,'
she confided in a whisper, 'I know I shall be.
As long as I have James as my husband and my
sister living just a stone's throw away at Oaklands House, I have everything that is important to me.'

'And soon a child of your own,' Arlette reminded her softly.

'Yes, and a child,' Marian said softly, caress-
ing her stomach with her hand. 'I do love James
so much, Arlette. I never dreamed I could be
so happy.'

'Indeed. Is there not proof of it shining in
your eyes?' Laughing lightly, Arlette embraced
her fondly. 'I am so happy for you, Marian, and
happy that you are my sister. You have become

very precious to me.' Holding her at arm's length, she looked at her seriously. 'And William?'

Marian's face fell. 'I am sorry about deceiving him and I deeply regret hurting him. But he has wished me well.' She looked at Arlette, her eyes questing. 'But what about you, Arlette— about you and William?'

Arlette stared at her, dumbfounded, and was certain her heart missed a beat. 'There is no me and William.'

'And you are sure about that, are you, Arlette? Ever since we were at Whitehall and I saw you dancing together, I have seen the way he looks at you—the way you looked at each other. William has never looked at me in that way.'

An embarrassed flush flaming in her cheeks, Arlette stepped back and looked away. 'I think your imagination has been playing tricks on you, Marian. Besides, I am practically betrothed to Sir Ralph Crompton. A marriage between us is important to Richard and Sir Ralph is growing impatient, waiting for my answer.'

'From what you have told me of Sir Ralph, he is far too old for you and should be put aside. You and William would be good for each other. You have spirit and that is what interests William— it is a challenge to his strength, his masculinity, that daring recklessness in him that attracts the ladies—I saw it happen at the Court in Bruges. I was not right for him. I was just eighteen when we became betrothed, while—according to gossip—he was no saint. He was a hard-bitten experienced man of the world and a soldier, whereas I was a babe in comparison. I can confess now that I was always apprehensive about becoming his wife. No, you are far more suitable for him than I could ever be. I know that my situation has caused a division between the two of you. Perhaps I should speak to him to try to rectify matters.'

'No, please don't, Marian. I would rather leave things as they are.'

'Well, in as much as I feel responsible for the two of you being on the cross, so to speak, I feel that I should. But if you're sure…'

'Yes, yes, I am.' Remembering the words William had said to her on parting that day in London—that she had shattered his trust in her and that it could not be rebuilt—she thrust the hurt those words had caused from her. That day something had been broken between her and William, broken and impossible to mend. 'There is nothing to be done, Marian. Nothing at all.'

Chapter Eight

When Arlette left Marian to await her husband, intending to leave right away, she was surprised to find William waiting for her. Unable to refuse his offer to take her home without causing a scene, she accepted. Just when she was learning to live, knowing she would probably never see him again, he had appeared and all her carefully tended illusions were torn asunder.

Inside the coach William settled himself into the upholstery, stretching his long legs out in front of him as much as he was able in such limited space. With a smile of contentment he folded his hands on his stomach and closed his eyes, composing himself more comfortably, as if he intended going to sleep.

Finding herself in such close proximity to this extremely diverse and complex man within

the warm, close confines of the coach, Arlette
was in danger of having all her rational thought
stripped away and a treacherous warmth was
slowly beginning to creep up her arms and down
her legs. Her entire body began to vibrate with a
mixture of shock, desire and fear—fear because
of the way he made her feel, of the sensual pull
he was exerting on her—but somehow her mind
remained in control. She glowered across at his
recumbent figure, indignant that he could look
so disgustingly relaxed while she was existing on
a knife-edge. She was determined not to let him
off lightly. He had hurt her deeply. He could hurl
whatever he wanted at her for all she cared. She
was not going to plead with him for forgiveness
because she had done nothing wrong.

Thankfully the journey to Oaklands House
took only a few minutes. Neither Arlette nor
William spoke until the dark outline of the house
came into view. The coach stopped at the bottom of a narrow flight of steps leading up to the
solid, double oak doors. When Arlette would
have risen to get out, William halted her.

'Don't get out, not yet. I beg a moment of your
time, Arlette.'

Arlette looked at him, wishing he had remained asleep. 'Beg? You?'

Drawing up his long legs and sitting squarely on the seat, he nodded. 'If it is necessary, I will go down on my knees.'

'Please don't do that. For a start there's little enough room in the coach as it is. Not only that—you would look quite ridiculous.' She sat down again, waiting for him to speak.

'Arlette, I've had time to think about what I said to you on our previous encounter and I want to apologise for the things I said to you. I should not have spoken to you like I did and I'm sorry if I hurt you. I do understand why you didn't tell me about Marian and James. Your loyalty to your sister is commendable, but you must realise that I believe in absolute honesty.'

'If that is the case, then perhaps you should have been honest with Marian and told her how you tried to seduce me on two occasions. Where was your honesty then, William?' she retorted sarcastically.

He merely looked at her and raised an eyebrow. 'You are right, of course. I should have told her the truth and, circumstances being what they were at the time, Marian would more than likely have rejoiced in my confession and encouraged our relationship. But I firmly believe that secrets and lies are corrosive and when you are holding something back you hold back a part of yourself.'

'I agree with what you say, but sometimes people keep secrets for other reasons.'

'And those are?'

'To protect the people one cares about.'

'And you were protecting Marian.'

'Yes, of course I was, as you did when you failed to tell her about us. Perhaps what I did in your eyes was wrong, but when I became Marian's confidante—which is what I was and I feel no shame in that—it had nothing to do with hurting you in any way. So, if you cannot come to terms with what I did, then I am sorry. You have made it plain that it will always be a barrier between us, so I will live with it. It was my choice and I have no regrets.'

'As it was my choice when I decided to make Marian my wife. I should have seen when Sefton appeared at Court to see his father the subtle change in her. Had I truly loved her, I would have sensed it,' he said quietly. 'Her eyes lit up whenever he was present, but I put this down to girlish fancies and put it from my mind.'

The door to the house opened and a finger of orange light shone down the steps. Hester stood in the doorway.

'I must go. Thank you for bringing me home.' Opening the door, she climbed out, turning and looking back at him. 'You are right. Failing to be open and honest is as damaging as a lie. The truth will eventually surface. Secrets and deceit will ultimately destroy a relationship's stability. Goodnight, William.'

Alette's instinct was to withdraw, for she had to ask herself what she was doing caring so deeply for someone who had turned their back on her when she needed them most. She remembered the passion of his embrace, the joy, the fun of being at Court and, most of all, the unmistakable love for him in her heart before he had thrust her away. Just now, as she climbed the steps to the house, she wanted him to call her back, to hold her tight, to ease the pain of her loss.

But that wasn't going to happen.

Arlette would have been extremely perturbed had she been given an insight into William's thoughts as he watched her walk towards the house. Arlette had grown into a natural temptress: alluring, lovely, entrancing and untouched. He found it hard to explain the appeal of this young woman he had brought to London when she had been just thirteen years old. Now Marian was married to James Sefton and he was to return to Arlington Court, he had seriously begun to consider marriage and Arlette was the lady of his choice. Proud and wilful she might be, he admitted to himself, but she was too lovely for comfort. She projected a tangible magic aura and, when he had held her in his arms, he had felt her vibrant inner energy and appetite for life. Her beauty in her home setting and on that day she had attended Whitehall Palace had fed his gaze and created a warm, hungering ache that would not be easily appeased by anything less than what he desired.

He did not pause to understand the reasons for what he was about to do. He wanted her and that was reason enough. Something must be done to prevent her marrying Sir Ralph Crompton. It did occur to him that, because of the recent rift that had sprung up between them, she might oppose him, but he was vainly assured of his own ability to lure her into his arms. But with wisdom born of experience, he realised he would have to tread with caution. On their initial confrontation when she had made him aware of Marian's infidelity, he had not wanted her to rebel and oppose him so fiercely. He would approach Hester and offer marriage to her sister with typical speed and resolve, and take it from there.

Arlette walked past Hester into the house. William told the driver of the coach to wait when he saw Hester approaching him.

'William, have you got a moment?' Hester asked.

'Of course,' he replied. 'What's troubling you, Hester? You look worried about something.'

'I'm concerned about Arlette.' She turned and looked at the doorway, where Arlette hovered, waiting for her. 'I can't talk now. Will you come to the house? Perhaps tomorrow if it's convenient? Arlette is to visit Anne with some items I promised her. She should be gone for most of the day.'

William's mouth set in a grim line. 'What is it that is so important? Is Arlette in some kind of danger, Hester?'

She gave him a strained smile. 'I sincerely hope not, but I have to protect her. You will come?'

'Yes, of course I will. There is something I have to speak with you about, too—something that concerns Arlette. I will come about midday.'

Hester hurried back to the house and as William continued on his way he wondered what on earth Hester wanted to talk to him about.

'How was the wedding, Arlette?' Hester asked as they went into the house, closing the door.

'It went well. Marian made a wonderful bride. I really wish you had come, Hester. She would have liked you to be there.'

'I doubt my presence would have made a difference. Besides,' she said, lowering her voice lest anyone be listening, not that it would have made any difference if they had been, 'Lady Sefton and I don't exactly see eye to eye. We are neighbours and live in harmony providing we keep to our own houses. She is not an easy woman to like—in fact, I don't envy Marian her mother-in-law.'

True to his word William arrived at Oaklands House the following day. The house was quiet, Hester alone in the parlour clearly awaiting his arrival. William studied her with a slight frown. Despite her attempt to appear unaffected by her request to see him, he could see that Hester was as tense as a tightly coiled spring.

'Thank you for coming,' she said when they were both seated. 'I have need of your assistance, William. Indeed, there is no one else I can turn to.'

'My curiosity is aroused. It is clear that you are extremely worried about something. Of what help could I possibly be? You said it concerns Arlette.'

She nodded. 'I believe you are to leave for Warwickshire shortly.'

'That is what I intend. Now Marian is wed there is nothing to keep me here and I am impatient to reinstate my presence at Arlington Court.'

'Would you consider taking Arlette with you?' Hester asked quickly, quietly, lest she be overheard. 'I know it is an imposition to ask this of you, but Sir Ralph Crompton is the weight of my problems. He is becoming more and more persistent. He harries Richard at every turn. Indeed, it is so bad that Richard goes out of his way to avoid him. Richard knows nothing of this. He owes Sir Ralph a debt of long standing. He fears that Sir Ralph is about to call in that debt should he not get his way.'

'Arlette has made me aware of this.'

'Then you will know that she is being forced into it against her will and I can no longer stand by and watch her being made unhappy by it.' She looked at William hard to lend strength to her words. 'Arlette is dear to me and deserves better. It is imperative that she leaves London and I beg your discretion. It is the only way I can think of to save her from a marriage that is abhorrent to her. Should Sir Ralph find out what I intend doing, he will do his utmost to stop her.'

'Are you not afraid of what he will do when he finds out he has been thwarted? I doubt your husband will agree with what you plan to do.'

Hester took a deep, determined breath. 'I will deal with that when it happens. My main concern is to remove Arlette from Sir Ralph's reach.'

William held her gaze as he considered her request. She had taken him by surprise. 'It all seems very complicated, Hester. Little wonder you are concerned. Of course I will do what I can to help Arlette. Mayfield is not out of my way, if it is your wish that I take her to Blanche until something has been sorted out with Mayfield Hall. But I have something else in mind and it does not include Blanche. Before we go any further I think I should tell you that I wish to marry Arlette.'

'I see. Forgive me if I don't appear to be surprised. I have seen the way things are between the two of you.'

William smiled. 'In the light of my recent betrothal to Marian, I know this is all rather sudden. Indeed, it is so sudden that even I am quite astonished. But Arlette is perfect. What I have to offer is worth your consideration, Hester.'

'I know that and, knowing your intentions, it makes what I am asking of you easier.'

'Of course it will not be acceptable for the two of us to travel to Oxfordshire alone. She is no longer a child and it would be most inappropriate.'

'Yes, I can see that. Then what do you suggest?'

'That I make Arlette my wife before we leave London.'

Hester nodded slowly, giving it some thought. 'I approve of that, providing Arlette is in agreement.'

'As my wife, she will be out of Sir Ralph's reach once and for all.'

'That is what I want.'

The silence that followed was long and heavy. Hester studied him gravely for a moment, then she smiled thinly. 'I see you have it all worked out.'

'It may seem that way, but I haven't, not really. Everything depends on me being able to persuade Arlette. Now Marian is married to James

Sefton I am a free man. I care for Arlette deeply, Hester. I love her very much.'

'I have seen that for myself and you would not wish to marry her if you did not, and—maybe I shouldn't say this—but I believe Arlette is more than a little in love with you, even though she may not know it yet. When she found out you were betrothed to Marian, it affected her very badly.'

Silently William wanted nothing more than to make Arlette his wife, but when he asked her, he hoped she would not think he had been coerced into it to keep her out of the clutches of another man. He would have to convince her that he had intended proposing marriage before he had spoken to Hester. He got to his feet.

'Forgive me, Hester, but I must think about this. No part of this dilemma is remotely easy for me. I have a feeling she will not take kindly to my proposal of marriage if she believes it has been prompted by nothing more than to prevent her marrying Sir Ralph Crompton. Her resentment will be great indeed and I doubt she will forgive me.'

'Oh, I think her pride might take a bit of a battering initially, but she will soon see the sense of what you are offering.'

William glanced at her. She appeared to be deep in thought. Encouraged by her approval, he continued to press his suit. 'I am a wealthy man, Hester, and prepared to settle any sum you care to name on Arlette, which may go some way to settling your debt to Sir Ralph. I promise you she will have no cause for complaint as my wife. Her life will be replete and I will give her every luxury in life within my power to grant her.'

'Then what can I say? I know the two of you will be very happy together. Will you come back soon?' Hester asked as he made for the door.

He turned and looked at her and nodded. 'Yes. I realise the situation is urgent. I will come to-morrow, about this time. Will Arlette be here?'

'Yes.'

'I will speak to her then.'

When Arlette returned from her walk by the river the next morning, Hester came out of the house to meet her. Her face was animated, as if she couldn't contain her excitement.

'Hester? What is it? Has something happened?'

'Oh, yes, Arlette. It has. Something quite wonderful. We've had a letter—a letter from Thomas. After all these years he has written.

He is alive and well. Can you believe that? It is wonderful news.'

Arlette stared at her in amazement. 'Thomas? A letter? But—I can hardly believe it. How is he? What does he say?' The words tumbled out of her mouth.

'That he's coming home.'

'Home? But where? Where will he go?'

'Why, Mayfield, I expect. The estate may have been sequestered, but in Blanche's last letter she told us that the old man who lived there has died so the house is empty.'

'But that doesn't mean it will be returned to us.'

'Let Thomas deal with that when he gets there. The main thing is that he is alive and coming home. And he has a wife and child—a son. What a wonderful day it will be when he is back at Mayfield.'

Arlette went about her work with a happy feeling. After so many years of not knowing what had happened to Thomas, he was coming home.

What Arlette had not expected was that Sir Ralph would come to the house that day. Hester was sitting out in the garden. Arlette was alone in the parlour. She sat on a stool by the window doing some mending. When he entered she rose, putting her work aside. She felt the hair bristle in the nape of her neck as, with a quiet confidence, she faced him.

He made no move to approach her. Despite the repugnance he inspired in her, her face gave no hint of this. She looked presentable in a snug-fitting olive-green woollen gown and a lace cap covered her hair, but it would be lost on Sir Ralph. He could barely keep his lusting gaze from straying from her beautiful face to her softly rounded breasts and tiny waist. But suddenly he seemed to recollect himself and pulled himself up straight, a hard gleam replacing the sexual desire in his eyes.

'Sir Ralph! You take me by surprise. Richard is in the garden with Hester.'

'I have something I wish to discuss with him, but I am also here to see you.'

'Oh. I see. If you will excuse me, I will let Richard know you are here.'

When she made a move to pass him he reached out and grasped her wrist.

'There's no haste, Arlette. I've been generous and more than patient, awaiting your answer to my proposal of marriage.'

She looked at him haughtily. 'I apologise for

keeping you waiting, Sir Ralph, but my time of late has been taken up with my sister's marriage to James Sefton. I've had little time for anything else. Please let go of my wrist.' Roughly he thrust it away. Much as she would have liked to rub her sore flesh, she would not give him the satisfaction of letting him know he had hurt her.

'You do realise that if you refuse me the consequences will be dire for your brother-in-law. I can make life very unpleasant for them.'

Although she was quaking inside, Arlette faced him with outward calm. 'I will not be bought, Sir Ralph,' she said, her eyes bright with indignation, 'or blackmailed into marriage to you.' She tossed her head in defiance. 'Very well. I will give you my answer. I have considered your proposal seriously and questioned your suitability as a husband for me. You fall short. I will not tie myself to a man I do not love—a man I know I can never love—so please do not embarrass either of us further by prolonging this meeting.'

Suddenly he laughed softly, his eyes dark and heavy-lidded with desire. It was as though her resistance excited him. Smiling with wicked enticement, he reached out once more and gripped her arm, pulling her close. What he intended evoked within her a shuddering revulsion.

'Come, Arlette, why so coy? By all accounts you were not so when you were at the Court of Charles Stuart.' His voice was low and coercing. There was an evil echo in his soft laughter which escaped Arlette as her mind darted about wildly to find a way to distract him from his amorous intent. 'I want you, Arlette. I can't get you out of my mind.' He positioned himself so that she could not get past him.

'It would appear I have come not a moment too soon,' a deep voice rang out. 'The lady does not appear to welcome your advances. Would you force yourself upon her when she is clearly unwilling?'

Sir Ralph let go of Arlette's arm and spun round, furious at the interruption.

Arlette also turned and looked at her rescuer, relieved to see William, who came to stand between them, his handsome mouth curled with distaste. Arlette hadn't seen him since the wedding. Until that moment she had struggled to banish him from her thoughts, but she had not succeeded. It was like being on a hazardous obstacle course of emotions that left her confused. Secretly she had missed him more than she would have believed possible, for how could she ever forget how volatile and attractive this man was? Instantly there was a resurgence in her of the magnetism that drew her whenever she was with him. It burned into her ruthlessly, making her heart turn over. In this relatively small parlour and towering over Sir Ralph's diminutive figure, power exuded from his tall frame.

A muscle twitched in his cheek, which it always did when he was angry. He had never met Sir Ralph Crompton, but he knew he was not mistaken that this was indeed the man responsible for the bruises he had seen on Arlette's arm. He could never stand a bully and it was plain to see that, if he hadn't arrived when he had, the man would have forced himself on her.

He looked at the angry assailant and spoke in a biting calm. 'Good God, man, can't you restrain yourself? I believe you are Sir Ralph Crompton, the man whose proposal of marriage Mistress Dryden has just rejected.'

Sir Ralph froze and shifted uneasily, his eyes wary as they surveyed the threatening figure whose identity he knew instinctively. Had it been anyone else he would have replied with equal anger. As it was he glowered at him, his righteous indignation replaced by smouldering malevolence. It would not help to make an enemy of a man as powerful and important as Lord William Latham—a man who had the ear of Charles Stuart. It galled him that his own power and influence, which had sustained him in his familiar world, had begun to wane since the Royalists had arrived in London. 'I would advise you to mind your own business, sir.'

'But I am making it my business,' William replied in a low, meaningful voice, trying to keep his fury at bay. 'It is clear Mistress Dryden does not share your lust. What did you intend? To ravish her under her sister's nose?'

'Certainly not. I proposed marriage to Mistress Dryden. I have waited long enough. I have come for her reply.'

William smiled thinly, raising an eyebrow. 'I applaud your excellent taste, but allow me to answer for her. Mistress Dryden is to marry me.' Behind him Arlette's eyes opened wide with shock. He heard her gasp, but did not turn round. 'She is to be my wife.'

'You!' The exclamation exploded from Sir Ralph's lips. 'So the gossip was true. You were consorting when she went to Whitehall Palace. She is promised to me.'

'You're mistaken. Miss Dryden is of an age to decide for herself who she will and will not marry. Her decision not to accept your proposal was final. Now save yourself further embarrassment and leave.'

Arlette cast a glance at Sir Ralph. His fists were clenched by his sides, his face contorted with anger. The look on his face as he glared at William told her that he wanted blood. She had seen that look before on their last encounter, when he had failed to get his own way and bruised her arm. He looked at her with icy stillness and fear spiked through her when she read the fury in his eyes.

He stepped away from them when Hester chose that moment to enter the house. She halted on seeing the three of them, their faces telling her that all was not well. Sir Ralph looked furious.

'Why, Sir Ralph. We were not expecting you. Is it Richard you have come to see?'

Sir Ralph's face darkened as he glanced at the three of them before settling on Arlette. 'You little slut,' he breathed. 'You gave him more than a kiss, didn't you?'

William took exception to the slur and stepped towards him, while Arlette exclaimed with fervour, 'No! I did not!'

'Watch your tongue, Crompton,' William warned, his tone low and deadly. 'I bore witness to the bruises you left on her arm from a previous encounter. Lay another finger on her and I swear you'll rue the day you ever offered for her.'

Standing quite still, white-faced, Sir Ralph cast a wary glance at the taller man. Then his gaze sliced back to Arlette. 'Is it true? Are you to marry him?'

Taken completely off her guard by William's announcement that they were to wed, Arlette was considering her answer when William's patience snapped.

'Damn you, Crompton. Stop badgering her.' Turning then, his jaw set in a hard line, William reached out to take Arlette's hand in his own, raising it to his lips in a tender gesture. He glanced down at her pale, startled face before again fixing his eyes on Crompton. 'Miss Dryden has done me the honour of agreeing to be my wife. Now leave. You have got what you came for.'

Sir Ralph stepped back, glancing at Hester. 'I will call again to speak to Richard,' he said tersely, moving quickly towards the door. 'Good day.'

At William's blatant falsehood, Arlette felt her

cheeks go from white to crimson. She felt as if she were being swept along on the crest of a violent wave and was in imminent danger of drowning. William had thrown her a lifeline, one that had taken her wholly by surprise. Withdrawing her hand, she stepped back.

'Thank you, William. Your arrival was most timely, but there was no need to go to such lengths as to tell Sir Ralph I am to be your wife.'

Hester looked at Arlette with a strained expression. 'What did Sir Ralph want?'

'My answer to his marriage proposal. I told him I wouldn't marry him and then William appeared'

'Did he touch you?'

Arlette shook her head. 'No.'

'That's a relief. William, thank goodness you arrived when you did and I thank you for coming so promptly.'

Arlette stared at her. 'You sent for him, Hester?'

'Yes, I did.'

'For what reason?'

Taking Arlette's hand, Hester pulled her down beside her on to a settle. 'I have become deeply concerned about Sir Ralph's persistence to make you his wife. Already he has started to work his spite on Richard. He can be vicious when roused. I spoke to Richard about my deep concern and you may be surprised when I tell you that he is in agreement that it would be best for you to leave London.'

'And the debt Richard owes him? He will call it in, you know that.'

'Yes, we do. Knowing you are to marry William, Sir Ralph will be feeling thwarted, but I know many of Richard's associates thought it was wrong for him to lust after a girl half his age. He is not well liked and there will be many who will rejoice in his embarrassment.'

'You will do this for me—you and Richard?'

'Yes. You are my dear sister, Arlette. I want what is best for you and it is not seeing you as the wife of Sir Ralph.'

'But what of you, Hester? I don't want to leave you at this time. You will have need of me when it is time for the child to be born.'

Hester laughed to allay her concern. 'Arlette, I have a house full of servants I can rely on. Do not concern yourself.'

'I still don't like leaving you. But—what has this got to do with William?'

'He is leaving for Warwick shortly and I think you should go with him, as his wife.'

Arlette's eyes flew to William. 'But—I thought you were jesting when you told Sir Ralph we were to marry.'

He shook his head. 'I have never been more serious of anything in my life.'

Angry at his arrogant assumption that she would simply fall in with his wishes, something inside her rebelled. She got to her feet, an indignant flush mantling her cheeks. 'Your arrogance amazes me. You haven't asked me to marry you. How dare you assume that I will. Since I was not present at this meeting you had with Hester, perhaps you would be so good as to enlighten me.'

'I saw Hester yesterday. Before I go any further, I will tell you that I had already decided that I would ask you to be my wife before I came. Your sister is concerned about you, Arlette. I think she is right. You would be better away from London at this present time.'

'I had thought you could go to Mayfield, perhaps stay with Blanche,' Hester said, clearly worried that Arlette was about to turn her well-laid plans upside down. 'That was before William told me he wanted to ask you to be his wife.'

'I can still go to Mayfield. If William is to go to Warwickshire, then he can take me. He doesn't have to marry me.' She looked at him.

'You and I have travelled the journey together in the past without mishap. Now we are no longer at war the journey should be even easier.'

'As my wife.'

'No, William. What you said to me on the day you found out about Marian and James cannot easily be set aside and will always stand between us. If you expect me to meekly abide by your wishes and do your bidding, then you are either jesting or insane. I would be grateful if you would escort me as far as Mayfield. Be assured that I shall endeavour not to be troublesome or an encumbrance and to do my best not to disrupt the journey in any way.'

William raised his brow in an arrogant arch. 'It would be appreciated. I do salute your courage and your boldness for undertaking such a taxing journey.'

'As far as Mayfield. We've had a letter from Thomas. He is to come home at last to Mayfield.'

William stared at her in amazement. 'Thomas? You have heard from him?'

'He is to return to Mayfield Hall with his wife and child. What he will find when he gets there is anyone's guess. It would be a relief to us all if a member of the family is there to welcome him home and explain everything that has hap-

pened during his absence. He will be unaware
of our father's demise.'

'He is well, I hope.'

'Yes,' Arlette replied. 'At least his letter gave
us hope to believe so.'

'Then I shall look forward to seeing him.'

'You will, if you take me with you.'

William looked at her. Her flesh gleamed rich
and warm and his head was filled with the delicious scent of her. Something quickened that
had lain dormant since he had last seen her. It
was a good feeling, but he did not intend nour-
ishing it lest it weakened him.

Arlette stood still, feeling suffocated by his
nearness. He watched every line of her face as
he considered the request, every fleeting expression. It pricked sorely that Arlette had to wait
for his reply and, had the cause been less desperate, she would have told him to forget it and
stormed off.

'Well, William,' she prompted. 'Do you agree
to let me travel with you? I promise you I will
give you no cause for complaint,' she hastened
to assure him. 'You won't even know I'm there.'

As he cocked an eye at her, he smiled, thinking she would be hard to ignore at any time.
'Common sense tells me you spell trouble, a

heap of it, but I know how eager you are to go to Mayfield.'

'Thank you, William,' Hester said, casting Arlette a cross look. 'I cannot tell you how relieved I am to hear you say that. I wouldn't trust Arlette with anyone else, but I sincerely hope you will give consideration to William's marriage proposal, Arlette. You will be compromised if you accompany him as a single woman.'

'How can I consider it when he hasn't had the temerity to ask me?' she quipped. 'When do you hope to leave?'

'Two weeks, three at the most.'

'Then we will make sure Arlette is ready,' Hester said, getting to her feet, thinking that William would have more chance of persuading her sister to accept his proposal of marriage without her looking on. 'Now I'd best go and tell Richard what has been decided.'

A silence fell between them, broken only by Hester's heels on the stone flags as she walked towards the door. Arlette looked at William. His broad shoulders and clear-cut profile were etched against the green fields beyond the window. Watching Hester's retreating figure, he suddenly turned and caught Arlette's appraising eye. She saw his face and felt her heart give a sudden leap. If only everything could be normal between them and that wretched business with Marian had never happened. William's eyes were fixed on Arlette's face. It was he who broke the silence.

'Is it decided, Arlette? Will you go with me to Arlington Court as my wife? Can I persuade you to accept?' Suddenly he grinned, moving to stand in front of her. 'It wouldn't be difficult. I only have to take you in my arms to kiss you into submission.'

Arlette stepped back, eyeing him warily. 'You wouldn't.'

One dark eyebrow rose in a measuring look and an almost lecherous smile curved his lips. 'Would you care to put it to the test?'

'No, I would not, and don't you dare. That is blackmail.'

He laughed. 'Call it what you will, Arlette, but if blackmail enables me to kiss you into submission then I am in favour.'

Arlette flushed, unable to quell the peculiar sweet stirring of pleasure his words caused. He meant it, she knew, and she was flustered by his possessive remark. His proposal tugged at her heart, despite the current rift between them. She longed for him to reach out and draw her into his arms, but she had erected barriers and there they would remain until she was of a mind to remove them.

'I can vouch for my sister's concern regarding Sir Ralph, but when I recall your less than gentlemanly treatment of me when you found out I had kept Marian's affair from you, you must forgive me if I doubt yours. I told you then that I refuse to be second-best. Don't you understand, William? You are asking me to be your wife for all the wrong reasons. You make a mockery of me.'

William gazed at her, noting the soft confusion in her searching eyes. 'You are not second-best, Arlette. Never think that. I want you. No man of sound mind could resist so much temptation set before his eyes. You have captured my interest and I have become hopelessly entangled in my desire.'

His eyes never left her—they seemed to scorch her with the intensity of his passion. Arlette was bewildered by it and lowered her gaze, afraid to meet that penetrating stare. She was already too well aware of the beguiling quality of his smile. 'You can't force me to marry you if I don't want to. Even if you drag me to the altar, you can't make me say I will.'

William smiled, recognising in her answer the same kind of hostility when he had tried to negotiate with fellow soldiers in unfortunate circumstances. Exactly like those soldiers Arlette felt powerless and in her pride felt the need to retaliate by making things as difficult as possible for him. 'What a proud, foolish woman you are,' he murmured. 'I won't have to force you. There's no reason why matters should not be amicable between us, Arlette. I feel that as my wife life would be more endurable, and pleasant.'

Arlette looked at him warily. 'Really! How?'

'Like this,' he murmured, pulling her close, his arms slipping easily about her and crushing her to him. Bending his dark head, he captured her mouth in a soft, compelling kiss, warming and penetrating to the depths of her being. His mouth forced her lips apart, his tongue teasing.

Arlette tried to turn her head, afraid that her will and her anger would crumble beneath his onslaught, but he held her in a gentle, but unyielding, grip, his hands boldly passing over her waist, her hips, possessively. For a moment her body responded eagerly, then mingled anger at his impertinence and horror at her own swift reaction caused her to stiffen in his arms.

William dragged his lips from hers and looked

down at her, noting the tell-tale flush on her cheeks.

She seethed with anger and humiliation. 'You are asking me to enter into a binding contract to change my life, something that will determine my entire future.'

She tossed her head back and William was alarmed to see not only anger, but what looked like a mixture of contempt and—what was it?—could it possibly be anguish?

'You are taking it for granted that because I allowed you to kiss me on more than one occasion I will marry you. It's not like that for me.'

'Then remember this. I know how you feel when you are in my arms. I have seen it in your eyes and how you reacted, and if you think you can watch me walk away, you are mistaken.'

There was a warning underlying the lightness of his words and Arlette knew that he spoke in all seriousness. The deep timbre of his voice reverberated in her breast and she gave up trying to discern what his faults might be. But she needed to preserve all her resources for herself if she expected him to see reason. How could she accept his offer? Of course she wanted to marry him. Her heart cried out for it. There was nothing she wanted more than that—but not like this. Not when he was fresh out of a betrothal to a woman who had rejected him—not when she would always be his second choice.

She was still standing close to him, the look in her eyes telling him she was her own woman and if he thought he could bully her into doing his will then he could think again. But she could feel his eyes on her, feel his penetrating gaze on her face, feel his presence with every fibre of her being and a growing warmth suffused her, melting her wariness. 'Has it not occurred to you that I might appreciate being asked to marry you? Am I not to have a say in the matter, an important matter that will affect my whole life?'

'Of course you have,' he murmured, taking her arms and drawing her close once more. 'But what are you afraid of?' he asked, his voice deep and husky.

She stared up at him, her mouth agape, his tall form making her achingly aware of her own vulnerability and helplessness. He was going to kiss her again, she knew it. 'I'm not afraid,' she whispered, her voice holding a desperate appeal as she took a step back.

His response was to draw her back. Raising her hand, he kissed her fingers very gently. Her heart was pounding a deafening beat. She was tense and still, her brain racing as she tried to think of a way out of this.

'William, please, I—'

'Arlette,' he murmured, 'be quiet.'

Looking into her eyes as he caressed her fingers with his mouth, he could feel her melting, feel it in the way her fingers trembled.

'But I—'

He stopped her words with his thumb gently pressed against her lips. 'Be quiet.'

Chapter Nine

The tone of his voice was so soft and inviting that for one mad moment Arlette almost surrendered. She felt herself tremble with the need that he always invoked in her when he was close, but she must not let him come closer. 'You cannot mean to do this.'

Taking her shoulders, he drew her lithe form towards him, capturing her in a fierce embrace, his eyes feasting on the delicate creaminess of her face and her shining hair. 'I mean it,' he whispered, his mouth against hers. 'The attraction between us has been denied for too long, my love. I think we need to reach an understanding before I leave this house today.'

'There is nothing to understand,' she whispered, suddenly afraid of the purposeful gleam she saw in those heavy-lidded eyes looking down at her.

'There is, Arlette,' he said as his lips caressed her cheek. His hands sank into the thickness of her hair, holding her head immobile as his mouth slanted across her lips and devoured their sweetness, languidly coaxing and parting, his tongue probing and plundering the honeyed cavern, as if he had an eternity to explore and savour. Pleasure rolled over his body, pleasure turning to desire. He wanted to taste her, to run his fingers through the silken mass of her hair. Within seconds his loins stirred.

The sweet urgency of it made Arlette lose touch with reality. It filled her soul. The embers that had glowered and heated her rebellion earlier now burned with passion, her protestations having become raw hunger. It was a kiss so exquisite that whatever conscience she had left died, as she became imprisoned in a haze of dangerous, terrifying sensuality over which she had no control.

Sensing this might be the moment to press his suit, he dragged his lips from hers and looked down at her upturned face, which was flushed a glorious pink. 'Your eagerness astounds me. Nothing you can say or do will change that. You do want me, Arlette,' he told her with a knowing smile. 'You cannot deny it.'

She swallowed nervously and stared at him, memories of his passion, his gentleness and restraint filling her mind, and added to that were memories of her own urgent desire. She opened her mouth to utter a denial, wanting to hurt him, to humiliate him, but her conscience chose that moment to assert itself and strangled the words in her throat. She had gloried in his kiss and she could not bring herself to tell him otherwise.

'Yes, William, I do want you,' she replied fiercely. 'I want you so much that it's unendurable.'

William tenderly caressed her cheeks, relieved when she didn't draw back. 'My poor little Arlette. It needn't be. It could be something quite wonderful if you would let it.'

It was his tone, not his words, that conquered her. 'I know,' she whispered shakily.

'Then don't fight me. You will tire yourself out with the effort. In the end you will succumb to what is in your heart and you will not want to fight me any more.'

Arlette breathed deeply, looking at him steadily. 'You are so sure of that, aren't you, William? You are so arrogant in your assumption.'

William's expression grew serious. He looked at her steadily. 'Apart from Marian—a situation which you understand fully—you are the only woman I have offered for. You are the woman I want to spend the rest of my life with and I will not be satisfied until you are my wife. Surely that must count for something in your estimation of me.'

Arlette swallowed and averted her eyes, feeling confused, her spirit still bruised from their harsh altercation that day he had discovered Marian's infidelity. Rather than stir up old hurts, she said, 'Yes, of course it does.'

William tilted her face to his. 'It was wrong of me to assume you would fall in with my plans without talking it over with you first, Arlette, and your reaction was exactly the reaction I would expect a proud, rebellious, lovely young woman to make. I apologise,' he conceded quietly. 'I have behaved badly. I deserve your anger, but not your dislike.'

To Arlette's mortification, tears stung her eyes. 'But I don't,' she whispered. 'Please don't think that.'

'I know you don't,' he said with feeling. Sensing her trepidation, he took her hand gently in his. 'So, Arlette, are you willing to plight your troth to me? To be my wife? Unless you would prefer to accept Crompton's suit?'

'No, of course not, although you know just how close Richard is to ruin and how advantageous a marriage between us would be for him.'

'I am aware of that. Despite the wars and the drain on Royalist coffers, I have come out of it better than most. I am not a poor man, Arlette. I have offered your brother-in-law a sizable stipend to be paid for your hand upon execution of the agreement,' William informed her. 'It will go a long way to shoring up his financial situation.'

Arlette looked calmly into his eyes. 'That is indeed generous of you, but when you put it like that, so matter of fact it might be a business proposition you are talking about, I feel that I am in exactly the same situation as when Sir Ralph proposed marriage. I will be marrying you to save my sister's husband from ruin and for no other reason.'

Contemplating her flushed cheeks, he placed his finger beneath her chin and tilted her face to his. 'If I thought that, then I would withdraw my offer, but I believe your feelings for me go beyond mere fondness. What I feel for you exceeds anything I have felt for any other woman. I want to make you my wife. In my heart there is no one who matters as much as you do. That is the power you have over me. As my wife, you will be in a situation far removed from that which would have existed had you married Crompton. So what is your answer to be?'

When he traced his finger along the flesh of her neck, she closed her eyes, awed that a hand which had dealt death so skilfully with a sword in battle could be so infinitely tender. She was disappointed that he hadn't answered her question as she'd hoped he would. Perhaps he was still feeling the hurt of Marian's deception and found it difficult to commit himself fully. But it was enough—for now. In time she was confident that love would grow.

The air was charged between them. She gazed into his eyes. They had darkened to a stormy dark blue. A tremor went through her. She could feel the pull of his masculinity. How had she allowed him to defeat her so easily? The realisation awed and frightened her. It excited her, that she, who had convinced herself she had no influence over anything in her life, had the power over the very man who was offering her and her family a lifeline.

'I cannot believe you are asking me this. Here we are, standing on the edge of a very different future than either of us had planned. Yes, yes, William. I accept. I will marry you.'

He saw tears shimmering in her eyes and he smiled. 'Thank you. And now I have something to give you—something Marian wanted you to have.'

Arlette watched as he removed a plain gold ring from his pocket and, taking her hand, he placed it on the middle finger of her right hand. Knowing just how much this would mean to her, he was visibly moved as he raised it and pressed it to his lips, looking down into her eyes which were bright with unshed tears.

'This was your mother's wedding ring, Arlette, the ring your father placed on her finger on their wedding day. Marian feels it is only right that you should have it.'

Arlette stared down at it, feeling a hard choking lump rise in the back of her throat. Her heart swelled with a great wave of tenderness and love for her mother, who she had known for such a short time, but who she was sure had thought of her with love.

'Thank you, William. I will treasure it always.'

'Now I think we had best inform your sister that we are to wed. We have a wedding to arrange before we can leave London.'

Arlette's mind was spinning with a welter of

emotions as she went out into the garden to find Hester and Richard. For all the intensity of William's kiss, she knew that he desired her—he had told her so, but would he ever tell her that he loved her?

The following days were filled with wedding preparations. Arlette saw little of William, who had much to occupy his time at Whitehall since he was to leave London the day after the wedding. Everything was rushed and planned and contrived to make the occasion a memorable one. Hester insisted that she must have a new wardrobe. At first Arlette maintained that it was an unnecessary extravagance, but soon realised that it was quite useless voicing her objections when Hester and Marian were being carried along on the crest of some enormous wave.

She was measured up for garments and accessories that were required to complete the extensive wardrobe of a lady of quality. Richard, unable to believe the satisfactory way everything had turned out and that William's generous stipend would rid him of the debt he owed Sir Ralph Crompton once and for all, was puffed up with gratification and provided the fine fabrics for Arlette's gowns. William intended leaving London immediately after the wedding, in which case the gowns would be sent on to Arlington Hall when completed.

The wedding was a quiet affair with a gathering of family members and a few friends. William was unable to believe that the exquisite young woman in a gown in ivory satin and silver lace was his wife. With her large blue-green eyes and her hair cascading in abundant golden curls and framing her enchanting face, she was a vision of radiant, breathtaking beauty.

'You look exquisite,' he murmured when she took her place beside him at the altar, raising her hand to her lips. 'Are you ready to become my wife, Arlette?'

Her gaze fixed on him. There was a splendid radiance about his dark masculine beauty today, his glowing skin clean shaved, his black hair drawn back and secured at his nape. He held her gaze steadily, and after a long moment she felt a softening inside her and she slowly yielded.

'Yes, William, I am ready.'

Then it was over. The wedding feast held at Oaklands House was a truly joyous affair and Arlette felt herself truly blessed to have both her sisters present. The only person missing was

Thomas and it was her hope that they would soon be reunited when she reached Mayfield Hall.

It was with regret that William returned to Whitehall after the celebrations, forgoing their wedding night. His conscience smote him that Arlette had been denied a period of courtship and by tacit agreement they had decided to wait until they took up their life at Arlington Court before becoming man and wife in every sense.

Arlette could feel herself relaxing as they left the bustle of London behind. She had bade farewell to family and friends who had gathered to see them on their way. She was particularly sad to say goodbye to Hester and Marian and hoped all would go well when the time came for their babies to be born. To spare the horses they rode at a moderate pace. Arlette found herself enjoying her husband's easy ways and casual banter. His charm, wit and manners were those of one born to wealth and position. What she had feared would be a tense, unpleasant journey was becoming enjoyable.

William was not unaware of the change in her mood. Riding beside her, he glanced sideways at her, cocking his handsome brow as he gave her a lengthy inspection. 'Why, Arlette, I do believe you are smiling.'

Looking across at him, she was unable to prevent her smile broadening. 'So would you, had you endured ten years of Commonwealth rule and seeing nothing at the end of it but to be wed to Sir Ralph Crompton. To suddenly find myself set free is a wonderful feeling.'

William laughed. 'Free? Do you forget you have a husband already, Arlette?'

She glanced at him, smiling. 'How can I do that when you are right beside me? I'm already enjoying the adventure, which is stirring the life within me and I am sure will carry me forward to some exciting future, although what it will be like as your wife living at Arlington Court, I really have no idea, but something tells me it will not be dull.'

Her enthusiasm brought a smile to William's lips and a gleam of admiration in his eyes. 'That is an extremely daring proclamation.'

'Prior to this, the most daring thing I have ever done is to allow you to take me to the Court of Charles Stuart.'

William's smile broadened at her exuberance, his teeth gleaming white from between parted lips. 'I shall never forget it. I recall your enjoy-

ment of the occasion and how we danced together. In time I will take you back as my wife
and we will dance again at the King's Court.'

Kicking her horse into a gallop, she laughed.
'I live in hope, William, that it will not be long.'

The day spent travelling, the numbing fatigue
of heat and hypnotic movement, fresh air and the
scent of the countryside and rhythmic pulsing
of a million insects took their toll on Arlette. It
was a tiring and entirely new experience for her
and her euphoria diminished somewhat. With the
dusky twilight and a cool breeze that had sprung
up, they stopped at a coaching inn where they
would spend the night.

Outside the inn William dismounted and
helped Arlette down. Whenever they had stopped
earlier and he had offered his assistance, she had
coolly and stubbornly rejected it, afraid of coming too close. But at the end of their day's ride
she was more fatigued than she had expected to
be and almost fell into his arms in her eagerness
to find some food and a bed, where she might
creep beneath the feather comforters and sleep
the night away. Having decided that there would
be a short period of courtship until they reached
Arlington Court—unless, he had quipped, with a

wicked gleam in his eyes, he found he could not resist her and was unable to help himself—true to his word he arranged to take separate rooms.

When Arlette had eaten she left William to enjoy an ale by the fire, unaware that she had drawn the attention of one of the patrons. The man had watched her eat her meal and say good-night to her companion, taking particular note when he heard her say she hoped he would have a good night and she would see him at break-fast. Having been allotted a cosy chamber be-neath the eaves of the inn, leaving her window open because it was a warm night, clad only in a shift she climbed into bed and soon drifted off to sleep.

She didn't know what woke her, but there was a change in the atmosphere in the room. Opening her eyes, she had the disquieting no-tion that something was wrong. The air had be-come tense. For a moment it held her in a deathly chill and she could feel the blood in her veins freeze. Pushing herself up with her elbows, in the glow of the candle she had left burning, she was shocked to see the silhouette of a man standing in the open doorway. Her body went rigid. The flame of the candle flickered as a light

breeze came through the open window and light
and dark shapes moved around the room. Sounds
of people still about drifted up to her from the
ground floor of the inn, indicating that the hour
could not be all that late. In her tired mind her
first thought was that it was William, but when
he came further into the room and closed the
door, she could see it was not.

'I don't know who you are, or what you think
you are doing, but get out of my room before I
scream.'

'Come now, a pretty girl like you. You caught
my eye when you entered the inn. I heard you say
goodnight to the gentleman and thought maybe
we could… Come now, be nice to me,' the man
crooned, his voice thick with drink.

Immediately Arlette scrambled out of the
opposite side of the bed to the man. She made
a dash for the door, but he reached out and
grasped her arm, making her cry out in pain as
he roughly pulled her back, flinging her on to the
bed, and swooped down on her. A fierce struggle
ensued between them. She lashed out and kicked
him with all her strength, her stomach heaving
at the stench of his sweat and foul breath.

With panic born out of desperation, Arlette
gave him one almighty push. Surprised, he fell

on to the floor, hitting his head on the corner of a large wooden chest. With her heart pounding and blood drumming in her ears, she shuffled to the edge of the bed and looked down at her assailant. He lay stretched out on the carpet, blood trickling from a wound on his scalp. Thankfully he was still breathing and grunting softly. Not wasting a moment, she took his feet and began dragging him to the door, praying he wouldn't come to his senses until she had dragged him out on to the landing and closed and bolted her door.

As those patrons staying at the inn began to drift off to their chambers, it might have been the mellowing effect of the brandies he'd consumed, but it seemed to William, seated before the fire with his long legs stretched out, that he couldn't get Arlette out of his mind. His thoughts were pleasurable as he allowed his thoughts to dwell on her. He loved the way she had ridden beside him, uncomplaining about the heat and the long hours in the saddle. He loved her spirit—and she had so much spirit.

After another glass of brandy, thoroughly sick of agonising over his emotions that were draining him, William felt his gaze drift idly towards the stairs. Despite the lateness of the hour he wanted to see her—to make love to her—which was something he could only think about. Already he was regretting the period of abstinence he had suggested, giving her time to adjust to their hasty marriage.

Now he was beginning to straighten out the confusing array of emotions that had been beating at him since he had found out about Marian's affair with James Sefton, he wanted to talk to the woman he had tried so hard to deny when he had first become aware of it. The matter had yet to be addressed properly, and the sooner the better.

Shoving himself out of the chair, he crossed the room to the stairs and wearily climbed to the upper storey to the room across from Arlette's. He idly wondered how she would react if he were to enter her room. He smiled, knowing perfectly well she would show him the door. The landing was dimly lit and he had to adjust his eyes when he saw a white-clad figure struggling with what appeared to be a body.

Many years as a soldier had conditioned him to react to any situation with lightning reflexes, but now all he could do was stand and gape. 'Arlette? What the hell—?' He stared at her, his eyebrows arched in surprise. He was no longer smiling.

Panting with her efforts she looked to where he stood. 'Well, don't just stand there,' she blurted out. 'Give me a hand. This imbecile thought he could take advantage of me. Thank goodness he's full of ale and was unable to react fast enough when I pushed him off the bed.'

William went to her aid, taking over the task of pulling the man further down the landing and propping him against the wall. 'What did you hit him with?'

'Nothing. I pushed him and he hit his head against the chest in my room. He will be all right, won't he?'

'I imagine so,' William said, taking a look at the man's head. Already he was beginning to move his arm and rub his head. 'He'll have one hell of a headache when he wakes up.' He went back to her. 'Leave him where he is. He'll find his own way back to where he came from.'

Taking her hand, he drew her inside her chamber and closed the door. She sank on to the bed, crossing her arms over her chest, her head bowed, her hair tumbling about her shoulders. Crouching down in front of her, he took one of her hands.

'Look at me, Arlette,' he demanded in a tone that prompted obedience. Slowly she raised her head to look at him. 'Did he hurt you?'

She shook her head, oddly touched by his concern. 'No. When he appeared in my room and closed the door I was afraid to begin with.'

'Are you still?'

She shook her head. 'All I feel is anger at what he meant to put me through. He shouldn't have been in my room. He deserved everything he got.'

At the vehemence with which she spoke, William had great difficulty in repressing a grin. 'Poor man. Had he known he was about to face a voracious female instead of a docile dove, he would have avoided your door like he would a plague. Wait. I'll go and see if he's come round.'

Opening the door, he peered out, just in time to see the man stumbling quickly away down the landing, groaning and holding his head. He watched the pathetic wretch go, sorely tempted to go after him and beat him to within an inch of his life for daring to lay hands on Arlette, but he thought better of it. Nothing would be achieved by thrashing a drunken man and drawing attention to themselves.

William returned to find Arlette standing by the bed. She looked shaken. 'You did the man no harm. He's gone now.'

'Thank goodness.' Unconsciously Arlette's

eyes were drawn to William. Suddenly her heart quickened. There was something about the way he was looking at her that sparked the hot blood within her. It was difficult for a young woman not to admire a man who was built with such perfect proportions as he was.

William moved towards her. Curling his fingers around her chin, he tilted her face up to his. She was calmer now, her eyes large, dark and soft. He stood looking down at her upturned face, a purposeful gleam in his dark eyes. 'Would you open your door to me, Arlette, should I come knocking in the middle of the night?' he murmured huskily, his eyes burning into hers as he reached out and lightly brushed away some wisps of her hair that clung to her face. 'And you cannot really blame the man— whoever he was—for seeking you out, looking as you do. I can well understand how he felt.'

'There's no excuse for his behaviour,' Arlette retorted, doing her utmost to hold on to her crumbling composure. 'And I trust you will have no need to come knocking on my door in the middle of the night until we reach Arlington Court.'

Without looking at him she walked past him to the door, but suddenly William's arm went round her waist and he pulled her back against his hard chest.

'I don't have to go, Arlette,' he murmured, turning her round to face him and slipping his fingers through her hair on either side of her face, his gaze settling on her lips, moist and eager. 'I have needs. I need you.'

It seemed a lifetime passed as they gazed at each other. In that lifetime each lived through a range of deep, tender emotions new to them both, exquisite emotions that neither of them could put into words.

'You can't…' Arlette gasped, seeing the workings of his mind and unable to say more, because at that moment, as though in slow motion, unable to resist the temptation Arlette's mouth offered, slowly William's own moved inexorably closer. His gaze was gentle and compelling, when, in a sweet, mesmeric sensation, his mouth found hers in a kiss that shocked her senses alarmingly.

The kiss was long and lingeringly slow. Holding her in his embrace, William tightened his strong arms about her. Pressed against him, she seemed so utterly female, warm and fragile and vulnerable. His heart ached with the fear of what the intruder might have done to her. The thought of Arlette knowing a moment's terror was too agonising for him to deal with. His senses were invaded by the smell of her. It was the soft fragrance of her hair—the sweet scent of roses mingled with a musky female scent—that made his body burn. William was caught totally unprepared by an unabashed display of emotion, felt reason and control swept away by the fervent ardour of her embrace.

Arlette's resolve was weakened by the exhaustion of the journey and her body driven on by the need to be close to him. She felt the strength of his arms and the warmth of his masculine body. She made no effort to free herself from that tight circle of his arms and William had no intention of letting her go while she was content to remain there. She could feel the hard muscles of his broad chest and smell his maleness. A tautness began in her breast, a delicious ache that was like a dangerous, honeyed warmth.

Her body melted against his and his hands held her close. On a sigh she welcomed his hand stroking her nape as they sank on to the bed. Her breath came in hard, shallow gasps. Through the clothes separating their hungry flesh she could feel the heat of him and found herself yearning for the unknown. Her whole body aching, she slipped her hand inside his shirt and placed light kisses on his neck before finding his lips once more. A strange, alien feeling fluttered within her breast and she was halted for a brief passage of time when she found her lips entrapped with his once more, and though they were soft and tender, they burned with a fire that scorched her. Closing her eyes, she yielded to it, melting against him.

William tasted the sweet, honeyed softness of her mouth, finding himself once more at the mercy of his emotions, when reason and intelligence were powerless. Savouring each intoxicating pleasure, he gloried in her innocence, her purity, painfully aware of the trembling weakness in her scantily clad body pressed against him.

His conscience chose that moment to resurrect itself. Expelling a ragged breath and out of sheer self-preservation, he flung himself away as he fought to reassemble his senses and bring his desire under control. What was he doing? He berated himself for treating Arlette as he would one of his sexually experienced women he had known throughout his years of soldiering. But she was not like them. She was his wife. She was uncompromised and untainted. Suddenly he pulled away from her, rolling back to the other side of the bed, his eyes open wide.

'William...' Arlette murmured when she felt him pull away from her. Kissed and caressed into almost unconscious sensibility, she opened her eyes in a daze of suspended yearning, awakened passion glowing in the velvety depths of her eyes. Suddenly she felt empty and afraid, embarrassed by her forwardness and unable to understand why he had left her. She didn't want him to stop kissing her. With her heart pounding, she propped herself up on her elbows. His eyes were translucent in the ghostly candlelight, his lean features starkly etched. 'Please don't go.' She slipped across the bed to him and lay her head on his chest. 'Why must you thrust me away?'

For a long moment neither spoke. William's gaze was smouldering, his breathing ragged, the throbbing ache in his loins reminding him how much he wanted to make love to her. With her hair tumbling around her in a glorious silken mass, she lay like a beautiful pagan goddess among the ruins of her bed. He drew her head away from his chest as she placed soft, tantalising little kisses against his throat. It was a provocative movement and she was too innocent and inexperienced to be aware of the devastating effect it was having on his already ravaged self-control. Riven with guilt, he raised her hand to his lips and pressed them to the soft centre of her palm.

'The reason is because although I want you very badly, I promised you a period of grace before I make you my wife in every sense. I will do my absolute utmost to abide by that. I will not break that agreement by seducing you the first time we stop for the night,' he said, getting off the bed.

'I understand,' she whispered, wanting to conceal how deeply she was affected by what had just happened between them.

William reached out and gently caressed her cheek, then he turned. Her eyes followed him out of the room. Not until then did her mind come together from the far reaches of her senses where it had fled the instant William had taken her in his arms.

In his chamber and with the landing separating them, William took stock of what had just happened. He could not deny that he wanted Arlette more than he'd wanted anything in his life, more than he could believe possible. For the time he had been back in England, the tension and explosive emotions her nearness elicited, and being unable to give way to his feelings because of his betrothal to Marian, had been hell. Like a siren in Greek mythology whose singing was believed to lure sailors to destruction on the rocks, Arlette's reappearance in his life—the very knowledge of knowing she was his wife and within reach—had lured him into her arms and her vulnerability had finally broken all bounds of his restraint.

After a fitful night and eager to be away, William went to Arlette's room to see what was keeping her. There was no reply to his knock so he gingerly opened the door and looked inside. She was sound asleep. Her hair tumbled about the pillows and her eyes were closed, her long dark lashes lying like soft shadows on her rose-red cheeks. Her sweet lips were parted as she breathed softly, her chest rising and falling evenly beneath the covers, which hid the tempting roundness of her breasts. As William was about to wake her he lingered, looking down at her in wonder, savouring this moment of peace and reluctant to wake her. Studying her carefully, he thought that in sleep she looked more like a child than a woman, harmless, innocent and uncommonly lovely. It was reluctance that he touched her shoulder to wake her.

Opening her eyes, she looked up into William's dark blue eyes.

'Come,' he said gently. 'The sun's been up two hours or more and it's time we were on our way.'

Still extremely tired and aching in every limb, Arlette forced herself to sit up, not even questioning his presence in her room as memories of the night before came flooding back.

'I'll get dressed.'

'How are you, Arlette?'

'Fine, considering the night I've had.'

'I apologise for my behaviour, Arlette, but I acted as any gentleman would when he knew a lady to be in distress.'

Recalling exactly how it had been, how he had held her firmly against his hard chest and caressed her with his warm and dangerous lips, rendering her almost helpless, Arlette felt her cheeks suffuse with hot colour.

'I was not in distress. I was angry because that man had the audacity to enter my room. Besides, it was more than that and you know it,' she told him with a trace of indignation. 'For the duration of our being together, I would be obliged if you would restrain your ardour and do not be-

have in that way again. You did say there would
be nothing of that nature between us until we
reached Warwickshire.'

'But you were tempted.'

William's smile was infuriating, and the
warm sensuality of his voice almost stole Arlette's breath. If he was trying to destroy her resistance, he was succeeding admirably. At that
moment some indefinable alchemy made them
extremely aware of each other and their eyes
became caught in that age-old way of would-be
lovers. Arlette's vulnerability was laid bare for
him to pierce the guard she had resolved to keep
on her emotions.

'When you were in my arms I felt it in your
response. Do not deny it, Arlette.'

'Am I so predictable?'

'You are to me. Now get dressed and come
down and have some breakfast.'

On a sigh, reluctant to leave her warm cocoon,
Arlette shoved the covers back and swung her
legs out of bed, unaware as she did so that the
bodice of her shift gaped open to reveal the ripe
plumpness of her breasts, unconscious of the delightful vision she presented.

Not quite out of the door, William turned and
looked at her once more. 'It is not my intention

to hurt you, Arlette,' he said, speaking softly, his eyes feasting on the glorious exposure of her breasts and admiring the slender shapeliness of her legs before she hastily covered them with a sheet, 'and for the time being I shall try to keep my ardour under control, no matter how my desire for you might overwhelm me.'

'Thank you,' she uttered tightly. 'Now will you please leave and let me get dressed.'

Meeting her gaze again, William lifted a querying black eyebrow. Arlette could only wonder at his thoughts as she struggled to maintain her composure beneath his perusal.

'Would you like me to stay and assist you? I am more than willing to oblige you.'

Arlette flashed him a look, seeing a flurry of wicked thoughts coursing through his mind. 'Certainly not,' she replied. 'Now please go away.'

'Why? Are you afraid of letting me come too close? Are you afraid that, because I have you here alone, I will force you to submit to my evil desires and rob you of your innocence?'

The husky resonance of his voice almost snatched Arlette's breath away and suddenly she was unsure of herself. 'Yes, I am,' she admitted. 'After your assaults on my person last night, I believe I have good reason to be concerned.'

William laughed, his teeth flashing white from between his parted lips. 'At least you're truthful. But I didn't assault you. The feelings were mutual.'

Irritated by his dalliance, getting out of bed she crossed to the door and pushed him out on to the landing. 'I think it's time you went to prepare the horses, so out you go and leave me alone, you compromising rogue. I will dress in private.'

When he had left her Arlette gathered her clothes together and dressed. After breaking her fast, mutely she followed William outside, coming awake the moment she felt the fresh, early morning air on her face. Taking a deep breath, she mounted her horse and followed William out of the inn yard.

Chapter Ten

As their journey progressed, Arlette felt a strange security in the presence of her companion. He knew the villages and byways well, having travelled them many times when he had been a boy and he had accompanied his father to London. Looking large and forbidding astride his large bay horse, with a pistol at his belt and a sword hanging from his saddle, he would instil caution in the meanest robber.

A lightening of spirits seemed to come over them both. Perhaps it was because they were conscious of nearing their destination, or because the very fact that they were alone was weaving a spell around them, but whatever the reason Arlette felt a whole new world inviting her to explore, becoming pleasantly aware of the beauty and strangeness all around her.

Riding beside William, she listened in silent admiration as he ardently pointed out places of interest to her. It was clear to her how much he loved England, how much he had missed it, for it was like wine to his soul. They rode into a quiet valley sheltered by trees. A stream tumbled its way through the centre. Unfastening the bag containing the food William had purchased from the inn before leaving, they left the horses to graze and found a secluded spot beneath the trees.

Arlette sat on the grass in the shade, her back propped against a stout tree. The day had all the drowsy beauty and heady scents of midsummer, which drifted into her senses. She munched her bread and cheese in silence, forever conscious of William's quiet presence within her reach. Appreciative of the view, she gazed along the length of the valley. Enthralled, a feeling of peace engulfed her. Allowing her thoughts to dwell on what had occurred at the inn and William's ardour, in a sense she became like someone who had fallen under some kind of enchantment. Unbeknown to her the air and the exertions of the ride had brought colour to her cheeks and her face had softened, her lovely eyes glowing jewel bright.

'This is a lovely place,' she murmured, turning to look at her companion. When she caught his eyes she sensed he was feeling exactly as she felt, that the place had cast its own special enchantment on him, too.

Having eaten his fill, William was lying on the grass, his head propped up on his hand. His gaze did an appreciative sweep of the land spread out all around him. 'It certainly is. I've been away so long that I'd almost forgotten how beautiful England is. How I longed for this when I was fighting on the Continent or kicking my heels in Bruges.'

'You were gone a long time, William.'

'Not by choice. It wasn't what any of us would have chosen, but it was far better than living in England under Cromwell's rule.'

Turning towards her, he eyed her casually. Something in his expression made Arlette's breath catch in her throat and look away. A warm glow spread inside her and she felt a brazen longing to be as close to him as she had been the previous night. She liked being with him—just the two of them. She was beginning the think this self-imposed abstinence was silly. She desperately wanted to experience the passion he could offer her, the kind of passion she had never known existed until he had come back into her life. She knew she was falling in love with him and she wanted him to be with her always, to be there when she woke in the mornings, for him to touch and kiss her again, for him to go on saying he loved her over and over again.

William lay still, contemplating Arlette's profile. She was totally at ease and unaware of the watchful interest of his eyes. He watched as she rested her head back and licked her lips as if savouring the last crumb of bread. He could not move. He could only stare at the upward curve of her mouth and the exposed creamy flesh of her throat. Gazing at her in rueful reflection, memories of what had occurred between them the night before assailed his consciousness. He recalled how it had felt to hold her close, how, when she had risen from the bed, the neckline of her shift had gaped open to reveal the soft plumpness of her breasts and high peaks of the lustrous, rose-red nipples.

The recollection stirred and raked the red-hot embers in his mind. His eyes dark and brooding, leisurely he reached out and trailed a finger gently on the flesh of her forearm exposed beneath the sleeve of her gown, his memory ex-

panding, the vision bringing a smile to his lips
and a narrowing to his eyes, and he could see in
his mind's eye the look on her face when she had
responded angrily to the intruder who had entered her room, her eyes as vindictive and sharp
as a bird's beak that could pick a man's bones
clean. But now he saw how soft and flushed her
face was in repose, her thick lashes making soft
shadows on her cheeks and her hair a glorious
halo of golden light.

Arlette was acutely aware of William's gentle touch on her arm. The intensity, the warmly
intimate look in his eyes held her transfixed,
its warmth igniting a flame within her blood.
Her delicately beautiful face was framed by her
halo of hair, shifting in the gentle, warm breeze
blowing up the valley, and the effect of William's
gaze was vibrant and alarmingly alive.

'Should we be getting on our way, do you
think?' she asked, having no wish to leave this
lovely place.

'There's no hurry. We haven't spoken two
words together since we began to eat.'

'You want to talk?'

'It would be nice.'

'Why, what is it, William? Having an attack
of conscience, or is it guilt?'

'Both,' he replied with a harsh, embittered laugh. 'We haven't spoken of that unpleasantness when I found out about Marian's infidelity. I have thought long and hard about it. I should not have said the things I did—for which I can only apologise and pray you will forgive me. If I could only take back those terrible things I said to you, I would. The guilt I feel where you are concerned is because I wanted you from the moment I saw you again on my return to England, when I was betrothed to Marian.'

She looked at him steadily. 'I cannot forget the things you said to me, even though I know they were spoken in haste and anger. They were hurtful and distressing. You need to understand why I didn't tell you about Marian and James. I tried to persuade her to tell you herself. I didn't want to be the one to tear your life apart because I didn't want to hurt you.'

Getting to his knees, he moved closer to her, putting his hand under her chin and tilting her face to his. He was thankful she did not resist. 'I do understand—more than you realise.'

'Your pride was badly hurt by her betrayal.'

'Yes, it was,' William acknowledged quietly. 'How perceptive you are.'

'Not really,' she replied. She loved him enough

to see what was in his heart. She sighed, tilting her head to one side. 'I'm a romantic, William, and when I look into the eyes I want to gaze into for the rest of my life, I want them to be clear, to see straight into your heart without the trace of a shadow between us. I realise and understand why you reacted as you did when you found out about Marian and James and I can't pretend that it didn't hurt. I didn't find that easy to deal with. Now it's up to you to deal with it.'

'I will. I have. Your devotion and loyalty to Marian was commendable, Arlette. You were within your rights not to tell me something she had told you in confidence. I would expect nothing less of you. Had I not been so blind and my time taken up with affairs concerning the retrieval of Arlington Court, I would have seen for myself what was happening right before my eyes. When I found out, my anger was all consuming. I should not have taken it out on you and I have hated myself ever since with a virulence that was overwhelming. I should not have put you in the position of demanding that you betray Marian's confidence and Marian should not have asked it of you. You were placed in an impossible situation, I know that. I was betrothed to the sweetest girl, yet it was you I wanted, and

I hated myself for betraying Marian. Can you imagine how that made me feel about myself?'

'You told me you didn't trust me.'

'As a matter of fact I would trust you above all others. Nothing could change the way I feel about you.'

'And yet, feeling like this, would you have married Marian?'

'No. Even if she hadn't been in love with Sefton, I doubt I would have gone through with it. You have feelings for me, Arlette, that I know.'

'Yes, I do, but giving you my love is giving you the power to break my heart. I trust you will not do that.'

William's eyes narrowed. 'If you think that, then you don't know me very well.'

'Well enough to have formed an opinion.'

'Favourable, I hope, and if so we could get to know each other better.'

Arlette looked at him steadily. She knew what he was suggesting and was ashamed of the temptation this presented. The two days she had spent with him on the road had rubbed her emotions almost raw and the solid wall she had built around herself in their defence was beginning to erode. One look from him could do immense damage to her heart and her mind, which was already a battleground of emotions. The thought of him held close against her, unencumbered by clothes, made her body tremble. She felt a sudden rush of anticipation and denial, and more than a little pleasure. Her pulse beat frantically in her ears. The corners of his mouth lifted in a ghost of a smile and he reached out and traced the line of her lips with the tip of his finger. A quivering began deep inside her and she knew she should protest, that she should pull away, but she couldn't. She watched him in silence, bathed in the sensation of his featherlight caress.

His hand moved to her jaw, to caress her throat. Then, slowly, he pulled away, leaving her in the aftermath of sensations he had created, bereft and wanting more.

'I think it is time we were on our way,' he said, getting to his feet and holding his hand out to help her. She took it and stood before him, confused and frustrated. 'We have some way to travel before we stop for the night. Tomorrow we shall reach Mayfield.'

They reached the inn where they were to spend the night as the sun was sinking on the horizon. It was not a large inn and it was a busy night for the innkeeper. Only one room left, he told William. William turned and gave Arlette a questioning look. For a long moment his gaze held hers with penetrating intensity. It was as enigmatic as it was challenging and, unexpectedly, Arlette felt an answering frisson of excitement. The darkening of his eyes told her that he was aware of that response. Something in his expression made the breath catch in her throat and the warmly intimate look in his eyes was vibrantly, alarmingly alive. As they continued to face one another, she craved his lips against hers, her body within his arms, without thought to the consequences. She stared at him, aware how transparent she must look. As if he had read her thoughts he turned back to the innkeeper. Without a qualm William told him they would take the room.

They had eaten their supper in virtual silence, each of their minds focused on the night ahead. When she had eaten Arlette excused herself and went to the room ahead of him. She tried to gather her courage as she waited for him to come to her. She stood there for several moments in an agony of uncertainty. And then he was there.

William felt a deep need to know Arlette, to learn all there was to know about her, what she liked and loved, but he would save that for another day. All he could think of at that moment was taking her to bed and making love to her.

'Come here, Arlette,' he said quietly.

Her body reacted to the deep caress in his voice and her traitorous legs moved slowly forward. His arms went round her and he held her with infinite care, bringing her in close contact with his lean frame, savouring the warmth of her body against his and the softness of her hair beneath his jaw.

Impatient to be closer still, buckles and ties were unfastened and clothes hastily disposed of. William's eyes coursed down the supple curves of Arlette's body, over the proud swell of her breasts and narrow waist, to the beckoning curves and soft, secret hollows and shadows of her hips. Her voluptuous bloom of womanhood evoked in William a strong stirring of desire. He could not believe how much he wanted her, that the body his own had so fiercely craved for so long stood in front of him. His hand reached out and gently traced the outline of her hip, his fingers moving over her slender waist and on to her breast, cupping its fullness.

'Have you any idea just how lovely you are, Arlette, how adorable you are, of how much I

want you?' he murmured huskily. Her hair had
come loose and lay in disarray about her shoulders.

When William reached for the shoulder of
her shift and Arlette's fingers closed over his,
he thought she was stopping him, but she took
hold of the skirt and pulled it over her head. He
thought he should stop, but Arlette's exposed
breasts, plump and pink-nippled, mesmerised
him and compelled him to lower his mouth to
the satiny flesh. His hands caressed her, leisurely
arousing her, stroking her breasts and moving
downward over her belly. Arlette's whole body
began to tremble as his lips descended to hers.

They stood apart, gazing at each other as
though they had not seen each other before.

William had never made love to a woman who
wasn't willing. She only had to say no and he
would stop. He looked at her face. 'Is this what
you want, Arlette? Are you certain?'

She nodded, taking his hand and placing her
lips on his open palm. 'I do—more than anything. Just the two of us, here, in this room.'

He smiled. 'Two lonely people finding solace
in each other's arms.'

'I would like to think it is more than that,' she
murmured, losing herself in those blue eyes, now

hazy with desire. 'I care for you so much, William. I know that each time I see you. I feel it each time you touch me.'

Slowly his hand slipped about her waist as he drew her body against his and kissed her gently, amazed and intrigued by the mixture of innocence, boldness and fear which fired this woman. One thing he was sure of, he would make her body sing before he was done.

His lips descended on hers, the kiss increasing his craving to a blaze of hot need that he found hard to restrain. Slipping his arms beneath her legs and shoulders, he lifted her into his arms. Carrying her to the bed, he laid her on the covers. He stood looking down at her, unable to believe she was here with him. He studied the arch of her eyebrows, her cheekbones and round, firm chin and soft lips, her eyes large and dark as they watched him steadily. Unable to help himself, he leaned over and placed a reverent kiss upon her lips.

Every nerve in Arlette's body was alive to his touch. She ached for it. Was this carnality? she wondered. Lying beside her on the bed, William slipped his fingers into her hair as he pressed her to his hard, lean body. She closed her eyes, breathing in the scent of him. Her pulse quickened as their lips met and she pressed herself closer still, melting into him until it seemed they were just one being. She succumbed to a hunger she had experienced with him before. She shivered as his fingers strayed over the soft, silky smoothness of her inner thigh. She cried out and her breath came in short gasps as his fingers coaxed and gentled her. She clung to him, sliding slowly into a dark abyss of desire.

Heedless of what he was doing, William urged her to give him back the sensual urgency he was offering her, driving his tongue into her mouth until she began to match the pagan kiss. He kissed her again and again, lost in the heady beauty of her. By God, she was lovely and he wanted her with a fierceness that took his breath away. An uncontrollable compulsion to make love to her overwhelmed him and he kissed her until she was moaning and writhing in his arms and desire was pouring through him in hot tidal waves.

His hands stroked downwards, over the curve of her hip, and then upwards along the velvet softness inside her thighs. She gasped, reflexively tensing her muscles and clamping her legs together. William felt her resistance and groaned.

'Arlette, please, my love,' he said huskily, his

face taut with restraint. 'Trust me. Relax. Don't ask me to stop, for I fear I cannot.'

Above her Arlette could see his face was hard, his eyes dark with passion, and yet there was so much tenderness in their depths that her heart ached. But it was the desperate need she heard in his voice that made her respond.

'Please don't stop,' she whispered emphatically. 'I want you...'

His blood spilling through his veins like molten lava, William covered her with his body and lowered his hips between her thighs, seeing the sudden panic in her wide eyes when she felt the probing, burning heat of his maleness intruding into her delicate softness.

'I'm sorry, Arlette,' he whispered, his hands moving behind her and raising her hips. 'This may hurt, but not for long.' He knew he must be gentle lest her fear destroyed the moment and, when he entered her, he was ready to be as patient as she needed him to be.

Arlette wrapped her arms around his neck, pressing her face against the base of his throat when she felt the unrelenting pressure against her tight, resisting flesh, feeling his rigid hardness inch its way into her soft warmth. Her heart began to beat to a new, frantic rhythm that suffused her with an expanding warmth. The pain of penetration was but a brief discomfort that she forced back as she became aware of a driving need to appease an insatiable hunger. He held her close and began to move, gently at first, but the violence of their passion consumed them both. Arlette gasped at the sensations she was experiencing, sliding her arms about his neck and pressing her soft breasts into the mat of hair that covered his chest, pulling his head down to hers.

William touched her lips, drinking in the glory of her, his hands cupping her buttocks, bringing her closer as he began to move. Amazement etched her flushed face as he met her stroke for stroke with vigour and the blossoming pleasure in Arlette's loins intensified and swept her on with the promise of still greater heights to reach. In the room behind the fluttering of the curtains, among the rumpled sheets overflowing the bed, they shared a furious passion, the sounds coming from the inn below mingling with the laboured rhythm of their breathing and the salty taste of sweat on their skin.

An eternity later William raised his head, the blood pounding in his ears. Arlette stayed in his arms, her cheek against his chest, her body pressed to his, trembling in the aftermath of the most explosive, inexplicable passion she had ever felt.

Gradually Arlette's breathing became even and the sounds from the inn below began to penetrate her drugged senses. Collapsed, spent, she lay supine in his arms, her chest rising and falling. The whisper of a sigh escaped her as she nestled close to him, wanting to hold on to this moment in time lest she lose some portion of it to the oncoming forces of normality.

'Dear Lord, Arlette,' William murmured, curling a tendril of soft golden hair around his finger, marvelling at the wonder of her, for her surrender to him had been complete and unconditional. 'You are wanton beyond belief and quite magnificent.'

Completely captivated by the intimate look in his eyes and the compelling gentleness in his voice, Arlette swallowed and said, 'So are you.'

William's hypnotic gaze held hers as his fingertips stroked her cheek seductively, sliding along the line of her jaw to her lips. From the first moment he had taken her in his arms he had known they were a combustible combination and what had just passed had been the most wildly erotic, satisfying sexual encounter of his life. Whatever Arlette had felt had been real and uncontrived. 'Do you regret what we have done?' he asked.

Saturated in the passion she had experienced, Arlette could not pretend, because she wanted to remember everything that they did together. She wanted to think about it, linger on it, close her eyes and squirm with pleasure at the thought of those hot, blissful moments they had made love. She wanted to dwell on each and every detail. Rolling on to her stomach and propping herself up on her arms, she looked at him. Her face burned where his lips had caressed her tender flesh. The dim light of the lamp cast its glow over his long, lean body stretched out on the bed beside her.

'You did nothing wrong, William. It was my choice. I have no regrets. I am your wife now, in every sense. Are you shocked by my behaviour?'

William gently smoothed her tumbled locks from her face, tracing his finger down the soft curve of her cheek. He gazed at her with something akin to awe and reverence, feeling humbled by her beauty and her unselfish ardour and uninhibited giving of herself.

'On the contrary. Would you like me to tell you what I like most of all?'

'Please do.'

'I like the way your body fits into mine so perfectly and that it is attuned to what I want.' Tenderly he kissed her lips. 'I like to have you near me and it is my desire to have you near me every morning I wake. How do you feel?' he asked, his voice gentle, his gaze so tender that Arlette's heart contracted.

'Rather wonderful,' she murmured, placing her lips gently on his chest. 'I never imagined for one moment that making love could be so pleasurable.'

He smiled tenderly into her upturned face, bending his head to caress her lips lightly with his own. When his mouth left hers his hooded eyes smouldered with renewed desire as they moved with leisured thoroughness over her delicately hued curves, his loins already hardening in demanding response to her nearness.

'Now, speaking of pleasure…'

Arlette's mouth curved in a sublime smile while his eyes grew dark and sultry. The heat of his gaze set her blood on fire and set her heart racing with sweet anticipation. She snuggled down so that they were facing each other, the soft flesh of her body lying against his. She lifted one leg and wrapped it around him, her eyes languid at the thought of what was to come. 'There's more?' she murmured.

'Absolutely,' he murmured, nuzzling the hollow in her throat where a pulse was beating a tantalising fast rhythm beneath her soft flesh. 'The night is not over and I intend to make the most of you while I have you in my bed. There is much I have to teach you before I can let you sleep.' He moved against her, his body rousing, responding again to the softness of her.

Arlette giggled softly and snuggled closer. 'Then teach me,' she whispered. 'If you think some lessons will prove beneficial, then I promise I will be an apt pupil.' Her sensual lips quirked in a half-smile, a rosy blush covering her soft cheeks.

William revelled in the sweetness of her, touching and kissing her with all the skill of a virtuoso playing a violin, as if he had all the time in the world. She had the body that was created for a man's hands and a mouth that positively invited his kiss. She had given him exquisite pleasure and, when the moment of his release came once more, he couldn't have said who clung to the other more desperately. It was as though the very life source was being wrung out of him. He had turned her into a passionate, loving woman, a woman to fill his arms and warm his bed and banish the dark emptiness that had been a part of his life for so many years, a woman to fill his life with love and laughter. What more could a man want? What more, indeed.

As the night had drawn on they had loved and slept. When dawn came, sending a glimmer of light into the room, William considered his slumbering companion. Her tousled head rested against the pillows, her lips slightly parted and her eyelashes shadowing her cheeks. Her body, warm and soft, was curled next to his. Her nearness filled his senses with the delicate essence of her. It was pleasurable to watch her sleeping, to fix her image in his mind. Leaning over her, he placed a soft kiss on her cheek.

On a sigh Arlette opened her eyes and stretched her lithe young body. She had a pleasant feeling of well-being and contentment. She felt a different person from the one who had left London. William had awoken feelings inside her that she had not known existed. She was no longer a naive young innocent but a woman, with a woman's wants and needs. What she felt for him she couldn't begin to analyse or understand. It was mysterious and consuming, a highly volatile combination of danger and excitement. Her face exploded in a blaze of scarlet when she thought how she had lain with him and she felt the pleasurable wanton feelings tearing through her again at the memory.

Resting his arms on either side of her, he kissed her lips gently. 'Time to get up, Arlette. I trust you slept well.' There was a small quirk of a smile on his lips as his gaze lingered on her lips.

Arlette gazed up at him, finding it difficult to hide her treacherous heart's reaction to the deep timbre of his voice. Why, she wondered, did she feel different from the way she had felt yesterday? Why could she still feel his hands on her bare flesh and his kisses on her lips?

'You're dressed,' she said, struggling to sit up. 'Have you eaten?'

'Not yet,' he replied. 'I waited for you. When we've had breakfast we'll be on our way. We should reach Mayfield by midday.'

With her bags secured and once more in the saddle, Arlette mounted her horse for the last few miles of their journey. William wheeled his horse in time to catch Arlette's eye. There was a sudden duel of glances as his eyes invaded hers, drawing her to him, drawing her in, and she felt again the sudden heat of suppressed passion. They were yards apart, yet in some strange way they seemed joined together.

'Ready?' he asked, his lips curving in a smile.

She nodded, urging her horse on.

Arlette enjoyed the experience of going back to Mayfield, somewhere she was at once familiar with. The woods and fields and meadows buzzing with the sights and sounds of insects, the village that had once been important to her, all evoked distant memories that rushed at her the closer they got—memories of her father sitting in his study or by the fire, a smiling Hester helping cook in the kitchen or the buttery, Thomas's incessant teasing, memories of herself riding her pony along the country lanes and Blanche, how she would wrap her motherly arms around her and instantly make her feel safe and loved.

And then they came to Mayfield Hall on the outskirts of the Mayfield village, that gracious, noble house where Arlette had been born and had spent the happiest years of her life. At first appearance with smoke curling up from the chimneys the house appeared to be occupied. They dismounted and stood staring at it. Ivy ran rampant up the walls and the windows looked back at them like staring empty eyes.

'It would appear someone is in residence,' Arlette said.

'So it does. I'm curious as to who it can be.'

Arlette turned her head and, reaching out, took his hand. 'I never thought this moment would come,' she said with feeling. 'When I last saw Mayfield I was with you. I never thought we would return together. I feel that this is a special moment for us. It seems we have come full circle.'

Leading their horses, they walked closer. The door opened and a man stepped out.

'Thomas!' Arlette gasped. 'Oh, see, William. It's Thomas.'

Immediately she took to her feet and, holding her skirts high, she ran towards him. Thomas had clearly recognised her and, after a moment's pause, he hurried to meet her halfway, lifting her off her feet into his arms and swinging her round before planting her in front of him and taking her face between his hands.

'Arlette, I cannot believe it is you. Why—just look at you—all grown up.' He hugged her again before looking beyond her to her companion. His mouth broke into a broad smile. 'William? William, you made it.' Breaking his sister's embrace, he covered the distance between them, sweeping the taller man into his arms.

'Arlette is my wife, Thomas,' William proudly informed him when they finally drew apart. They had parted on the most wretched of days when they had been taken prisoner after Worcester and the feelings and memories this evoked moved them both. 'We are on our way to Arlington Court, but we could not pass so close to Mayfield without coming here. We knew you were to return, but had no idea you would be here already and that you appear to have taken up residence.'

'I arrived three weeks ago and, as you will see, there is much to do.' He looked at his close friend who had his arm about his sister's waist and burst out laughing, which lightened the moment. 'Good Lord! Look at the two of you. Married! That is good news, indeed, but Arlette is still a girl to me.'

'If you think that, then your eyesight is sadly impaired, Thomas,' William said, giving him a brief, rakish smile. 'Your sister is a beauty, a rare jewel and quite unique, and I strongly suspect that she has the courage to pit her will against any man—including me. I have also discovered she has a temper and an unpredictable disposition, is wilful and often argumentative.' This earned him a mock scowl from his wife and amusement from Thomas.

'That is our father's fault. Being the youngest she was his pet. He indulged her every whim and allowed her far too much freedom.' He gave his sister a hug to soften his words.

'Before you say anything else, Thomas, it's worth bearing in mind that I am now your brother-in-law.'

Thomas grinned and winked. 'Now that is something to celebrate, as well as your marriage. After so many bleak years and the end of the Commonwealth, it is time for celebrations. A new age is upon us. The King sits upon his throne and England is at peace. Whether Charles Stuart will be a good king only time will tell. But come inside. Constance, my wife, is just putting our son down for a nap.'

They sat in the hall with the sun shining through the diamond-paned windows, lighting up the hall, and, with her brother's presence, memories assailed Arlette, reminding her of happier times, a house that had held much laughter and love.

'I can't believe we're here at last,' she whispered.

Reading her mind, Thomas smiled at her. 'As soon as I arrived in Oxford, discovering the house had been sequestered and the family living in it deceased, I went to see our lawyer to lay claim to the estate and set things in motion to have it returned to our family.'

'So is it official, Thomas?' Arlette asked.

'It is. The estate is back in our hands. Now,' he said, looking towards the stairs and getting to his feet when a smiling young woman appeared, 'here's Constance.'

Epilogue

∿

They had stayed at Mayfield Hall one week before setting off for Arlington Court. Arlette was overwhelmed when she saw Blanche again, much older but still the same loving woman who had been more like a mother to her in the past. Her nephew was an adorable child and, before leaving for Arlington Court, they promised to visit often.

Arlington Court was a large, lovely old Tudor house with turrets and tall chimneys in the Warwickshire countryside. Arlette loved it at once and the turmoil of emotion and events of the past weeks were put behind them. The previous unwelcome occupant had moved back to London, hoping to escape the King's retribution for being a man who had been one of those responsible for his father's execution.

Arlette settled down into her new home, knowing she had so much to look forward to.

* * *

Hester and Marian wrote often with news of London. Sir Ralph Crompton, who had married a wealthy widow close to his age, had turned his back on Richard after calling in the debt. Richard, whose business was thriving under the patronage of returned Royalists and the generous settlement William had given him on his marriage to Arlette, paid it in full. Hester and Marian were both delivered of their babies in the same week. Hester had a son and Marian a daughter James doted on. In the months that followed, to Arlette's delight she conceived their first child. It soon became evident, after their son was born and then left babyhood behind, that he had inherited his father's charm as well as his looks.

William walked arm in arm with Arlette in the garden in the evening quiet, their young son running ahead of them on wobbly legs. Bees and insects hummed and butterflies flitted among the flowers. Apricots and pear trees espaliered against the warm brick hung with golden fruit. They spoke of many things—of their home and the King and their lives at Arlington Court. They spoke of their second child that was growing in Arlette and soon, before too long, they would go to Mayfield Hall to visit Thomas and Constance. Hester and Marian and their respective families were to join them. It was to be the first family gathering since Thomas had come home.

'You're excited about going to Mayfield, Arlette, and naturally so,' William said.

'I cannot wait to see Hester and Marian. It seems so long since we left London. It will be a happy family gathering. The children will inject new life into the old place. And soon there will be another. Have you thought of whether you'd like a son or a daughter this time?'

William's gaze did a sweep of her expanding belly. 'I haven't given it serious thought. I'd like to have at least one of each. A daughter who looks like you would be nice.'

They paused and looked proudly at their son and then faced each other. With the old glint in his eye and the familiar sardonic smile, William cupped her face in his hand and gently kissed her lips, a kiss filled with both promise and content. It filled her with a sweet melody, a blending harmony of memory and desire that defied the telling because words were not enough to capture or define.

Arlette smiled. 'I love you, William.'

'And I you, my love. Never doubt it.'

* * * * *

MILLS & BOON

Coming next month

AN UNCONVENTIONAL COUNTESS
Jenni Fletcher

'It's strange, but you might be the only person in the world who *can* understand.'

Anna felt her pulse quicken at the words. It was the same thing she'd thought when she'd told Samuel how she felt trapped, as if they truly *could* understand each other. As if maybe, despite everything, they might be a good match after all, just as the Baroness had said. The way he was looking at her now suggested he thought so, too, but how could that be possible? She was a shopkeeper and he was an earl...*maybe*. Or maybe not. There was an equal chance that he might remain a captain.

'I do understand.' She tried to keep her voice normal. 'Only my mother told me recently that bitterness and resentment weren't very attractive qualities. Shall I repeat her lecture?'

'Did it make you feel any better?'

'No, but it did make me think. Now I want to let go of the past and move on, wherever it leads me.'

'Wherever...?' He echoed the word as he lifted a hand to the side of her face, his fingers sliding gently across the curve of her cheek and beneath her chin, tilting it upwards. The touch sent a thrill of heat coursing through her body, making her feel as if every inch of

her skin was blushing. Thank goodness they were outside in the dark. Although they really shouldn't be. Not together and certainly not touching like this. No matter what he said about understanding each other, there were still too many obstacles between them. Only it was becoming hard to hold on to that thought.

'We ought to go in.' She swallowed nervously. 'You said it was time for supper.'

'Did I?' He moved closer, his jacket brushing against the front of her dress. 'I can't remember.'

'Yes. I don't think…'

Her words faltered as his arms closed around her waist, enveloping her in a feeling of strong masculine warmth. She didn't move or resist, too surprised to do anything as he leaned in towards her, his mouth moving slowly towards and then hovering above hers, so tantalisingly close that it was hard to believe they weren't already touching. She could feel the warmth of his breath as it skimmed across her cheek…and then there was a sensation of cold air as he moved to one side, gently grazing the edge of her mouth.

Continue reading
AN UNCONVENTIONAL COUNTESS
Jenni Fletcher

Available next month
www.millsandboon.co.uk

Copyright © 2020 Jenni Fletcher

COMING SOON!

We really hope you enjoyed reading this book. If you're looking for more romance, be sure to head to the shops when new books are available on

Thursday 23rd January

To see which titles are coming soon, please visit

millsandboon.co.uk/nextmonth

MILLS & BOON

JOIN US ON SOCIAL MEDIA!

Stay up to date with our latest releases, author
news and gossip, special offers and discounts, and
all the behind-the-scenes action
from Mills & Boon...

 millsandboon

 millsandboonuk

 millsandboon

It might just be true love...

GET YOUR ROMANCE FIX!

MILLS & BOON
— *blog* —

Get the latest romance news, exclusive author interviews, story extracts and much more!

blog.millsandboon.co.uk